ENTICING THE ENFORCER

WITTMORE U

ANGEL LAWSON

For jocks that double as human exclamation points.

FOREWORD

Welcome back to Wittmore Hockey!

I'm excited to bring you Jefferson and Ingrid's story but first, let's get a few things on the table. Two years ago, like so many of us romance lovers, I was enthralled, entertained and just joyful about the revelation of Taylor Swift and Travis Kelce. I think that I was here for the joy, the distraction, the real life football + pop star romance during a particularly challenging place in my life. TnT felt like a sports romance book coming to life! How could I resist!?

Is that parasocial? Ugh, I hope not. I'm a fan but admittedly somewhat superficially. I'm definitely that person that lets everyone else do the hard work and then I watch the reels later explaining all the Easter eggs and secret sauce. I'm probably more impressed by both of their talents and business abilities than anything else. (And Taylor's ability to shoot crack into my veins lyrically), but look, as I was plotting out the final two books in the series I was absolutely, positively inspired by Taylor and Travis for this book. I hope you see that for what it is, reveling in the happiness and not in any kind of gross, invasive way. I save that for the Barons.

Otherwise, there aren't any real content warnings in this book, just a steamy and sexy romance for my hockey lovers!

Happy Reading!
Angel

1

I ngrid

IT'S nights like this when I understand why musicians use drugs. I always feel high when I'm on stage. It's a natural rush that comes from performing. It's the crash after that makes me feel a little lost. That's when I want to reach for something to keep the feeling going. Since I don't use drugs, I tend to channel that energy into something less destructive. Writing another song. Eating a greasy cheeseburger. Taking a run. And if luck is willing, spending the night with my boyfriend and getting that dopamine hit between the sheets.

Tonight was only a rehearsal. Tomorrow, after the concert, will be a million times worse.

And due to my ex, right now I'm shit out of luck.

I roll over and grab my phone off the hotel nightstand.

Another hotel, another arena, another town I'll barely get to see. Don't get me wrong, I'm living my dream, but after months of being on tour, it's all starting to blur. I lay back on the bed and look around the room. Even I can admit that this one has a unique vibe. The boutique hotel is on the edge of Wittmore's campus, and each room is decked out in collegiate swag. Pennants and framed images of the campus, the football team, or hockey team hang over the walls. Even the soap in the bathroom is in the shape of their mascot, a badger.

The suite is up on the top floor, and Madison, my assistant, is in the second bedroom, while Marv, my security guard, is most likely out in the common area.

There's a saying, "Even in a crowd, you can feel alone." That's how it is sometimes—with the fans, my Flock, as they call themselves, my assistant and best friend, Marv, and the other members of my team. They're always here, but once we settle down for the night, there's always a little restlessness. A touch of isolation that never seems to fade.

I know it's that feeling that drives me to open my phone, and do the thing I've promised not to–check out Jake's ChattySnap account.

Big mistake.

He's smiling in every post. That smile I used to wake up to. Holding a guitar in one, a new girl in the other. I scroll faster, like speed will lessen the sting.

Nope.

I back out of the app before I spiral. Open a browser instead. Search: *Wittmore's best hamburger.*

First thing that pops up: *Serendee Cult Disbanded After Leader Captured and Jailed.*

Okay... not what I asked for.

Second: *Wittmore Hockey Team Heads To Frozen Four For The Second Year In A Row. Will They Clench It This Time?*

I swipe into the images, and that's when I see it. A shot of the team, mid-celebration, black and yellow jerseys, mouths open in a cheer. My eyes drag past the blur of bodies until they lock on one number.

#23. Jefferson Parks.

And just like that, the static in my chest fizzles.

I remember the note. The one taped to his locker in the dressing room I'll be using for the concert. It's folded neatly, tucked inside my purse. This time I get off the bed and cross the room, digging in my designer bag for the folded-up piece of paper.

No phone number. Just:

"Not trying to be that guy, but I'd kick myself if I didn't say something. If you ever want an escape, a behind the scenes tour of Wittmore, or to learn how to skate without falling on your ass–I've got you."

—Jefferson #23

I don't know why I let Marv give me the letter. Fans try to reach out to me all the time. Letters, notes, posters, songs, artwork, little trinkets, and jewelry. Most are sweet. Encouraging. But some? A fucking nightmare. People are psycho out there. The parasocial relationships are real, and we have to be careful.

But here I am, with the note in my hand. I flop back on the bed, open my phone again, and stare at the screen for a few seconds. Then, heart thudding, I swipe over to ChattySnap.

He's got a public profile. A few hockey shots. A dumb reel of his shirtless, tattooed teammate jumping over a couch in their house. And one recent photo of him, sweaty and laughing, leaning on his stick at practice.

He looks fun. Easy.

Hot.

I hover. Then hit the DM arrow.

IngFlock: *Got any suggestions for a really good hamburger?*

I hit send before I can overthink it.

Then I drop the phone on the bed beside me, exhale, and flop back on the pillow like I haven't just DM'd some college hockey player I barely know.

Okay, maybe I've officially lost it.

Or maybe, just maybe, I need a burger.

And a reason not to look at Jake's feed again.

2

J efferson

THE TATTOO on the inside of my bicep burns, a steady throb that flares every time I move. The boys and I each got an 'M' inked to represent the last four years of Wittmore, living in the Manor, and becoming more like brothers than team or housemates. A few more days, and our days playing hockey at Wittmore will come to an end. A few weeks after that, we'll graduate, and we'll each split off toward our future. Both Reese and Axel are free agents, hoping to get a spot on a professional roster, while Reid is already locked in with a contract in New York as well as a successful side hustle in design.

Me? Like Reid, I drafted early and have a spot waiting for me down in Florida, which meant I've had two primary focuses in college: playing my best and having as much fun as I can before life gets serious.

The air has a warm edge tonight. Spring is close enough to taste, even up here in the North East. Streetlights buzz overhead, casting golden halos on the sidewalk. Students pass in packs, laughter echoing down the brick alleyways that cut through this town like veins. I'm going to miss Wittmore. The past four years have been epic. We were so close to winning the Frozen Four a year ago, but didn't quite have what we needed to secure the trophy. We were all a lot wilder back then. Reese's relationship with his ex was rocky as hell. Axel spent more time focused on partying, rebelling against his preacher father, than he did on the ice, and Reid... well, Reid just needed to catch a break.

The three of them are all in a better place, settled down with the kind of girls you lock down with a ring on their finger. Me?

Well.

I've spent the last four years having a killer time. Frat parties, sneaking into sorority row, puck bunnies, and dominating the ice. Unlike the others, keeping a balance isn't a problem for me. I play, I fuck, I win, and do it all over again the next day.

A couple heads my way: the girl in an Ingrid Flockton t-shirt, little silver feathers hanging from her ears. And the guy? He's wearing a Wittmore jersey. Number 23. It never gets old seeing my name and number on the fans, but I keep my hoodie pulled low. It's too close to the championship, and I don't feel like talking about it.

They pass, too into each other to notice me. He's got his arm around her waist and kisses the side of her neck. I've got my hands shoved in my pockets, my bicep aching beneath the fresh ink.

I like feeling that little tinge of pain. I get why Axel is addicted to getting tattoos. There's definitely a dopamine hit that comes with it. Most of all, it was a distraction from facing the idiot move I pulled earlier in the day.

The note to Ingrid Flockton.

Yep, *the* Ingrid Flockton

I've been listening to Ingrid Flockton since I was fifteen years old and hiding in my brother's beat-up Jeep. She was already famous back then–this untouchable, ethereal voice coming through the speakers, singing about sneaking out of bedroom windows and broken hearts. I didn't know what half of it meant, but God, it hit hard.

Now she's twenty-two, like me, almost a decade into a career most people couldn't even dream up, and she's somehow only gotten sharper. Bigger. Wilder. Her third album, *Holy Feral*, broke records like they were glass under her lace-up boots with five number-one singles, two sold-out world tours, including one she just extended for a few additional shows. She's won Grammys. She's played Glaston-bury barefoot in the rain. There's a fan theory that her fourth album was a coded love letter to a popular celebrity. I believe it. She makes everything sound like a secret you're lucky to hear.

And yeah, I get that it's a little weird for a guy like me to be into a pop star like this. I'm a hockey player. I get in fights, lift weights, drink beer, and fuck sorority girls, but Ingrid Flockton?

She's a fucking goddess. Gorgeous with her long, shiny hair usually tinted pink or blue, whatever she's feeling at the moment. She's tall, at least five-eleven, and the way she carries herself on and off the stage looks strong. There's no fragility there. Other than in her words.

I want to meet her. Kiss her. Give her a few moments of bliss in an otherwise crazy life. She's been on the top of my list–yes, an actual list–of people I want to have sex with since I made it. I've crossed off a few others: the captain of the cheer squad, the Easton goalies' (now ex) girlfriend. That hot mom who always hung out at our neighbor-hood pool.

Yeah, when I want something, I go for it.

That's why I left the note on my locker door after Coach told us to clear everything out for the show tomorrow. The show I'm missing because I'll be in Chicago prepping for the Frozen Four. Every player knows the motto of Wayne Gretzky. "You miss one hundred percent of the shots you don't take."

Ingrid Flockton is coming into my house?

Yeah, I'm taking my fucking shot.

I'm halfway down the strip when my phone vibrates in my pocket.

I ignore it at first. Could be anything. Could be Coach. Or a teammate. Or my brother telling me not to do something dumb in Chicago.

But something nudges at me.

When I finally pull it out, I see the notification.

ChattySnap: New message from IngFlock.

My heart actually stutters. Like missteps. Like when you hit the boards a little too hard and lose your breath for a second.

I stare at the screen.

Got any suggestions for a really good hamburger?

I read it twice. Then a third time.

It's her.

Ingrid Flockton. *The* Ingrid Flockton.

I exhale, almost laugh. Her profile icon is a falling feather.

She got my note.

I never expected her to actually read it. I wrote it half as a joke. Folded it up and stuck it to the vent of the locker room on the way out the door. Figured someone would throw it away or her security would toss it before she even saw it.

But now...

Fuck. I swipe my thumb over the keyboard, thinking for a second. Then I type:

Best burger in town's at the Badger Den. If you want the Jefferson Parks Special, you'll have to show up in person. Comes with fries and zero paparazzi.

I stare at it for a beat, a thin coating of sweat beading on my neck. Jesus, since when does Jefferson Parks get nervous about sliding into some chick's DMs? I suck it up and hit send.

A slow grin pulls at the corner of my mouth.

It could be nothing. A bored pop star looking to fuck around with an idiot fan. Someone on her team who gets off on catfishing.

Or maybe Ingrid's ready to play.

Either way, I pass the pizza place and make my way to the Den. Reese, our captain, gave us specific instructions not to go out tonight.

Zero fuck-ups because the bus leaves early as hell, and the next few days are the most important ones in our lives.

But now I've got something just as interesting as a win.

I've got her attention.

3

I ngrid

It's barely past ten, and I've already lied three times tonight.

First to Madison. I told her I needed fresh air and wouldn't go far. Second to Marv. I said security could stand down, that I was exhausted and not planning to leave the hotel. And third to myself, when I stood in the bathroom mirror, pulling on the worn gray high school hoodie Madison left hanging on the back of the door, and tucking every strand of lavender-streaked hair beneath a faded Yankees cap.

I told myself I wasn't really going.

But I am. Every step away from the hotel is proof.

I wince as my sneakers hit the sidewalk, feeling the tender blisters on the back of my heels from the boots I wear on stage. The pain is worth it though. I look amazing in those boots. Like always, I push the pain aside and duck away from the buzzing streetlight. I've performed all over the world, in big cities and massive arenas.

Wittmore is small, but there's an energy from the student population that gives it a bigger feel. More worldly. The old brick buildings are pretty, and have alleyways that smell like pizza or stale beer. It's the kind of place that would've made me ache when I was sixteen, stuck in green rooms and dressing rooms and rented-out luxury suites. College life: classes, dorm rooms, frat parties... a whole life where I didn't wake up every morning, worried about what the tabloids were saying or the weight of employing hundreds of people who help form and shape my career.

According to the map on my phone, The Badger Den is only a few blocks from campus, the kind of college dive that's never seen a reservation and wouldn't know what to do with a vegan menu. From the tags on socials, it appears to be a hockey bar–the spot where the team and fans hang out during and after games. I'd looked it up after he messaged me, just to see if it was walkable. It was. Too walkable. Stupidly close. Close enough that I've been wandering for half an hour trying to talk myself *out* of this.

Because what the hell am I even doing?

Meeting a fan?

Definitely.

Meeting a hot, six-foot-five hockey player who wants to carve a notch in his bedpost? Who wants to tell his friends and teammates he hooked up with Ingrid Flockton?

Probably.

I looked him up. There's no way he doesn't know everything about me, so I should know something about him, right? From the sports blog I found, Jefferson Parks' is an 'enforcer,' whatever that means, and stats include:

Height: 6'5"
Weight: 230 lbs
Shoots: Right
Year: Senior
Team: Wittmore University Badgers
Position: Right Wing / Enforcer
Post College Commitment: The Surge: Jacksonville, Florida

The photo gallery gave more insight. His hair is sandy blond, the lines of his face chiseled, except for the crooked slant in his nose. His lips are way too soft looking for a man. Solid fuck-boy features. A man who knows what he wants.

Which would track. He did leave the note on his locker. Not through a friendly security guard, or an attempt to get to Madison. Not with an ask for a selfie or a shoutout, or a ticket upgrade. Just a scrawled line on folded paper, like we were in high school. It was cocky. Sweet. Weirdly sincere.

It was a huge swing and, yeah, I'm the kind of girl that likes a man who takes initiative. I spend every moment of every day making decisions and being the boss. Beyond that, it made me feel seen.

Which is ridiculous. I know it's ridiculous.

I'm *Ingrid Flockton*. I've sold out stadiums. I've lost my voice from singing under purple spotlights. I've bared my soul publicly, one line at a time. I've dated a guy whose face is on the cover of *Rolling Stone* and still somehow managed to feel lonelier next to him than I do tonight, anonymous and hidden in my best friend's hoodie.

Jake always said I needed someone to "tone me down." As if I was too much. Too loud. Too pink. Too passionate. I wrote *Thirteen Steps to Disappear* after we broke up. He thinks it's about addiction. My therapist thinks it's about grief.

It's actually about me and how easy it is to lose yourself one step at a time. Allowing others to erase you. Control you, which is probably why I just want one night that *isn't* a headline.

I stop at the edge of the alley that curves toward the bar. There's a cluster of students out front, someone laughing too loud. My stomach flips. Maybe I should go back. Maybe I've already pushed this too far. I could just say I got lost. Say I needed a walk. Say–

"Hey."

I spin, heart in my throat, but it's him.

Jefferson Parks.

He's even taller in person, taller than me, and let me tell you, that's as rare as it is a fucking turn on. He's all shoulders and messy hair and a dimple that ruins me on sight. His hoodie is half unzipped.

In one hand, he's holding a brown paper bag that smells like salt and grease and something deeply unfair.

"I figured you might chicken out," he says, shrugging as if not a big deal. As if I'm not a sideshow freak in a traveling circus.

I blink. "I was about to."

He shrugs. "Good thing I intercepted."

Then he lifts the bag.

"Jefferson Parks Special. Double cheeseburger. Bacon, avocado with crunchy fried onions on top. Fries. No paparazzi. You want to hang out somewhere not swarming with people?"

I hesitate. Only for a second.

Then I nod.

Because, although I do know who I'll be tomorrow, up on that stage, giving everything I have to people I've never met, tonight I want to experience something different. Something I don't know how it will end. Right now, I'm just a girl in a borrowed hoodie, standing in front of a boy who brought her dinner.

And for once, that's enough.

～

He doesn't wait for me to speak again—just turns like he expects I'll follow.

I stare at his back, his broad-shouldered, ridiculous wing-spanned back, until he turns and says, "Coming?"

No! I want to say. I almost do, because what the hell am I doing?

This is crazy. No. It's fucking dangerous.

I've had stalkers before. Mentally disturbed fans. Parasocial relationships that blur the lines of reality. But for some insane reason, I just nod and take a step after him, my long legs working double time to catch up with his even longer ones. Why? Because I'm curious. Because I'm hungry. Because, despite all the good reasons to stay put in the safety of the hotel, I'm starting to think the suites and tour buses and arenas are starting to suck the very life out of me.

We walk side by side in silence for the first block, the only sound between us the shuffle of our sneakers on pavement and the crinkle of the brown paper bag swinging gently from his fingers.

He turns us off the strip, passing a street of large houses lit up like Christmas. Greek letters hang over the doors. There's a guy in a backwards cap yelling from the second-floor porch while holding a red plastic cup. Down below another group stands around a wooden table, and one of them lets out a half-hearted "*Wooo!*" before recognizing Jefferson and shouting, "Good luck, Parks!"

"Bring home the trophy!"

Jefferson lifts a hand at the guys, but makes no move to join them.

"Are you in a frat?" I ask, trying to sound casual, like I understand this world.

"Not a chance," he grins, flashing that dimple. "Although I guess my team is pretty close to a frat. We're like brothers; we live and party together. We're there through thick and thin."

"That makes sense. I get close to the people I work with, too."

"Those guys..." he gestures to the frat boys who are back to playing some game on the tabletop. "They're fans. Hockey is very popular at Wittmore, I'm pretty well known on campus."

Across the street are similar houses, although bigger and cleaner. No tabletop games or couches in the yard. A girl exits her car by the curb, and I look away quickly, but it's unnecessary. Her eyes skirt past me and land squarely on Jefferson. That's a first, but I think I get it. He's got a magnetism. And from what I can tell from the way his shirt stretches across his shoulders, a killer body. "Hey, you."

"Chantel," he says, eyebrow raising.

"I heard Reese issued a no-partying rule tonight?"

"No partying here," he says, positioning his body between me and the girl. I realize he's keeping her from being able to see my face. "Just showing a friend around campus."

"Well," she tilts her head, "if you end up looking for a place to crash tonight, you know where to find me."

"Will do," he says, flashing her that grin. "See you around."

Even after we're a house away from the girl, I tug my hoodie lower, pulling the brim of my cap down. "That happen a lot? Girls inviting you to 'crash' at their place?"

"Pretty often," he replies with zero shame.

"Is that what you think is happening here? That your little private tour and greasy hamburger will lead to a hook up? A one-night stand with Ingrid Flockton? A way to get tickets? An autograph? Details on what really happened with me and my ex to sell to the tabloids?"

He stops and looks down at me, a piece of blond hair falling in his eyes. "Babe, if I wanted in your pants, I would've brought condoms, not fries."

A beat stretches between us, and I feel stupid and out of my depth, which rarely happens to me. Usually, I'm the one in control; I make sure of it, but at this moment, out on the cold street in Wittmore, I'm anything but in charge. Also? Marv is going to kill me. I narrow my eyes. "How do I know you're not going to murder me?"

"Jesus, you sound like my roommate's girlfriend," he mutters. "I'm a hockey player, not a psycho."

"That's not *entirely* reassuring."

"Well, statistically speaking," he says, deadpan, "you're more likely to be murdered by a pop star than a college athlete."

I let out a laugh. "Where'd you hear that?"

"Probably on ChattySnap. But hey, if I was planning to kill you, I wouldn't have paraded you across campus."

Fair. He's not exactly hiding me, and true to his initial letter, this *is* a tour of Wittmore. I swallow my concerns as we turn a corner and step off the main road. The noise fades, replaced by the occasional sound of campus life. Wittmore unfolds in front of us—wide lawns, old buildings, glowing lamplight washing the sidewalks in warm gold.

He points to a red brick building on our left. "That's the comms building. My second home, basically. I'm a journalism major."

I blink. "Wait—really?"

"What, don't I look like the sensitive, ethical media type?"

"I just assumed your major was... gym."

"Ouch."

"You know what I mean. You exercise for fun."

He chuckles, not offended. "Yeah, well, turns out I like writing almost as much as checking guys into the boards. If this hockey thing doesn't work out, I'm hoping to end up in sports media. Maybe TV."

"That actually makes sense."

He tilts his head, looking at me. "Because I have a face for print?"

God no. He has a face that could be plastered on the cover of magazines and not just the sports ones. But the cocky smirk tugging at his mouth tells me he knows that. "I think it's smart to have a second skill." I look away from his exquisite jawline. "So where are we going?"

He flashes a grin, a little secretive now. "You'll see. But I promise it's safe, quiet, and has no frat bros or sorority hos."

A laugh slips out. "You did not just say that."

"I'm pretty sure I did." Jefferson glances down at me with that lazy grin that should probably be illegal. "The arena."

"You're taking me to the one place I've already been and will perform in tomorrow?"

"I told you. It's safe and quiet. No Ingrid Flockton fangirls or boys allowed," he says, then winks. "Well, maybe one, but you reached out to me, and I brought food." He then holds up a plastic card. "As a senior and alternate captain, I have a keycard, which gives me access twenty-four seven."

I snort, thinking of the private clubs I've been to, the exclusive memberships. "I'm not sure that's as impressive as you think it is."

He leads me around the back of a wide brick building with a heavy metal door that clicks open when he swipes a card. It's a different entry point than where I came in earlier with Madison and Marv, and a part of me notes that I should point out the breach before the concert tomorrow. But then I'd have to admit why I know about this and decide to file it away for later.

Inside, the hallway smells like leather, cleaning supplies, and that heavy scent that can only be identified as testosterone. I was here six hours ago, doing mic checks and sound tests, pacing the stage in platform boots while Madison fought with lighting techs, and I pretended my chest wasn't tight just being there. I remember thinking it felt too *echoey*, too impersonal. But now, peering through the glass window that looks into the space, without the stage lights and thumping sound systems, it feels different. Still. Dim. Almost like the place is holding its breath.

Jefferson continues past the rink, that I know is now covered with flooring and a stage. Instead, he leads me through a side hallway and into a room labeled *Lounge*. It's nothing fancy–a couple of couches, a scratched-up air hockey table, a vending machine missing most of its candy, and a big screen TV that takes up the majority of the back wall. He gestures to the couch. "Welcome to the inner sanctum."

"Very elite," I murmur, collapsing onto the cushions with a grateful sigh. "Smells like body spray and victory."

"More like sweat and Febreze," he admits, walking over to a refrigerator and opening the door. The inside is filled with water and sports drinks. He grabs two water bottles and sets them on the table, then sits next to me. "But we've had a hell of a run. A few more days and we'll go down in the history books as either winners or losers."

Something tells me Jefferson Parks doesn't like losing.

He opens the bag and starts handing me food. I unwrap the burger and it's just like he said, double cheeseburger, bacon, avocado, the works–and it smells absurdly good.

"Holy shit," I say around the first bite, barely managing not to groan. "This is... dangerous."

Seriously. I think my mouth is having an orgasm.

"I'm not stupid. You want to impress a goddess, you show up with the best food in town."

I give him a look. "You call every girl you meet a goddess?"

He grins. "Only the ones who sell out stadiums and make me feel things I didn't know songs could make me feel."

My cheeks warm under the hoodie, and I look down at the fries like they've suddenly become fascinating.

"How long have you been listening?" I ask even though I know it's tricky territory. One wrong word and this whole fantasy dissolves.

He shrugs, then leans back, chewing a huge bite of food. Everything about him is big. His jaw, his hands, his legs stretched out into the room. "Since I was fifteen. Your first album. A girl I had a crush on played it nonstop, and at first, I wanted to stab myself in the ear–"

"Talk about ouch."

"But," he continues, "after a while, I started listening to the words. I'd go sit outside in my brother's Jeep and put *Lace & Lead* on repeat until I knew every line. It just felt like, I don't know, you knew how to put all those feelings into words. Like the songs got there before I did."

I stare at him, stunned by the honesty in his voice.

Most guys either fanboy too hard or pretend they've never heard of me.

Jefferson Parks isn't trying to do either.

He's just here, telling me his story.

"What about you?" he asks, like it's his turn. "What made you want to do this? Music?"

I chew slowly, then swallow. "It wasn't a choice, really. I mean, I've always loved it. Writing. Performing. I was that kid who sang in the mirror and cried at bad commercials. But it's also, I guess, what I was good at, even when I was younger. It made sense when everything else didn't."

"And now?" He takes another bite.

"Now I'm *really* good at it. Maybe the best in my generation," I admit with zero pretense. The downloads, the album sales, the merch, and sold-out venues... I don't have to prove myself. It's all there in black and white.

"But..."

Our eyes meet. I can tell in this light that his are a bluish gray. "But, I'm just not sure I *like* it all the time."

"Too much pressure?" He asks like he understands it.

"Sometimes. Maybe more like, there's too much noise," I say. "Everyone wants something. Everyone's always watching. Waiting for you to slip. Sometimes I just want to go out for a burger without someone selling the photo five minutes later."

"Well," he says, "Since I'm supposed to be getting ready for the biggest games in my career, the last thing I need is for someone, primarily my captain or coach, to know where I am and what I'm eating–so no cameras. Your secret is safe with me."

I smile. "You're not what I expected."

"Let me guess," he says. "You thought I was some loud-mouthed jock hoping for a selfie and a blowjob?"

I snort-laugh so hard I almost choke on my fry. "Pretty much."

"I mean," he chuckles, reaching for his drink, "I wouldn't say no, but I'm not just that."

"No?"

"No. I'm incredibly skilled at *giving* oral, not just receiving, I'm remarkably humble, and," his head tilts toward the game table, "I'm very good at air hockey."

At the oral comment, I choke on my water. This guy. His ego is massive, possibly the biggest I've ever encountered, which says a lot coming from the industry I'm in and the men I've been exposed to over the last decade.

"Remarkably humble," I repeat, plucking a fry between my manicured nails.

The room feels warmer. Closer. Like we've carved out this little bubble of unreality.

"You gonna sing *Lace and Lead* tomorrow?" he asks, quieter this time.

I nod. "It's on the set list."

"I can't believe I'm missing it." Something flickers across his face–disappointment, maybe. Then he leans in just slightly, not enough to scare me, just enough to make my breath catch. "I guess you'll just have to play it for me another time."

$$4$$

J efferson

"You were right," she says as I walk her back to the hotel, our shoulders brushing every few steps, "you are very good at air hockey."

A normal guy would have let the woman he's interested in win, but I'm not a normal guy. I put myself out there. You either take Jefferson Parks for who he is, or you don't.

That being said, I can't tell if Ingrid likes me. Not yet.

Me? Well, my pulse is doing this stupid pounding thing, like I just took a slap shot to the chest. I want to kiss her. Hell, I want to do *way* more than kiss her. I'm living out a decade of locker room daydreams, and late night jerk off sessions. She's right here, laughing at my dumb jokes and stealing my fries like she's not the most famous woman I've ever breathed next to.

Like she's not Ingrid Flockton. Number one on my sex list.

For once, my brain is working better than my dick. Because as much as I want to press her up against any and every available surface to show her just how not-boyfriend-material I *could* be... I know better.

Ingrid may be famous. She may be experienced. But she's also ready to run at the first wrong move. Tonight is a one-off for her. A fun little escapade so she can still feel alive. But it's not real. I can feel it in the way she smiles too quickly, in the way she glances over her shoulder like she's keeping tally of every exit.

And if I want more than just dinner and a walk across campus–if I want *her*–I've gotta play it right.

"Okay, I've got one," she starts, "pre-game superstitions. Do you have any?"

We've been going back and forth like this all night. Comparing our lives. Ingrid's a mega-rich and famous rockstar. I'm a popular hockey player on my way to the NHL. Is it even? No, but there are still some things in common, and she's right, superstitions are part of it.

"I have a few," I admit. "Nothing drastic like when Axel grew a pornstash earlier in the season during our winning streak." I grin, thinking about our goalie and his horrific facial hair. I'll give it to him, he committed. "But yeah, I have a lucky pair of socks, and my mom always texts me before the game, and..."

"And what?"

We're walking down the sidewalk, and I glance over at her. "No sex the day of the game."

"Seriously?"

I shrug. "Yep."

"Wow. Okay."

"What about you?" I've slowed, trying to keep this night from ending. "Any pre-show rituals?"

"Of course," she says, her pace easing to meet mine. "No speaking for six hours before the show–"

"To anyone?"

She shakes her head. "No one. Not even Madison–my best friend and assistant," she clarifies. "I have to protect my voice."

"Makes sense." We step off a curb and cross the road. The hotel lights are in the distance. "Anything else?"

"Cherry and pineapple gummy bears."

"Oh," I laugh. "Got it."

"What?" she tilts her head.

"You're one of those musicians. A diva."

She rolls her eyes, but the little smirk on her red lips tells me she doesn't mind the title. We're a half block from the hotel, and with every step I'm trying to work out how I'm going to leave this night, when she suddenly tugs on my sleeve.

"Listen–"

Before I can finish, she pulls me down a narrow side street, her hand tight on my wrist. It's darker here, quiet, the buzz of streetlights fading behind us. She spins, presses me back against the brick wall. She's so tall. Confident. Then her hot, soft lips are against mine, and she kisses me like she's trying to erase everything else–like she's starving and I'm the only thing left to eat.

It knocks the goddamn breath out of me, and Jesus, I want more.

When she finally pulls back, I'm blinking like I forgot how to use my eyes.

"What was that for?" I ask, voice low and hoarse. My cock twitches on my thigh.

She licks her lips, thumb brushing my jaw like she's memorizing the shape of me. "Because I wanted to."

Then she steps back like she didn't just short-circuit every working part of my body. And I swear–if she turns around and walks into that hotel like nothing happened, I might actually pass out right here in this alley.

She smirks like she's got the upper hand–and fucking hell, she does. "Just a kiss goodnight," she says. "You know... the end to a really fun, unexpected night."

My eyebrows lift. "'Fun' is one word for it. Doesn't have to end here, you know."

She doesn't take the bait, just smooths her hoodie over those long legs and gives me that pop star smirk. That untouchable look I've seen her give a hundred times on stage or in magazines. Except this time it's aimed right at me. And yeah, it does things.

"So that's all this is," I say, my hand trailing casually up and down her arm, thumb brushing the inside of her wrist like maybe I can flip the switch back on.

She nods once. "That's all this is."

There it is. No hotel invitation. No 'wanna come up?' Not even a suggestive wink. Just the cold, hard truth wrapped in a hot, soft package.

She steps back, already in motion. "Don't walk me the rest of the way," she says. "I don't need a headline in the morning."

Message received.

I raise both hands like I'm innocent–even though I'm very much not. "Wouldn't dream of it."

She turns, but before she gets more than a step away, I grab her wrist. "One more," I say, already leaning in and yanking that hoodie off, revealing her lavender hair.

The first kiss was hers, but this one is mine. I take it slow and cocky, like I'm trying to brand it in her memory. My hand cups the side of her neck, fingers in her hair, body lined up with hers like I've got nothing to lose–which I don't. We're in overtime, the clock is winding down, and like I've practiced for years, I'm taking the goddamn shot.

Thank Christ, she kisses me back, just enough tongue and teeth to make it sting when she finally pulls away with a soft exhale. That feeling in my pants? It's way more than a twitch. We've gone full hard-on.

"Thanks for the night out, Jefferson," she says, fingers slipping away from mine. "And good luck."

Then she's gone. Hood up, back across the street, slipping into the lobby of her fancy-ass hotel like we didn't just make out in an alley like two drunk college kids.

I watch her go, not even pretending to look away.

Yeah, when I reached out to her, I was hoping I'd end the night with a little more than a kiss. Thought maybe I'd get to notch the infamous Ingrid Flockton off my very short, very exclusive list. But weirdly, I'm not that pissed.

She was fun. Hot. Smart as hell. And even though I didn't get the ending I wanted, I still feel like I won something, even if I didn't win the game.

BY THE TIME we pull up to the team hotel in Chicago, I'm in the final three songs of Ingrid's last concert. Her fans record them in full and then upload them on socials so that everyone who wasn't there can watch the spectacle. And fuck me if she isn't a firecracker in those sequined thigh-high boots and sweeping dresses strutting across the stage.

Even though I'm fully immersed in the woman, I do successfully push every intrusive-ass thought about last night out of my head. How I had *one* shot and blew it.

Sure, I got to meet her and spend a little time with her, but I didn't seal the deal on the one thing I wanted most of all: crossing her off my list.

Turning off the video, I let Emerson, crammed in the seat across from mine, chirp about strategy for our first game tomorrow. I even allow Pete to fall asleep on my shoulder without elbowing him in the face.

Axel stretches as we unload, his shirt riding up to reveal the dark ink all over his lower abdomen. He looks around like we're about to hit the town for a night out instead of checking into a basic-ass hotel set up by the league. "Man, Chicago's got that energy," he says, inhaling deep.

"I feel like anywhere has more energy than the Texas suburbs," I say, reminding him of where he's from. His father is the preacher of a mega-church called Kingdom. He was set up to be the next in line before he finally told his controlling, dominating father to fuck the hell off.

I'm from LA, or just outside. My dad is in tech, a programmer who designed a system that only he knows how to implement. My mom is an artist–her medium is paint and collage. I'm used to big cities, but Chicago does have it's own vibe.

Axel laughs, slaps me on the back, and disappears into the hotel lobby with Reid and Emerson, already trying to figure out where they can grab deep dish pizza the size of their heads. Coach Bryant gave us tonight free, but curfew's locked for tomorrow. Not that it matters. We didn't come here for the pizza and nightlife.

We came here to win.

I grab my duffel and head inside with Reese, who's more focused on his phone than his feet. I don't even need to ask who he's texting.

"Twyler, I assume," I say, eyeing the little smirk tugging at his mouth.

"She just wanted to make sure we got in okay," he says, not bothering to hide the fact that he's so whipped for this girl he can barely see straight. "She gets nervous before big games."

"She gets nervous before *your* big games," I point out. "You're the one playing."

He shrugs. "Yeah. But she's invested."

That's one word for it. Twyler has been invested in Wittmore Hockey since she was assigned to the team for her training internship. She's been invested in *Reese* since the day they fake-kissed their way into a full-on relationship. My boy didn't just fall for the tomboy trainer. He jumped head, dick, and heart first.

The team's rooms are on the tenth floor, double queens, same setup we've had for every away game since freshman year. I throw my bag on the bed closest to the window, and Reese takes the one near the bathroom. Automatic at this point. No words needed.

"You think Coach'll go with the same line rotations tomorrow?" I ask while he kicks off his shoes.

"Probably," he says, pulling out his laptop. "Unless he's hiding a secret weapon we haven't seen yet."

"Doubt it," I snort. "You're the weapon, and it's not a secret."

He grins. I'm not wrong.

Unlike our power forward and star scorer, my job's not flashy. I'm not the guy with the most points or a highlight reel full of toe-drags and bar-down snipes. But you need someone to protect the puck? To clear the crease? To slam someone into the glass so hard they forget which way the bench is? That's me.

Every team needs a hammer. I just happen to be one in skates.

Reese flops onto his bed and flips open the laptop. I already know what he's doing, pulling up the latest film Coach Bryant sent over. He'll probably watch it ten times before he goes to bed. That's why he's the captain and the number one prospect at graduation. "You ever think about what happens after this? Like, after we win?"

"After we win?" I ask, arching a brow. "Not if?"

He shrugs again. "Confidence. Twyler says manifesting is important."

Jesus Christ.

"I'm hoping I'll be drowning in puck bunny pussy," I reply, since my one shot with my dream girl was a bust. "Women love victory." He rolls his eyes, but it wasn't that long ago that he was sowing his oats all over campus and would have been thinking the same thing. I stretch out on my bed, letting my muscles relax. "But I'm not thinking about that right now. One game at a time."

Reese nods, but there's a glint in his eye. He's not done. "You ever think about more than hockey? You know, in the future."

I look over. "You want me to say I'm gonna find a nice girl and settle down like you?"

"Couldn't hurt," he says with a grin. "One day, maybe?"

"Unlikely."

And I mean it. It's not that I *can't* be that guy. I just have no interest in becoming him.

My parents have been married since they met at Berkley. On paper, they're the dream team–Dad's the owner of his own tech business, works from home, controls his hours, doesn't own a suit. Mom's got that hippie vibe, her hands always covered in paint or ink. They've got money, stability, but the one thing they don't have? A single fucking thing in common.

I grew up watching them orbit around each other like two distant planets. Vacations where they never spent a minute together, each of them splitting off to their respective interests. My dad loves the outdoors and playing golf. My mom, museums and galleries. For as long as I can remember, they have acted more like roommates, not a couple.

Love? Commitment? Marriage?

That shit looks like a trap wrapped in a lifetime of monotony.

So no, I don't do girlfriends. I don't play house. If possible, I don't even bring them home. I've had plenty of hookups–sorority girls, puck bunnies, the occasional TA who should've known better. I don't promise anything. I don't text the next day. I don't let it get messy.

And last night?

I definitely don't *regret* it, but I'm not sitting here daydreaming about what could've been. It was a moment. A hot, unexpected, kind of unforgettable moment with a woman who's probably about to walk out on stage now. We kissed. It was good. Better than good. But she made it clear where the line was drawn, and I respect that.

Because that's all it was.

And honestly, I'm surprised at how okay I am with it.

Reese is back on his phone, probably updating Twyler on what kind of socks he packed. I pull out my headphones and queue up the same film Reese has open–Coach sent it to all of us. My mind shifts away from last night, back to the rink, to strategy, to faceoffs and power plays. I let the buzz of anticipation settle into my chest.

Tomorrow, it's game time.

And whatever that night was?

It's already behind me.

5

———————

I ngrid

The tour schedule gave us a rare breather today. No travel. No meet-and-greets. Just a wide, blessed window of silence. It's the chance to sleep in, answer emails, get in a little vocal rest, and maybe take a bath that doesn't jostle with every pothole like it does on the tour bus.

But something else kept me in Wittmore.

Hockey.

I'm used to fanbases. I have a massive one of my own, but just being in Wittmore exposed me to the fervor of the energy around college hockey. At the show last night, there were just as many hockey jerseys on the fans as there was Ingrid Flockton merch. The business side of me wants to know a little bit more.

And the girl who kissed Jefferson Parks two nights ago?

Well, maybe she wants to know a little bit more about the man who lit my skin on fire.

That's how I end up texting Mads, telling her to get dressed and to meet me downstairs. She didn't ask questions, showed up just as ready to get out of the hotel as I am.

"How did you find this place?" she asks after we're settled in a booth in the back of the Badger Den. Marv had plowed through the rowdy crowd, creating a path to get us to the booth. He came in early and spoke to the owner, who was happy to save a spot for us. There are TV screens hanging for every angle, but the largest is a massive screen above the bar playing pregame commentary for the Frozen Four semi-final. All eyes are on the TV. Except mine.

Mine are on the laminated menu, but my brain isn't really registering the words. It's replaying a kiss over and over, to the point that I think I may have a problem.

"Ing." Madison snaps me back to the present. "How did you find this place?"

"Oh, I just googled the best hamburgers in Wittmore and had one delivered to the hotel last night." It's shocking how easily that lie comes out. "Seriously, though, this hamburger is to die for. I've been craving it for two days."

I've been craving more of Jefferson Parks since the moment we said goodnight. That kiss. God. I've had guys kiss me. I've had guys who wanted something from me, but this was different. It was all heat and rough fingertips, the scrape of his jaw against mine, the firm hold of his hand under my chin, tilting my head exactly where he wanted it.

His other hand had been around my waist, but barely. Like he was holding himself back from grabbing me fully, throwing me over his shoulder caveman-style. There was a moment–just a flicker–where I thought he might, and the way my entire body responded was... intense.

And yeah. I noticed. The way he pressed up against me, the very obvious, *very hard and defined* evidence of just how badly he wanted me. He didn't try to hide it. That did something to me. Something Jake never did.

Jake always made me feel like a chore. Like loving me was just this... inconvenience. Like he was doing me a favor. I had to tiptoe around his moods, practically audition for affection. When we were together, it felt like being halfway underwater all the time, like if I spoke too loudly or wanted too much, he'd just let me drown.

Jefferson made me feel the opposite. Seen. Desired. Powerful.

And that was just from sharing dinner and a kiss.

The concert last night had been electric. My voice felt smoother, my body lighter, my moves more natural. I swear, the whole thing had this extra charge. Like kissing Jefferson flipped a breaker inside me. A man like that–big, cocky, a little dangerous–I can't help but wonder what it would feel like to go all the way. Would it leave me glowing like that again? Or completely wrecked?

Either option sounds great, honestly.

Our waitress shows up just as Wittmore hits the ice. She's cute, in a down-to-earth way, with a long blond braid, black leggings, and a Wittmore hockey jersey. Her green eyes are wide–fangirl wide–and she bites down on her bottom lip.

"I'm Shelby," her voice wobbles, "and I'll be your server." Then in a low rush she adds, "But can I just say that I love you and your music. I was at the show last night and it was incredible. And I promise not to act weird, but I just needed to say something so that I could get it out of the way and we could move on."

I laugh. "It's fine. And I'm glad you enjoyed the show."

She bounces on her toes a little. "It was so great. Amazing really." She breathes in and exhales. "Okay, would you like to hear our specials? I think–"

She turns, flashing the back of her jersey.

"Rakestraw-slash-Wilder?" Madison asks, amused. "What, couldn't pick just one?"

The girl rolls her eyes playfully. "That's my brother *and* my boyfriend. My brother made this because, as he says, 'family comes first.'"

She uses finger quotes, and Madison barks out a laugh, but my ears perk up. Rakestraw and Wilder. I know those names.

Jefferson mentioned a few of his roommates in passing the other night. "So who's who? Your boyfriend and your brother?"

"Axel Rakestraw is my older brother. I moved out here about a month ago and have been staying with him." Her cheeks get a little pink. "But Reid Wilder is my boyfriend."

"You didn't want to go to the game?" Madison asks, nodding at the TV. "It looks like a blast."

"They told us not to come unless they make the finals. Superstition or whatever. So now we just sit here and 'manifest.'"

"'We'?" I ask, lifting a brow.

She tips her head toward a high-top table near the window. Two girls sit perched on stools, both leaning forward, eyes glued to the game. They're in full Wittmore gear.

"That's Twyler," she points to a cute girl with a dark ponytail. "She dates Reese Cain, captain of the team. And Nadia is my brother's girlfriend."

I take in her friend. Her shirt is low cut, tits straining at the V, but the name across the back is definitive: RAKESTRAW 01.

"We've formed a bit of a weird support group."

A support group for girls who love hockey players.

"Oh," Madison says. "You're WAGs."

Wives and girlfriends of athletes. The college version at least.

My eyes skip between the three of them for a moment. How normal they look, sitting in this bar, dressed up to support their men. Like, they *own* this part of their life instead of avoiding it.

Jake never even came to my shows, and he absolutely refused to walk a red carpet.

Mads notices my silence. "You okay?"

"Yeah," I lie, turning back to the menu. "Just hungry."

She gives me a long look, but doesn't push it. And I'm relieved to change the subject by ordering. Shelby scribbles mine down, then grins. "That's funny–our friend Jefferson orders the same thing every time. Burger, bacon, avocado, and crispy onions on top. The kitchen started calling it the Jefferson Parks Special."

My stomach flips.

Madison perks up. "Wait–who's Jefferson Parks?"

I manage a casual shrug, masking the flush in my cheeks. "Just one of their players, right?" My voice is breezy, but my chest pounds. What if she figures it out? That I met up with him two nights ago?

"You know, he'd freak out if he knew you ordered this. He's a huge fan."

I wait a beat, but if she knows anything, if Jefferson told her anything that happened between us, she doesn't let on and excuses herself to go drop off our order.

"I think this is a first," Madison says after taking a sip of water.

"What's a first?"

"That we've been out and people are more interested in a game on TV than you."

I laugh, but she's not wrong. The bar is so involved in the game that no one even notices us. It's nice and it's not long before I find myself drawn in, trying to follow it on the big screen. The puck moves so fast I can barely keep track of it, bouncing off the ice and boards-sometimes the guys themselves. The players speed across the ice on skates the way I own the stage in a pair of six-inch heels.

It's powerful. Magnetic. And my eyes desperately search for one name and number.

#23 Parks

The energy shifts in the room and I try to follow what's happening on the ice. Across from us the girl with the ponytail jumps to her feet.

"Oh, come *on!*" she shouts, loud enough that half the bar glances over. "You've *got* to crash the net there. Soft rebound like that and you're backing off?"

She throws her hands up, her dark curls bouncing with the motion, then presses her palms to the table like she's physically restraining herself from climbing over it. Nadia, across from her, doesn't even flinch–she's focused, arms crossed, chewing at her straw while her eyes track the puck like a hawk.

From our table, I glance at Madison. She blinks, lost.

"I need that girl over here to explain what the hell is going on," Madison mutters.

As if summoned, Shelby returns with a steaming basket of fries.

She sets them down between us with a dramatic flair, right as the buzzer goes off to signal the end of the first period.

Madison reaches for a fry and gestures toward Twyler and Nadia with her other hand. "Do you think your friends would want to sit with us? Maybe help us understand what we're watching?"

Shelby's green eyes go wide. "You want *Twyler* to join you during a game?" she whispers, like it's a dare. Then she bites her lip, clearly thrilled, and spins on her heel. "Give me one minute."

I watch her bounce over to their table and lean in between them. She says something low, and both girls freeze. Then Twyler whips her head around, mouth slightly open in disbelief, like she's making sure we're really talking about *them*.

Nadia arches a brow, skeptical but curious.

Twyler shrugs, grabs her cider and half-eaten hot dog, and nods toward us. "Guess we're relocating," I hear her say, as she picks up her tray.

Nadia follows with an amused smile, sliding her phone into her back pocket.

We make quick introductions, and although they seem to know me, they don't have a fangirl freak out, and I'm instantly at ease.

Twyler grins as she sits down beside Madison. "Sorry in advance. I get a little...invested."

"No problem," Madison says, shifting to make room.

"I just don't believe in letting injustice go unaddressed," Twyler replies, eyes narrowing at the overhead screen as they show a slow-motion replay of a hit. "Case in point–see that? That should've been a five-minute major. Guy *led* with the elbow."

Nadia takes the open seat beside me. "Reese is a big boy. He can take a few hits."

"Of course he can. It's not the hit. It's the principal!"

There's something electric about the way they join the table, like the volume clicks up a notch, the energy shifts. Even Madison softens, watching the two girls bicker playfully about power plays versus penalty kills. I find myself leaning in too, drawn by the easy knowledge and total lack of pretense.

"So wait." Madison asks, "What *is* a power play again?"

Nadia opens her mouth to answer, but Twyler cuts her off.

"Okay, so imagine you're in a horror movie," Twyler says, brandishing a fry like a knife. "There's a serial killer on the loose—"

"Oh my god," Nadia groans. "Why is it *always* murder with you?"

"Because it *works*," Twyler insists. "So there's five players on each side, right? But then one does something illegal–like, I don't know, stabs someone with their stick–and they get sent to the penalty box."

"Okay, I'm listening," Madison says, raising an eyebrow.

"So now it's five versus four. One team is down a player, think of them as trapped in a closet while the killer's roaming free. The team with all five? They're on the power play. They're supposed to strike fast, take the advantage. But sometimes?" She shrugs, leaning back. "They just creep around, wasting time like they forgot what movie they're in."

"That... actually helped," Madison says slowly, like she's still processing the details.

"Thanks," Twyler says, smug. "Now imagine overtime like a standoff with Michael Meyers..."

"Don't," Nadia warns. "Just eat your fries."

By the time the second period starts, we've rearranged the table. The fries are mostly gone, Nadia ordered nachos, and Twyler has claimed narrator rights to the entire game.

"Okay, so that's Wittmore in white, obviously. That's our goalie. Axel, number 01," she says with the camera pans over him in the goal. "His saves are epic, and he uses his body like he's a wall. Then you've got Reese, our captain, number 15. He's the one flying up the ice right now–total beast in transition."

"Not to mention Twyler's boyfriend," Nadia says.

The camera flashes a still photo of him on the screen along with his stats. He's incredibly goodlooking.

"Which one is Shelby's boyfriend?" Madison asks.

"Number eight. He's a defender," Twyler says, then points to Nadia's jersey. "He also designed that logo on her shirt."

I've seen the little retro style badger on different shirts since I've been here and a big display at the arena. I nod in approval. "He's talented."

"Oh, and that's Jefferson, number 23, playing right wing. Best hands on the team, easy." I catch the flicker of Jefferson on the screen and try to play it cool. Just a quick flash of him chasing the puck along the boards, but my body remembers too much.

"He's always so laid back," Twyler continues, "but don't let that fool you. He's brutal on the ice. Smart, fast, good with the puck–but he's also not afraid to throw down if he has to."

"He's a total charmer, too," Nadia adds with a roll of her eyes. "He's slept with, like, half the campus. But somehow, no one stays mad at him."

"Total fuckboy," Twyler says, fist tightening at a missed shot. "But Nadia's right, everyone loves him."

Part of me doesn't want to hear that. The other part, stupidly, already knew.

The game is intense. Wittmore is fast, brutal, relentless. The crowd in the bar roars with every goal, and when the final buzzer sounds with Wittmore up 4–2, the place explodes.

Shelby runs over with a scream and jumps into Nadia's arms, beer sloshing slightly from her glass. Twyler beams, her grin wide and pure joy. Everyone's celebrating. Cheering. It feels infectious.

I lean back against the booth, watching it all unfold. My burger is half-eaten, forgotten in the excitement.

"They move on, right?" I ask.

"Yup," Twyler says, breathless. "Next game's in two days–the Regional Finals."

Up on the screen, the camera man flashes to the guys celebrating on the ice.

I know this feeling.

The flood of adrenaline after a flawless set. The lights, the screams, the way your body hums for hours after you've given them everything and they gave it right back. That's what winning feels like. That's what it *does* to you.

I catch a familiar grin, Jefferson's cocky smirk, his helmet is off, his blond hair, now dark, soaked with sweat. He pulls a teammate into a hug and yells something the mic can't pick up, but I don't need to hear his words.

He feels it, too. That high. The rush. The fire of being on top and knowing you *earned* it.

And suddenly, there's something sharp and hot in the center of my chest.

Jefferson Parks loves winning as much as I do.

6

Jefferson

THE PLACE IS BUZZING—SHOULDER to shoulder with fans from the game, all riding the high of our win. Every table is packed, the bar is three deep, and the air smells like beer, sweat, and victory. Feels fucking good.

There's no actual drinking allowed, not this close to the finals. The food is greasy and hits the spot after burning thousands of calories on the ice. Most of the team is mingling with a fresh group of puck bunnies since we're not on our home turf. These are expert level bunnies, willing to come out for the Championship, happy to help celebrate our win.

I said *most* of the team. Reese, Reid, and Axel are tucked into a booth with overflowing baskets of food in front of them and wide-ass grins. No girls on their laps, no numbers being handed over, nothing but the sound of their laughter echoing under the music and clinking glasses. Whipped bastards. I tease them for it, naturally.

"Remember when you used to be fun?" I nudge Axel as I pass by.

He just flips me off and raises a chicken wing. "Remember when you weren't jealous?"

I smirk. "Jealous? Of your missionary sex and lack of mystery?"

"Monogamy's good for the soul," Reese chimes in with that smug, post-win glow.

"Maybe," I say, stretching. "But while you're doomed for a night of rubbing off to phone sex, I'm going to have the real deal."

They don't care. They're content with their relationships–safe with the thought of their girls back home. Me? I've got a little more energy to burn.

I weave through the crowd, letting the heat of the room settle into my skin. There's no shortage of hot women in the bar tonight–smiles flashing, eyes lingering. One of them slides into step beside me at the bar. Tall, blonde, clearly knows what she's doing. Her elbow brushes mine and she leans in close enough to smell her shampoo.

"You're one of the players, right? Enforcer." Her eyes drop to my lips and then back up. "Parks."

"That's me." I love being recognized. Especially by beautiful women.

"I saw the game. You guys crushed it."

"Yeah, we did."

She orders a drink and turns fully toward me, her body language loud and clear. Her dress is tight, her perfume expensive, her smile practiced. She's exactly the kind of girl who'd look good in my bed and slip out before breakfast. Low effort, clean break. Exactly what I was hunting tonight.

Then I notice it, when she lifts her glass, a fine-line tattoo peeks out beneath the strap of her top. A single feather, light and delicate against her skin.

It's not just any feather.

It's *that* feather.

Same one that's inked on Ingrid Flockton's tour posters, merch, album covers. Subtle, sure, but anyone who's ever lined up outside one of her concerts would know it. I sure as hell do.

My brain flashes back to Ingrid's body pressed against mine in that dark little corner of the street, the taste of heat on her tongue. How I was after that kiss.

Fuck.

I haven't messaged her since that night. Not because I didn't want to. I've opened that thread a dozen times. Typed things. Deleted them. She's famous. I'm a college hockey player. We live in different galaxies, and it's not like I expect her to orbit into mine.

The girl beside me takes a step closer. "So... want to find somewhere a little more private?"

Her voice is soft, her hand already brushing against my chest.

The 'yes,' is on the top of my tongue, but right as I open my mouth, my phone buzzes in my back pocket.

I check it without thinking.

IngFlock: Congrats on the game tonight.

Everything inside me pauses.

The room doesn't, but I do. The noise fades, the voice of the girl standing with me blurs, the heat between us cools in an instant. That message: simple, casual, *timed to perfection*, slices through the haze I've been chasing all night.

She was watching?

I look down at the message again. One little line has just opened the door to a hundred possibilities.

And suddenly, the last thing I want is a forgettable night with someone whose name I won't remember.

"I should get back to my team," I tell the girl, stepping away.

She pouts. "You sure?"

"Yeah." I slide my phone back in my pocket. "Something just came up."

When it's clear I'm not going to budge, she turns on her heel and heads over to a group of my teammates hanging by the bar. I cross the room and slide back into the booth.

"Did she blow you off?" Reid asks with a snicker.

"No," I state firmly. "She was DTF. I just realized that I've got a lifetime to screw around with puck bunnies and only a few more nights like this with you guys."

Reese grins. "You love us."

"So much," Axel adds, throwing his tattooed arm over my shoulder and giving me a side hug.

"It's okay, big guy," Reid winks, "we love you too."

TWO DAYS LATER, I'm sitting on the edge of a bench in the locker room, scrolling my phone as my teammates get ready for the game. Puck drop is in forty-five minutes. The energy in the room, a combination of pent up adrenaline and nerves, is overwhelming. One step closer to that Frozen Four title, baby.

Me? I don't do nervous, so I busy myself scrolling back over the messages from the last forty-eight hours, a stupid grin tugging at my mouth.

Jparks23: Does that mean you were watching?

IngFlock: Popped my hockey cherry.

I'd stared at that for a full minute before firing back.

Jparks23: How was it? For a first time.

IngFlock: Not as awkward as I expected. Little rough around the edges, but I was screaming by the end.

Jparks23: Wish I could've been there to see it.

The messages have spanned the past few days. The two of us firing off little shots while I've navigated practices, workouts and watching the other games. Ingrid was busy traveling by tour bus across the midwest.

Jparks23: When's your next show?

IngFlock: Tomorrow. Minneapolis. Too bad you can't come and pop *your* cherry.

Jparks23: Oh, sweetheart, I popped my Ingrid Flockton cherry a long time ago.

IngFlock: You've been to a concert?

Jparks23: Not that kind of cherry.

IngFlock: I'm listening…

Jparks23: I lost my virginity to one of your songs.

There was a pause long enough for me to wonder if I'd gone too far. Fuck.

IngFlock: Which song?

Jparks23: You'll have to guess.

IngFlock: Velvet Skin?

Jparks23: Nope.

IngFlock: Honey Drip.

I smile. That would have been a good one.

Jparks23: Wrong.

She kept trying, four more guesses, each one a miss. I learned one thing about Ingrid, she loves playing games too.

The last text came in an hour ago. A simple, *Good luck.*

I close the phone and center myself on the present. How the air smells like tape adhesive, menthol rub, and damp gear. A low bass line from Reid's speaker thumps under the chatter.

Across the room, Axel is taping his stick, head down in concentration, until he glances up. "Who are you texting nonstop? That phone's been glued to your hand since we got here."

I smirk, shoving it into my duffel. "Your mama."

He groans and rolls his eyes. "Original. My mother would eat you alive, spit you out, and then read Bible verses to you until you begged to be put out of your misery"

If he's waiting for a real answer, he's shit out of luck. I pull my jersey over my pads, tugging it down until it sits just right on my shoulders. My gloves hang open on the bench next to me, the palms worn in so they feel like a second skin.

I'm not just keeping this from Axel, I'm not telling any of them. Not about meeting Ingrid. Not about the kiss. Not about the late-night texts that make it hard to focus on anything else. Even if I did tell them, even if they *believed* me, the ribbing I would get would be merciless.

Hard pass.

The door opens and Coach Bryant steps in, clapping his hands once, loud, sharp.

"All right, men, settle down. This is it. You've been working for this moment all season. Some of you are here for the first time. A few others," his eyes flit over to Reese, "are here for a second chance. Whatever the reason, we're here to win it. Forty minutes at a time, all gas, no brakes. You play *our* game, and nobody's taking this from you."

"Hell no they aren't!" Reese shouts, rising up to set the tone as our captain. He's a good leader. A good man. I'm lucky to have played with him and call him a friend.

The rest of the team builds on that energy. Heads nodding, gloves slapping against knees. Axel yells, "Let's go!"

I roll my shoulders, feeling the weight of the pads, the stretch of the jersey.

As I stand, Coach Green, our trainer, passes by, gives my shoulder a quick, firm check. "Ready, Parks?"

"Always," I tell him, mouth curling into that game-time grin.

The tunnel to the ice is waiting. And for the first time in a long time, I'm feeling like I've got more than one kind of win to chase.

I STARE DOWN at center ice, hyper aware that we're in the third period, five minutes left.

We're up by one, but it's not enough. Not against Central.

It falls in a blink, but Reese takes the draw, wins it clean, snaps the puck back to Reid. I'm already in motion, cutting down the right side, looking for an opening. Reid feeds it to Emerson, who threads it across the neutral zone to me.

I take the pass on my blade, skate hard, and hear the crunch of their winger chasing me down. Dropping a shoulder, I fake the dump, and slide it behind me to Reese, because fuck yes, he's got a lane. He rips a shot from the top of the circle and it soars–

Clang. Off the post.

The rebound's chaos–sticks, skates, bodies colliding. I'm in the thick of it, trying to muscle their defenseman, Lennox, off the puck. He throws an elbow and I take it hard in the ribs.

Wrong move.

"Is that how you want it?" I ask, shoving him back, hard enough his helmet rattles. The puck squirts free, Emerson dives for it–but the ref's whistle cuts through everything. The game, the guys, the crowd, screeching to a halt.

"Twenty-three! Roughing!"

My stick hits the ice in frustration. "Come on! He–"

"Box. Now."

The refs don't give a shit that we're this close. This close to moving on. *This close* to taking the whole goddamn thing.

I skate to the penalty box with my blood running hot, adrenaline still tearing through my chest. The crowd's a blur of black, gold, and waving signs. Axel gives me a look from the crease–half 'calm down,' half 'good hit.'

I don't even dare look at Coach, although I can hear him. He's pissed. Both at me and the ref. At the risk. I drop onto the hard bench, lean my stick against the wall, and tug my helmet up. My eyes drift toward the premium seats as a distraction.

Wait. What the hell?

There's no mistaking Twyler, although I'm still not used to seeing her in the stands and not down with the players, icing muscles and wrapping sprains with our head trainer, Coach Green, by the bench. She's not supposed to be here. Neither are Nadia, *or* Shelby.

Yet there they are, crammed into prime seats, dressed out in Reid's Wittmore designs. Twyler's yelling something I can't make out– probably cursing me to hell and back for taking the penalty. Nadia's nervously shoving popcorn in her mouth, while Shelby leans close to her. On the far end another girl leans forward in a heavy black coat and black stocking cap that has a gold pompom on top.

Lavender hair spills out from underneath.

She's angled like she doesn't want anyone to see her face.

But I see her. Holy fuck, I see her. I drag my eyes back to the game, attempting to focus on the biggest moment of my life and not the woman in the stands.

Try, and fucking fail. She came to my game. She's sitting there in the cold glow of the rink, pretending she's just another fan. I can't smile. I *won't* smile. Not when the scoreboard says we're still in a fight and the ref's still arguing with Coach from center ice.

But my pulse? Yeah, it just shifted gears.

This game was already worth winning.

Now?

This just got a hell of a lot more interesting.

7

———

I ngrid

THAT RINGING in my ears isn't from a night on stage being surrounded by thousands of fans. It's because Wittmore wins and Twyler hasn't stopped screaming since the final buzzer.

Her energy is infectious and I'm carried along with it and the rest of the crowd as we pour out of the arena, black and gold flooding the streets of Chicago. I've never been on this side of the pandemonium. It's light. Wild. *Freeing.*

"Is this what it's like after leaving one of my shows?" I ask Madison.

She gives me a look. "Times ten. Plus, glitter, fairy wings, and *waaaay* more girls."

That tracks.

When I'd suggested we use the next break in the schedule to come to Chicago to see the playoffs with our new friends from the bar, Madison thought I was joking. Who decides to do something like that spur of the moment? Not Ingrid Flockton, at least not normally. I like a schedule. I like routine and predictability. Mostly because nothing in my life is ever routine or predictable–but none of that is my doing. That's the life of a pop star.

But ever since I slipped out of that hotel room in Wittmore, I've been craving it more: spontaneity of my own making. It's a rush.

Madison took care of the logistics: getting the girls to the airport and flying them in to meet us in Chicago. I'd been excited to see them: people who have nothing to do with my world, but seemingly have embraced me anyway.

Now, we're outside the arena, waiting in back where the bus idles and waits for the team. The air sharp with the sting of winter and adrenaline. As the players emerge, I'm hit with unexpected nerves. Not just because they're all massive, towering over family and friends like giants dressed in crisp button-downs and neatly pressed suits. No, my nerves are strictly personal.

What the hell am I doing here?

"How?" Reese demands the second he spots them. Before anyone can answer, his mouth is already dropping to kiss Twyler like he's been starving for it.

Axel doesn't bother with questions. Adorned in piercings and with tatt covered hands, he sweeps Nadia up, spinning her off her feet while she shrieks and laughs, legs wrapping around his waist.

Reid? He's impossible to miss in a moss green suit and vintage boots. On anyone else it would look ridiculous, but he owns it, the same way he takes one step toward Shelby and goes in for a kiss so deep they might never come back up. It's consuming. Public. Unapologetic. The kind of passion you can't mistake for anything else. The kind that doesn't care who's watching. Everyone in the radius knows exactly what these men are saying without words. With their hands gripping their women's hips, their mouths branding them, their last names stitched across the backs of jerseys.

Possession, pure and simple, and it goes both ways.

It's foreign to me. I'm used to the opposite: ducking out separate doors, slipping into different cars, lowering my head so the cameras don't catch me–catch *us*.

What I've known never looked like this. It looked like hiding. Drifting.

Jefferson hangs back from the chaos, giving each girl a hug, laughing at something Twyler whispers as she tugs at his shoulder like she's inspecting damage. He's casual. Cool. A contrast to all that heat happening just feet away, although the slate gray of his suit, the same color as his eyes, the way it hangs on his broad shoulders...

I'm feeling my own kind of warmth.

"What are you doing here?" Reese finally asks, his voice breaking through, eyes narrowing in suspicion. "Not that I mind, but you weren't going to come until the finals."

"We made some new friends," Shelby says, tipping her chin toward me, mischief curling her lips as she gestures like she's dropping a bomb. "One who happens to have a private jet and access to box seats."

And just like that, all of them are looking between me and Madison. Recognition flares immediately. Of course it does. My poster has been taped to their bedroom walls, my voice the vehicle for their emotions, and well, for one of them, the soundtrack for losing his virginity.

I still can't figure out what song it is and it's pissing me off.

Axel is the first one to speak, blurting out, "Holy shit, you're Ingrid Flockton."

"Shhh," Nadia hushes him. "Inside voice, babe."

He shrugs, but his expression is friendly. Twyler introduces me to Reese and Reid offers a wide eyed wave. The fourth in their crew, I catch watching out of the corner of his eye. Jefferson plays it so smooth, approaching me last. "Hi. Big fan."

"Same," I answer, schooling my expression. "Of all of you. That was an incredible win."

The circle of them tightens, warmth and noise pressing in as introductions fly–names I already know, but I let them say them anyway. Their energy is contagious, so bright and buoyant after the win, that for a moment, it almost feels like I belong in it. Almost.

Before the reunion can spin too far, a shout cuts through the night. One of the staff, waving toward the bus.

"Coach's rule. We have to ride back together," Reese announces, not even pretending to not be disappointed, Twyler still glued to his side like he'd never let her go again. "Where are you staying?"

The girls glance at me, hesitating, like they need permission. It's sweet–protective. But I cut in before the pause grows heavy.

"I have an apartment here," I explain, sliding my hands into my coat pockets. "I invited them to stay with me."

"Sweet," Axel's grin turns wolfish. "Slumber party."

Nadia rolls her eyes at him. "Ignore him."

"If you want..." The words stumble out before I can edit them, softer than I intend. My eyes betray me, darting everywhere but where I really want to look. Anywhere but Jefferson. "You guys are welcome to come over and hang out for a while."

"Really?" Reid asks, his grin easy and wide. "That would be awesome."

Even Reese seems into the idea, and from what I've heard he's all business all the time. My kind of guy, except maybe he's not. Because Jefferson, well, he doesn't answer right away. Just stands there, a half-step back, studying me through the shadows of the arena lights, unreadable. It's obvious he hasn't said a word to his friends about our night together, and I can't decide how that makes me feel.

AFTER THE HOTEL PICKUP, they pile into my SUV, Marv steady at the wheel. The boys have shed their suits and ties upstairs for more causal clothes. The laughter rolls easy as they stretch out like they own the space. Reese drapes an arm around Twyler, Reid sprawls across half the bench, Axel props his long legs on the console. Jefferson claims the window seat, quiet, the blond of his hair haloed by the passing lights.

By the time we reach my building, Madison's already arranged delivery from one of the best deep-dish spots in Chicago. No champagne. No beer. Just pizza stacked high, sodas clinking in glass bottles, and water–because they're disciplined. The next round of the Frozen Four is only days away.

"Is this Sarah Homes?" Reid asks, studying a large painting of bright flowers just inside the living room.

"You know her?" I ask, impressed.

"Yeah, I like her use of contrasting colors."

"Me too. It brings out a bold quality on fragile subjects."

He moves to the next painting and then to a grouping of photographs by an up-and-coming photographer that worked on my last album. Turns out Reid is a few weeks away from earning an art degree and has collaborations with the Wittmore Athletic department with some of their merch designs.

"I make most of my tour income on merch sales," I tell him. "That's a big deal for the university to use your work."

"I'm good at hockey," he says modestly, "but I love art and design."

"Send me your portfolio. I'd love to see it."

"Really?" He looks flabbergasted. "That would be incredible."

I'm learning these men have a little more depth to them than muscles and brawn. I lead us into the den where the guys are inhaling their dinner.

"Tell me about tonight," I say instead, dropping to the corner of the couch with my drink. "I don't know hockey the way you do. Walk me through it."

Their faces light up.

Reese leans forward, one hand on Twyler's knee, the other animated as he breaks down plays from the first period. "We owned the ice from the first drop. Their defense couldn't keep up," he says, eyes sparking. "We were living in their zone."

"Until you bricked that open-net shot," Reid mutters, smirking.

Reese shrugs. "Doesn't matter. We still scored first, didn't we?"

Axel cuts in before they can keep going, puffing his chest like a showman. "Scored first because *I* robbed Lennox in the second. Guy thought he had me glove-side, but nope." He snaps his hand in the air like he's catching the puck all over again. "Stone cold."

"Robbed?" Reid snorts. "You coughed up a rebound right into their stick. I had to save your ass."

Axel waves him off with a grin. "Details."

Reese laughs. "You two sound like an old married couple."

"Better married to me than letting Lennox light you up," Reid fires back, and Axel just smirks wider.

The conversation shifts toward the final tomorrow night. Their voices overlap, bold and certain, like they can already see it.

"We can't give St. Alden an inch," Reese says about the opposing team.

"They'll come in swinging," Jefferson comments. "They play dirtier than Central did tonight."

"Dude, I've been waiting to bring that up!" Twyler shouts. "You could've cost us the game."

His head jerks up, those gray, blue eyes narrowing. "He hit first!"

"Not enough to get tossed," she fires back, smug as hell.

"Lennox is dirty," Axel throws in, defending him instantly. "I saw it. It was a nasty hit."

"Still," Twyler presses, competitive to the bone. "You let your temper get to you and that's the kind of mistake they're looking for."

The back-and-forth spirals, playful but relentless. Finally, Jefferson growls in frustration and stands, hooking a thumb under his shirt, yanking the fabric up.

"You need proof?" he challenges. "Take a look at this."

The room stills and Twyler takes in the bruise blooming dark and ugly across his ribs, but that's not what steals the air from my lungs. It's the rest of him—every ridged plane of his torso, solid and carved like someone chiseled him out of marble. Not lean, dancer-thin muscle like I'm used to. Not the clean lines of my trainer, or the skinny-fit frame of Jake. Jefferson has mass. Power. Strength.

He's *thick.*

A man.

Lord.

Around me, the girls react to the bruise—grimaces, sympathetic noises, then back to their conversations, unfazed, because this is normal to them. They're used to bodies like this, to Greek-god physiques being revealed like no big deal.

But me? I can't stop staring. My throat goes dry.

"Ingrid."

I blink, snapped out of my trance. And of course the first thing I do is look straight at Jefferson's face and down to his small grin, the all-knowing, cocky little curve of his mouth, that says he caught every second of me looking. Heat licks up the back of my neck before I tear my gaze away.

Madison stands in the doorway, one brow arched. "Can you help me with something? In the other room?"

Grateful for the escape, I follow her down the hall to my office. The space is calmer, softer, with a full wall of windows revealing the city's glitter into the night, a plush chair by the shelves where I sometimes settle in to write lyrics. My first guitar, the one I got when I was eight, sits on a stand next to the chair.

"What's going on?" I ask, though I already know. She's been trying to get me alone since the plane landed.

She doesn't waste time. "These people are nice, Ing, but what are we doing? Who *are* they? Why did you essentially invite a group of strangers not only to a hockey game, but to your house?"

I exhale, running a hand down my arm. I get it. This isn't me. I keep my circle tight. Family, management, fellow performers. Not strangers from a college town. Not girls I barely met. Not hockey players that slide into my DMs.

But it doesn't feel wrong.

"I don't know," I admit, my eyes skating over the wall behind her. Gold records. Awards. Framed magazine covers. All the markers of success that used to feel like proof of worth. Now they just feel... hollow. Empty. "They're different. Fun and I could use a little of that right now."

"Ohhhhhh." Her eyes widen. "I know what this is about."

My pulse spikes. She knows. She knows about Jefferson. About me sneaking out. Shit. Marv will *kill* me. "It's not what it—"

"This is about Jake," she interrupts.

Jake.

The name slams into me like a brick.

"No." I straighten, collecting myself, sharpening my voice. "This has nothing to do with Jake."

"You're rebounding," she insists.

"With three girls from a college town back East?" I snort, trying to laugh it off.

"It's an escape," she says simply. "No cameras. No questions about what happened between you two. And zero chance of running into him like you would with your other friends."

She's not wrong. But she's not right, either.

Because yes, I'm running. Yes, I'm hiding. But it's not from Jake.

It's toward something. Maybe.

"For once in my life I want to just do something spontaneous that isn't about anyone else but me." I look at my friend. "Is that so bad?"

"No, babe." She reaches for me and pulls me into a hug. "It's totally normal to want that. I get it. But you don't know these people. I just want you to be careful."

What she doesn't say lingers between us, a heavy weight I've been carrying for a long time. People like me don't get to be normal. No matter how much we want it.

8

———

J efferson

INGRID'S APARTMENT IS EPIC. Like, the kind of place you see in glossy magazines stacked on the coffee table in a dentist's office: exposed beams, huge windows, velvet couches in jewel tones. My teammates are sprawled across them like they own the place, pizza boxes open, with SportsCenter running on the massive flat screen. Reid's already arguing about defense strategy with Axel, and Nadia is making Shelby laugh so hard she almost spills her drink.

They're having the time of their lives. Me? Not so much.

I'm sitting there, pretending to care about the highlight reel while my head spins. Ingrid Flockton. In my DM's. Then at my game. Now inviting us all over like she and I don't know each other, like I don't know what her tongue feels like in my mouth.

It's too much coincidence. Too much silence around what's not being said and hell, I just want to talk to her again.

The girls spilled most of the story on the way over; how on the day after her concert Ingrid was still in town and came into the Den for dinner. "She ordered the Jefferson Parks Special," Shelby said with a grin. Shelby is the other Ingrid Flockton fan in the group. We've bonded over it a little–like Reid and Twyler and their shared love of murder documentaries. Shelby and the guys know my secret. That there's a list I carry around with the names of women I want to fuck.

Ingrid is on the top of that list.

"Because it's amazing," I'd replied casually, despite the fact I've been strung tight since I saw her in the stands.

I'm trying to figure out how to get Ingrid alone when Madison reappears without her. Huh. I take the chance and slip out of the laughter and noise and into the hall. The place feels even bigger back here, ceilings soaring, rooms spilling one into the next. My footsteps echo on the hardwood until I hear something faint–a creak, maybe a shuffle–from a room to the left.

I peer in.

She's standing there by an antique desk painted this striking teal blue, fingertips brushing along the wood like she's trying to steady herself.

"Hey," I say, leaning against the doorway.

Her head jerks up, lavender hair curling down her shoulders. "Hi."

For a beat we just look at each other. No crowd, no music, no teammates. Just us.

"So this is a surprise," I say finally.

"I owe you an explanation." She twists her hands together, a rare sign of nerves. "Madison and I went to grab burgers at the Badger Den the other night, and Shelby was our waitress–"

I hold up a hand, stopping her. "No need to explain."

"Really?" she asks, eyebrows lifting.

"It's obvious."

A wrinkle forms between her brows. "Obvious how?"

I let a grin tug at my mouth, trying to play it off. "You're obsessed with me."

Her laugh bursts out, sharp and disbelieving. "Oh my god. You're absurd."

"Am I wrong?" I step further into the room, closing some of the distance between us.

Her smile falters just slightly, eyes flicking down to my chest before darting back up. She'd been checking me out earlier when I hiked up my shirt to show Twyler the bruise. Now? Damn, the heat that sparks there almost knocks me on my ass. I want to kiss her again. More than that, I want to press her back against that teal desk, taste her, get answers with my mouth instead of words.

But she's unreadable, half amusement, half something else I can't pin down. Is this about me? My teammates? Something bigger I don't see yet?

The tension stretches, thick enough to choke on.

And all I can think is: I'm in trouble with this girl.

Ingrid is the one to speak first. "That bruise," she says.

"What about it?"

"I have something for it." She starts toward the door, and turns, going deeper into the apartment. She stops at a bedroom. Massive. Colorful. Blush pink, more teal, soft green. Pure female, *mature*, not like the college dorms and tiny rooms in the Shotgun district we live in back at school. I've been in a lot of women's beds, but this one isn't just different because of the extravagance. It's different because it belongs to her.

Number one.

My eyes land on the bed, covered in a million pillows, iron scroll work at the head and foot.

A vision of Ingrid on all fours, her slim fingers wrapped around the iron headboard flashes through my mind and Jesus Christ.

Unaware of my fantasies, she dips into another room, this time a cavernous bathroom, where she opens a cabinet revealing dozens of labeled slots, organized and sorted like an apothecary. After running her finger over the labels she stops and pulls out a glass jar.

She turns to me. "Arnica–it helps with the swelling and inflammation."

I take the jar from her, the tips of my fingers grazing hers. "Yeah? What do you know about bruising?"

"What do I know about bruising?" she repeats with a look that can only be described as incredulous. "You're kidding, right?"

I lift my shoulders. "I mean, obviously you have amazing cardio and strength, but it's not like you're getting pummeled repeatedly by six-foot-four, two hundred and fifty pound men."

"Poor baby." She pouts, patronizing and dismissive. "You're right. My cardio and strength are incredible, but no one gives me pads and gloves. I'm out there in sparkly spandex and six-inch heels. I'm hoisted by ropes, carried by dancers, playing my guitar or piano for three hours straight. My blisters *have* blisters. My bruises are replaced by other bruises. My muscles ache, and then I get up and do it all over again."

"Well. Now I just feel like a dick."

"You should."

"Wow," I say, twisting the cap open just for something to do with my hands. "So not only are you talented and beautiful, but you're tough, too. Should I be intimidated?"

"Stupid men have made the mistake of underestimating me before." She leans back against the marble counter, bending one of those long legs at the knee.

"I'm not stupid, but I have been told I'm stubborn."

Her lips twitch, like she's trying not to smile. "You're unbelievable."

"Unbelievably charming?" I throw her my best grin.

"Unbelievably risky." Her eyebrow lifts. "Do your friends know you're back here? Do they know about us?"

"No," I murmur, softer, and the space between us suddenly feels too charged. "Does Madison?"

She shakes her head and takes the jar back. Unscrewing the lid she dips her fingers in and coats them in the cream. "Lift up your shirt."

I obey, though my pride bristles at the command. I want to be the one telling her to take off her clothes. The cotton pulls against my sore ribs, and I wince as the bruised skin is exposed. It's already ugly, shades of purple and green blooming across my side like someone's shitty art project.

Ingrid's eyes narrow, her mouth tightening, but she doesn't say anything. She just steps closer, fingertips glistening, and touches me. I suck in a sharp breath. Not because it hurts, though it sure as fuck does, but because her touch is nothing like the trainer's brisk, clinical hands. Hers are slow. Careful. Almost reverent. She spreads the cream in little circles, her fingers cool and gentle at first before warming against my skin.

Suddenly, I get why Reese is always letting Twyler check his boo-boos.

It's foreplay.

"This is pretty bad," she murmurs, eyes flicking up at me through her lashes.

"Part of the job," I say, though my voice is rougher than I want it to be.

Her fingers skim lower, tracing the edge of the bruise. My abdomen caves, ribs aching under the pressure, but the sting fades beneath another thought. She's touching me like I matter. Not like I'm a one-way ticket to being a WAG, but like I'm–fragile. Breakable.

No one treats me like that. Not the puck bunnies or sorority girls.

"You should take better care of yourself," she whispers.

I want to laugh it off, make some cocky remark, but my throat's too tight. Instead, I let her keep going, her hand moving slow, spreading the cream until my skin hums. The sharp chill mixes with the heat of her touch, a contrast that makes me shiver.

Her palm flattens over my side for just a second, lingering. We're close enough that I can smell her shampoo, sweet and clean, not some expensive perfume, but Ingrid herself. My pulse pounds.

"You're good at this," I note, because I need to say something, anything, before I do something stupid like grab her hand and kiss it. She goes still, just for a beat, like maybe she felt it too–that shift in the air between us. The crackle of energy. Then she smooths the last of the cream across my ribs, her touch lighter now, more like a caress than a treatment.

I can't look away from her.

"Thank you," I say finally, but it comes out rough, too full, like it's holding more weight than just gratitude.

She sets the jar down, her fingers leaving my skin, and it's ridiculous how much I already miss the contact, which is why I take a step closer.

She might bolt. But she doesn't move, and I swear the corner of her mouth curves up, just a little. "Is this a secret?" I ask, truly wanting to know. "This thing between us?"

"I don't know what *this* is," she admits, a little of the bravado failing.

I take a slow breath. "I know I want to kiss you again." Her eyes flicker, surprise, maybe a flash of the memory we both share–that one night, quick and easy, supposed to be nothing. A one time thing. I hold her gaze, not moving in, not pushing, but add, "I just don't know if I'm allowed."

The silence stretches, heavy with possibilities, before she shakes her head and laughs softly, breaking the tension. "Do you always ask permission before you kiss a girl?"

Fuck. It's a challenge pure and simple and Jefferson Parks isn't the kind of guy who runs from a challenge. My eyes drop to her mouth, and her breath stutters, the space between us shrinking until I can feel the heat radiating off her skin. She doesn't back up. Nah, she just stands there, steady, even as her fingers twitch like she's fighting the urge to reach for me. Then she exhales, shaky but certain, and tilts her chin up.

That's all the permission I need.

I close the gap in one motion, my mouth crashing against hers, hard and hot. The kiss is just as good as the first time–*better*–heated, desperate, full of every question neither of us wants to answer. *What is this? What does this mean? Where is it going? How?* She fists my shirt in her hands, pulling me closer, and I grip her waist, anchoring her against me like I might lose her again if I let go. Her tits feel incredible against my chest while my dick threatens to break loose.

It's fire and want and something dangerously close to trouble, and the only thing I know for sure is I don't want it to stop.

"Stop," she says, wrenching her mouth from mine. Her lips are puffy. Sexy. Her eyes wide. "We need to stop."

With my cock throbbing against my leg, I inhale and exhale, willing my body to slow down.

"Do we?" I ask, leaning down to suck a kiss on her jaw.

"They're going to wonder where we are," she explains, placing her hands on my chest and pushing me away, before turning to look in the vanity mirror to clean up her lipstick and smooth out her hair.

So it is a secret.

"Yeah, well, you're going to have to go out first." I don't hide the fact I need to adjust the front of my jeans. This woman gets me harder with one kiss than anyone ever has before. "I'm going to need a few minutes." Her lips form a perfect circle, the shock of finding out how my body reacts to her. As she passes me on the way to the door, I grab her wrist. "This isn't over, Ingrid."

To my surprise she doesn't argue, she just glances back at me one more time, leaving me and my boner all alone.

It's my second shower of the night, but this one had nothing to do with getting clean. I came home from Ingrid's apartment still hot and throbbing, needing to work off some of the pent-up want that's been building for days. It's one thing to have flirty little texts, but to have her in my hands, to have her mouth against mine... it's too fucking much and I ducked into the shower the minute we got back and stroked myself thinking about the way she looked at me–*touched* me. Her hands were gentle when they skimmed over the bruise, and my arousal was as much from the mere fact skin was touching skin, but the erotism of not taking it a step further.

Everything about her is so fucking hot.

It doesn't take long for the pressure to build. Not when I'm thinking about that soft pink mouth, or the feel of her tongue. Not when I'm imagining what her tits feel like in my hands, or how tight her pussy would clench around me when I'm inside.

That's the image that does it, and I come, painting the tile, while I let the shower drown out my heavy breaths.

"Jesus, Christ," I mutter to myself, hand flat against the shower wall. The water runs cold, and I bask in it, like a post game ice bath, cooling off my muscles. Reese doesn't give a shit–he was already Facetiming with Twyler when we walked in the room, hardly able to be away from her for a few minutes without checking in.

They're off the phone when I come out of the bathroom, my towel-dried hair a mess. My muscles are finally loose, but jerking off doesn't fix the knot in my chest. I already know the truth. I'm not going to settle down until I can fully have her.

Reese is sprawled out on his bed in shorts and a Wittmore T-shirt, scrolling his phone, TV flickering low in the background. He doesn't look up until I flop down on my own bed, dragging the comforter up over my waist.

"Crazy night," he says, setting his phone aside. "It's big enough we made it to the finals, but I still can't believe Ingrid freakin' Flockton brought the girls to the game." He makes a face. "That's insane, right?"

I smirk up at the ceiling. "Yeah, pretty wild."

Reese shifts onto his side, eyeing me. "You're not even freaking out. This is your celebrity crush, man. Years of posters, playlists, your 'number one' speeches. And she just shows up and you don't care?"

I roll my eyes, trying to play it cool. "Relax. It's not a big deal."

"Not a big deal?" Reese laughs, incredulous. "Bro, if I was single and Margot Robbie walked in and sat courtside, I'd be fainting. You're acting like she's just some random Kappa you met at a kegger who showed up at the game."

I force a shrug, leaning back against the headboard. "Dude, she's just a person, right? I'm not fifteen anymore. Crushes don't count in the real world."

Reese narrows his eyes, studying me like he's waiting for me to crack. "So you're telling me that you have a chance to hit that you'd pass because she's 'just a person.'"

"Shelby and the girls seem to like her. I'm not going to fuck things up for them."

That answer appeases him, slightly. He still looks skeptical when he turns off the light, shrouding the room in the dark. I close my eyes and bask in it: the win, the rush, but most of all the kiss that comes flashing back to me, the way the curve of her hips felt in my hands–

"You were gone for a while tonight while the rest of us were watching clips from the games."

"Seriously?" I say, rolling to my side and punching my pillow. "You're still on about this?"

"Yep," he presses from the bed next to mine. "*Both* of you were missing. You hit on her didn't you?"

Heat flickers in my chest, sharp and guilty, but the lie comes easy. "Nope."

"Come on."

Reese is my best friend. It's no surprise he doesn't buy it. I wouldn't.

"I didn't hit on her," I say smoothly, sliding lower into the bed. "I called my mom to let her know how the game went. You know how she is with the time difference. Figured I'd check in before she started calling us at 2 AM."

That earns a laugh, because it's happened more than once. Even so, it's obvious he's not sure. "Calling your mom, huh?"

"I swear on the trophy." I hold up a hand in the dark. "Didn't see or talk to her outside of everyone else. Chill."

"You really want me to believe, that you, Jefferson Parks, Wittmore's biggest fuckboy, is in your dream girl's house, she's *right there*, and you don't take a shot?"

"I know, it's embarrassing," I admit, because it *is* humiliating. Jefferson Parks, Wittmore's biggest fuckboy, is disappointed in himself. I was in her house and had her alone. Her bed was *right there*, and I didn't seal the deal. Sure, I got a kiss, but that's not what

Reese is after. My status as the campus playboy is in jeopardy. "It's like getting called up to the pros and sitting the whole game on the bench."

"Shit, man, that sucks..." Reese goes quiet for a beat before I hear him roll over, adding with the slightest laugh, "but I guess that explains why you needed a second shower."

9

I ngrid

THE GIRLS all crashed in my apartment that night–Twyler, Nadia, and Shelby sprawled across my ridiculous overstuffed couches and on the floor with blankets, while Madison slipped away to her own quarters like the responsible one she is. I love her, but she doesn't do sleepovers and giggling in pajamas.

We stay up long after the guys head back to the hotel, Reese not allowing anyone to miss curfew. They have what they call 'morning skate' and then their final game in the evening. It sounds like a packed day, but I can't talk, I'm usually up before dawn, already at work when the sun rises.

When everyone gets comfortable, I ask the question that's been burning at me.

"So...how did you guys actually meet your boyfriends?"

"You going to put this in one of your songs?" Shelby asks, more wishful than concerned.

"Maybe," I grin. "Honestly, I'm just curious. You guys all seem so happy."

Twyler snorts. "None of it came easy," she says. "Those guys were a mess when we got to them."

"Reese was hardly a mess," Nadia challenges. "Captain of the hockey team. Surely a first round pick for the NFL."

"Fucking anything that moved," Twyler adds, rolling her eyes. She doesn't seem mad about it, or even insecure. "I didn't even like him at first and he didn't like me, he told the whole team that he thought of me as a little sister."

I grimace. "Ouch."

"Then one day I'm in line at the campus coffee shop, getting my caffeine hit, the next thing I know, he's kissing me."

"What?" I ask, trying to follow. "He just assaulted you in the coffee shop?"

"Entitlement runs thick with these men," Nadia chims in. "He was trying to get his ex off his back and he thought sticking his tongue down Twyler's throat was the way to do it."

"Seems like it worked," Shelby says.

"Somehow that kiss turned into a full-on fake dating situationship, both of us using one another to get over past relationships," Twyler says all of this like it makes perfect sense. "Then the fake stuff got more real, and now here we are."

"Mine was worse. Axel and I had what we call an epic fuck up." I raise an eyebrow urging Nadia to continue. "A one night stand, turned friends with benefits, turned relationship." She shrugs. "The 'epic fuck up' turned out to be the best thing I ever did."

"What about you and Reid," I ask.

Shelby's voice is softer, more careful. "I grew up in a really strict home. My parents had already arranged a relationship and marriage with a guy at my church. I realized things were moving too fast for me and I came East to stay with Axel for a while. The first night here I met Reid–"

"On Valentine's Day," Nadia adds, grinning wide. "He thought she was one of Axel's former hook-ups coming for a booty call and kissed her."

"He didn't know who you were?" I ask.

"Nope." Shelby shakes her head. "And I may have had something to do with the kiss. I did initiate it."

"Damn," I mutter. The good girl vibe on Shelby is strong. I can't see her making a move like that. Although I was the one that kissed Jefferson first, so who am I to talk?

"Reid showed me that life didn't have to look like what my parents had planned for me. That I could actually choose what and who I wanted to spend the rest of my life with." Her cheeks flush pink. "He opened up my whole world."

Their faces glow when they talk about these men and it's like watching a living playlist of love songs I've written–except theirs are the kind that last, not the gossamer and fantasies I weave into lyrics. They're talking about real, steady, still burning love even after the dopamine fades. I've never had that. I've only ever gotten the sugar rush version. Sweet, addictive, over too fast, and leaving me in pieces.

There's a pause, then Shelby glances at me. "What about you? Are we going to talk about Jake or is that off limits?"

Normally, I'd laugh it off. Crack a joke. Redirect. But they're all so open, so honest, it feels wrong not to tell the truth for once. They don't need the backstory. That Jake's a musician too. Different scene. Edgier. He wears all black and is covered in tattoos. My world is pink and glitter, his is heavy riffs and shadows.

"Some of the stuff you've heard is probably true. That we'd been drawn to each other forever, like suicidal moths to a combustible flame. An obvious match except for the fact that the timing never worked. Either he was taken, or I was. Then finally, last Christmas, we were both free. It should've been perfect." I twist the blanket in my lap, remembering. "The years of pent up tension building to this one moment. We were older, more mature, had more stability. Why not? Right?" The laugh that bubbles from my chest is humorless. "It was anything but perfect, though. All those daydreams of finally being together were quickly erased. He didn't want me out in the world with him. We took separate exits from venues. Separate cars. He wanted me behind closed doors, which was fun in it's own way. We spent a lot of time naked and he gave me everything, but when it came to daylight, to being seen together, he acted...distant. Disinterested. Embarrassed, even. Like I wasn't the girl you claim in public, just the one you keep in your bed."

My throat tightens, but the words are out there now.

"Turns out," I continue, "he was talking to the media behind my back. Feeding them little crumbs–where we'd be, when I was leaving his apartment, even dumb things like what coffee I ordered. Making it look like we were sneaking around when in reality, he just didn't want to be seen with me. It made him look like the mysterious bad boy who landed a pop princess. Free publicity for his concerts. For me, it was just humiliation."

The girls are quiet. Not awkward quiet, just listening quiet.

"I think what hurt the most," I swallow, "was realizing he wanted me naked in his bed, not by his side. Behind closed doors, he'd drown me in attention, but out in the world? He was embarrassed of me. Embarrassed of pink and sparkles, of bubblegum pop songs. He wanted to use me to burn brighter, not actually stand with me." I shake my head. "Leaving him sucked. Really sucked. And keeping my mouth shut while the gossips dragged me, while his fans swallowed his version–that I wasn't good enough, too career-obsessed, too shallow–it's brutal. They think, that to me, he's just, I don't know... another hit song now. Another heartbreak on my setlist."

"Let me tell you something, Ingrid, he's not worth it," Nadia says, leaning forward, her dark eyes flashing. "Ask me how I know."

I glance at her, and the edge in her voice softens into something like solidarity. In an instant I feel it. She *does* know what it's like to be used by a man. I give her a grateful little smile.

"Yeah," Twyler says, hugging her pillow, "everyone knows Jake Merchant is a fucking poser."

"His nose ring is fake," I blurt.

"Oh my God," Nadia howls. "That's fucking hilarious."

"Told you," Twyler says smugly. "Total poser."

Shelby watches all of this with wide eyes, until she tilts her head. "So what's next then? Any new guys? An actor this time? Maybe one of those moody British ones?"

I laugh, shaking my head. "I think I'm holding off on dating anyone right now. Things are way too busy with the tour wrapping up. And honestly? I don't think I can handle another relationship for a while."

There's a murmur of agreement, like they all get it. For the first time in a while, I feel lighter, but when I look back at Twyler her expression is wary.

"What?" I ask her.

"Since you're being honest about musicians, please tell me the New Kings aren't douchebags?"

I saw the tattoo on her upper thigh when she changed into pajama shorts. I know from experience the pride of someone getting a tattoo inspired by you that they are a major fan. "They're pretty great actually. I got to see them play Coachella and it was pretty epic."

She grins, my history with Jake already forgotten, and leans forward. "Tell. Me. Everything."

"It was raining and they could have cancelled their set, but they didn't. They played the full set, soaking wet."

"I saw the pictures. I can't believe you were there."

"It made everything feel even more intimate, like they were committed. I love that about them. They are true to their fans."

Twyler clutches a pillow to her chest like she's holding on for dear life. "I knew it."

Nadia laughs. "Now you've done it. She's going to make us listen to their entire discography on repeat before bed."

"Correction," Twyler says, already grabbing her phone. "Live performances only. I need to experience this properly."

Shelby snorts, tugging the blanket higher. "Fine, but only if Ingrid does the commentary. I want the behind-the-scenes version. Did you meet them? Backstage? Anything juicy?"

I roll my eyes, but I'm smiling now. "No backstage gossip, just the rush of being in the crowd, singing at the top of my lungs. Sometimes that's enough."

Twyler's grin softens. "See? That's what I love. The feeling–not the drama. Their music really helped me through a hard time."

"Exactly," I say, hugging my knees. "Music should feel like that. Not like... shitty exes who are using you to get ahead."

For the first time in months, talking about him doesn't sting.

The girls chatter on, pulling up live clips, squealing when the crowd roars through the speakers, but my mind drifts. Not to Jake. Not to the wreckage he left behind.

To Jefferson.

To the hard press of his mouth against mine in the bathroom, the way he kissed me like we were the only two people on the planet. He makes me feel alive in a way Jake never did. Not like an accessory or a prize. But seen. Chosen.

I close my eyes and bite my lip, heart racing. Except... how is this different? We're still sneaking around. Still hiding in the shadows. The question twists in my chest, sharp and unwelcome. Is that my decision–keeping us secret? Or his?

THE NEXT MORNING the girls head out to see the city before the final game that night. I told them I'd meet them at the arena. Unfortunately, I have a full day of catch-up to do–even days off tour are workdays. I'm in sweats with my setlist propped against the mirror, humming scales under my breath, when the door bangs open.

Madison doesn't knock. When has she ever?

"You've been caught."

I blink up at her. "Huh?"

She strides in with the energy of a storm, iPad clutched like a weapon. One swipe and my face fills the screen.

"Oh my God," I mutter.

It's me. Sitting between Madison and Shelby in the stands, my stocking cap with the ridiculous little gold pompom pulled low over my forehead. I'm mid-cheer, mouth open, eyes shining, cheeks pink from the cold. Honestly, I look good. Alive.

But yeah. Busted.

"What does it say?"

Madison scrolls, then reads aloud in a faux-serious announcer voice: "*Was Ingrid Flockton really at the Frozen Four playoff games? At first it made no sense to see our favorite winged singer at a college hockey match, but we did a little digging...*"

She skims further, eyebrows rising. "Blah blah. Rehash of the last year. Then–ah, here we go. They haven't ID'd the girls yet, but it's only a matter of time. They're speculating you must know someone on the team. Family member, boyfriend, something."

I groan and bury my face in my hands. "The Flock is terrifying with their detective skills. They should be solving actual crimes instead of stalking me."

Madison shrugs. "Internet sleuthing is their Olympic sport. But this–" she taps the screen again, "this has traction. You're trending. It's not just the fan sites. The sports and pop-culture pages have picked it up."

I flop back against the couch, staring at the ceiling. My phone is on the cushion beside me. I reach for it, thumb hovering over the screen.

"I should probably give the girls a heads-up," I mumble.

"Tell them to ignore anyone that contacts them and to lock down their accounts," she frowns, "to protect you and them from the vultures."

My phone buzzes before I can open our group chat.

Jparks23

I freeze. The letters of his username glow up at me.

Madison narrows her eyes. "Who's that?"

"My dad." The lie tumbles out before I can think, and I flip the phone facedown. My pulse is hammering, traitorous because of Jefferson Parks. Number twenty-three. The reason my face looks so alive in those photos.

I chew my lip, heart pulling in two directions at once. On one side, the rising panic–headlines, speculation, the constant question of whether my choices are ever really mine, or if I'm just playing games. On the other, the memory of his mouth in the bathroom, the way he kissed me like I was just Ingrid, not Ingrid Flockton™.

And now he's texting me.

Jparks23: *You look good in the stands, Flock. Bright cheeks. Pom-pom hat. Real cute.*

My stomach dips.

IngFlock: *So you're one of the internet detectives then?*

Jparks23: *Nah. Didn't need to investigate. Had front row seats from the penalty box to you cheering for me.*

Heat climbs my neck. Madison is scrolling through comments, but her voice fades into the background. He didn't mention this once last night. Probably because he was too busy kissing me.

Jparks23: *Thought about you last night. Couldn't sleep. Should've been resting up for tonight's game, but all I could think about was your mouth.*

I press my lips together, trying not to grin like a complete idiot.

IngFlock: *Yeah?*

Jparks23: *Tell me you're thinking about me too.*

My throat tightens. Because I am. God, I am. Even here, with Madison two feet away and my whole career hanging on threads of discretion.

Me: *Maybe I am.*

Three dots pulse. Stop. Start again. Then–

Jparks23: *Not enough. I want details.*

I bite down harder on my lip, pulse racing, because if I give him details, I'll never stop. And that's dangerous.

Madison gives me a weird look. "Are you blushing?"

I tuck the phone under my leg. "Nope."

"Well, I'll talk to the rest of the PR team and see how they want to handle it–especially since we're going again tonight."

I trust my team to do the dirty work and I spend most of the morning curled up on the chair in my office with my guitar balanced across my knees, notebook open beside me. My brain has been churning with inspiration for a new song for days now and it's reached the point where I can't avoid it any longer. A few scraps of melody have been stuck in my head since we were in Wittmore last week, so I pluck them out, scribble lines, cross them off, and try again.

It's messy and unfinished, still needs a tighter bridge, but it feels good. This is the part I love: just me and the music without anyone watching. No cameras, no managers, no gossip pages posting about what I did last night.

By the time the sun starts sliding low outside the windows, I set the guitar aside and stretch out. Tonight I'm meeting the girls at the rink. That thought alone has my stomach fluttering. Not because of them, but because of him. I still haven't responded to his last text, and he hasn't messaged again, either. I know he's busy. I respect that. God, I love it. I love a man that has passion for his work.

I try to distract myself, flipping back to the notebook and tapping my pen against the page, but the words blur. I can't stop circling back to Jefferson. To that kiss. To the way he makes me feel alive in a way Jake never did. Seen in a way I didn't know I was craving.

This is dumb. He's hot. Sexy. Funny. Charming as hell and I deserve a little of all of that in my life, right?

My thumb hovers, pulse kicking faster than it should. I type, erase, type again, then finally let it fly: *If you win the game tonight, I'll show you what I've been thinking about in person.*

I hit send, drop the phone on the cushion beside me, and lean back with my hands over my face, heat crawling up my neck.

It takes less than a minute for the reply to come in.

Jparks23: *Angel, I was already planning to win. But now? Consider it done.*

10

———————

I ngrid

THERE'S no anonymity this time. Not even close. The minute I step out of the SUV, the press is waiting, lenses flashing like strobe lights at the club. Shouts of my name mix with questions I have no intention of answering. Marv muscles his way through security, clearing a path like he's parting the Red Sea. Madison stays glued to my side, her phone in one hand, her expression set to ice queen mode.

It feels different from the other night. That time, I slipped in unnoticed, blending in with my signature pastel hair tucked under the beanie and cheering like I was just another fan in the stands. Tonight, there's no pretending. Everyone knows I'm here, and worse– they're determined to find out *why* I'm here.

"Ingrid! Do you know someone on the team?"

"Ingrid! Have you always been a hockey fan?"

"Ingrid! Who do you think will win tonight?"

I give a small smirk, but no comment. Tonight isn't about me. We bypass the crowded concourse and head straight for the suite Madison secured. No more hanging out right behind the glass. Marv's insistence. Inside, the energy flips instantly. Shelby, Twyler, and Nadia are already there, buzzing like they've just walked into the VIP section of heaven.

"Did you see all this food?" Twyler is already at the buffet, a pile of snacks on her plate. She's dressed in Reese's oversized jersey and a pair of ripped jeans. "Nachos *and* sliders."

"Don't forget the open bar," Nadia adds, eyeing the bartender.

Nadia spins in a slow circle, her wide eyes taking in the private seating, the glass wall overlooking the rink. "This is unreal. Ingrid, you've officially ruined regular seats for us forever."

I laugh, shedding my coat and handing it off to Madison, who folds it with military precision and drapes it over the back of a chair. "Aren't the guys headed to the pros? I'm sure you'll get special seating."

"Yeah, but we won't be together," Nadia says, giving me a kind look. "So thanks for this. Really."

The puck drops, and the roar of the crowd filters through the glass, muted but still electric. Even from up here, the intensity thrums. Jefferson's out there on the ice, moving faster than my eyes can track, but I feel him like a magnetic pull.

I don't totally understand the rules: the constant line changes, the way the puck disappears into a scramble of sticks and bodies, but the energy is contagious. Every time someone slams against the boards, the entire arena vibrates.

"God, did you see that hit?" Shelby practically shrieks, gripping her beer like it's a stress ball.

"Clean," Twyler assures her, though she doesn't sound entirely convinced.

"That's the best part," Nadia adds with a smirk. "Controlled violence."

I laugh, shaking my head, but I can't stop watching Jefferson. When he's on the ice, the crowd reacts before I even know why, like they can sense something's about to happen. And it's not just him–it's the way he and his teammates seem to move as one. A sharp pass, a quick shift, someone always in position. It's choreography without music, perfectly timed and brutal all the same.

It reminds me of being on stage with my musicians and dancers, when everything clicks and the sound swells bigger than the sum of its parts. That unspoken rhythm, the instinctive give-and-take. Jefferson thrives in it. He leads, but he also trusts, and it makes them all stronger together.

I sip my drink and lean back in the plush seat, pretending I'm just here for a night with the girls. But every time the number 23 blurs past, I catch myself holding my breath. I think about that kiss, how the hands wielding that stick with such power were on me the night before–strong but gentle.

I fan myself with my hand.

"Are you okay?" Madison looks me over.

"Yeah, just a little warm in all these clothes."

She's barely watching the game, scrolling her phone.

Below, the puck whips across the ice, stick to stick so fast I almost miss it. Then Jefferson cuts toward the net, skimming past the St. Alden's defender, shoulders down, blades spraying ice as he pivots.

"Here it comes," Nadia murmurs, leaning forward with both hands braced on her knees.

It happens in a blur–the sharp crack of his stick, the puck sailing past the goalie's glove, the light flashing. The crowd erupts, a wall of sound so loud I feel it in my chest.

"YES!" Twyler jumps to her feet, her plate of food tumbling to the floor. Shelby and Nadia cling to one another in an excited embrace.

And me? I'm frozen. My heart's in my throat, my palms slick. Because Jefferson isn't celebrating with the guys who swarm him, not really. His helmet's still on, but his gaze lifts, and I swear he looks straight up at our box. Straight at me.

Everything around me fades, I can't hear anything over the rush in my ears. He's smiling–wild, unstoppable. I've never been so turned on in my life.

I sink back into my seat, trying to act like I'm not completely undone, but it's useless.

Two kisses and this man is fully under my skin. What happens if I let him in any further?

IT ALL COMES DOWN to the final moments of the game. Wittmore's up by one, and St. Alden's pulling every desperate move they have left. The intensity is not like anything I've ever felt before. Winning in my world isn't like this. The Grammys, the MTV statues, and gold records... there's no clock winding down, no other player breathing down my neck, fighting over the same little puck. This is raw. Heated. *Violent.* The puck cuts across the ice like a blade, a St. Alden's forward winding up with everything he's got.

He fires.

Axel drops low, pads snapping shut like a steel trap, and swallows the shot whole.

The buzzer blares.

For half a heartbeat there's silence–like the entire arena inhales at once–and then it erupts. Sheer pandemonium. Fans on their feet, screaming themselves hoarse, the sound shaking the rafters. White and navy towels whip through the air like a storm. Players swarm Axel, piling on top of each other in ecstasy. The pile grows as teammates from the bench join, everyone laughing and shouting over one another. Wittmore did it, they won the Frozen Four.

"Come on!" Twyler shrieks, practically vibrating out of her seat, clutching my wrist with manic excitement.

"Where are we going?" I ask, still blinking, still trying to make sense of the chaos unraveling below.

"Down on the ice to celebrate," Nadia says, already halfway to the stairs. Her tone makes it sound like the most obvious thing in the world.

"We can do that?"

"Hell yeah we can," Twyler grins, already halfway down the aisle.

I follow, Marv quickly catches up and he gives me that hard, don't-even-think-about-it look. "Ingrid, I don't recommend—"

I cut my gaze to him. "Just one night," I ask–no, beg. "I just want *one* night of normalcy."

But I know better. It's an impossible ask. Not even close to realistic. During intermission, the cameras found me, zoomed in tight, and splashed my face across the jumbotron. The crowd reaction had been split right down the middle. Some hockey fans weren't thrilled I'd infiltrated their sport. But the cheers had been there too, that ripple of excitement that always comes when I show up somewhere unexpected.

Madison leaned over after the third intermission and whispered, "They're saying you're sitting in the WAG box."

I'd shaken it off, but the weight lingered. Imposter syndrome heavy in my chest as we trail Marv, who nods us through security. We pile into a private elevator, then down a hushed hallway until we spill out into a tunnel leading straight onto the ice and the scene explodes before us. The players are involved in a post-game handshake line. Wittmore's team glides along the ice, shaking hands with St. Alden's, sportsmanship in motion, and the defeated team nods, smiles forced but respectful.

We're not allowed on the actual ice, but Twyler works her way to the edge of the wall–a part not walled off by glass. I don't miss the tears at the corner of her eyes when the captains–Jefferson included– lift the trophy high for the first time. The crowd roars. No superstition here, just pure joy. The captains pass the trophy down the line, and every player skates a lap with it aloft, grinning, sweat and triumph mixing on their faces.

The players are everywhere–sweaty, red-cheeked, towering on their skates. They're shouting, laughing, hugging, stopping for reporters. Pure joy and chaos.

And then they see us.

Reese makes a beeline toward Twyler. His dark hair soaked with sweat. He grabs for her and lifts her over the wall, spinning her around. "I knew it," I see her mouth. "I love you."

I glance away from the intimacy, and lock eyes with steel gray.

He sees *me.*

The world tilts on its axis.

Jefferson's helmet is off, blond hair damp and curling around his temples, cheeks flushed with victory. He's laughing with his teammates, but the second his eyes cut toward me, everything stops. At least, it feels like it does. The sound, the movement, the chaos–all of it fades under the weight of his gaze.

And in that split second, I'm exposed.

It's painfully, humiliatingly obvious: I shouldn't be here. Not on this ice, not in this moment, not in his world. The other girlfriends wear team colors, fitted jerseys with their boyfriends' numbers. They belong. They've earned this spot.

Me? I'm just... me. Too shiny. Too loud. Too *other.*

I don't belong.

"Ingrid."

My eyes snap away from his–away from Jefferson's easy grin, the sweat still dripping down his temple–to the reporter calling my name.

Marv is already there, sliding between us like a shield, all business as he shuts it down with a clipped shake of his head.

In the same breath, Jefferson's coach claps a heavy hand on his shoulder and steers him back toward his team.

Just like that, the moment splinters–him pulled one way, me the other.

But you can't really break something apart that was never together in the first place.

11

____

J efferson

HOURS LATER, after the arena finally kicked us off the ice and out of
the locker room, we're back at the hotel, the team's celebration in full
swing. Exhausted but still humming with adrenaline, I sink onto one
of the couches in the lounge, letting the noise wash over me. Plates of
food litter the tables. Drinks flow for the over-twenty-one crowd. The
guys are loud, laughing, replaying moments from the game with that
messy, joyful energy only winners know.

My parents were at the game, proud and congratulatory, and after
catching up, they went back to the hotel with some of the other families in town. My phone has been buzzing all night. Family and friends
sending their congratulations. Old teammates from the Junior's
league, my high school coach, and a dozen puck bunnies back at
Wittmore. The latter is letting me know they're up to celebrate when I
get back to town.

Those aren't the messages that catch my eye. They're nice enough, but the alerts I've set up keep flashing. Ingrid's name pops up, over and over. The news that she was at the game tonight, sitting with the WAGs, has ignited a wildfire online. Comments, articles, gossip–the level and speed that it traveled... well, it's fucking insane.

"Me!" I want to shout. *"She came to see me!"*

There's not a goddam thing I can do or say about it. Not if I want her to trust me.

Not if I want to see her again.

I keep going back to the last text she sent me. *If you win the game tonight, I'll show you what I've been thinking about in person.*

That line alone makes my chest tighten. Makes the entire night sharper, more electric.

A coach from Florida, the team I'm committed to playing professionally next year, sidles up. "Congrats, Parks. You were on fire tonight. Bring that kind of energy down to the Surge and you might have a second trophy to your name."

I shrug, trying to downplay it. "There'd be no bigger honor than winning the Cup for the team, sir."

The truth? I *was* on fire tonight. Every shift, every hit, every sprint down the ice had a purpose beyond just the team. Winning for Wittmore, giving Reese the victory that slipped through our fingers last year, making Coach proud of taking a chance on me four years ago... that was all part of it.

But the real fire? That came from her.

The girl up in the stands, the one with the pouty lips, the purple hair tucked under a hat. The one who had my attention the moment I saw her. I wanted to impress her. Prove that I was worth noticing. Worth showing up for, risking exposure.

Worth *her.*

I can still see her, mid-cheer, eyes wide, hands gripping the glass, energy spilling into the arena like it was part of the game itself. The goal I scored tonight was for her. Every shift I threw my body into, every hit I took, every sprint. I wanted her to know I was capable. That I could rise to the challenge. That I was worthy of someone as special as she is.

And now, sitting here, surrounded by food, laughter, and the leftover chaos of our victory, I can't stop thinking about what happens next. About that text. If that was serious or just part of the game.

I scroll my phone again, trying to stay casual, but the thought of her has me wired tighter than any game-winning buzzer. Tonight isn't just a win for Wittmore. Tonight is personal.

I watch her across the lounge, sitting at a table with the girls, laughing and leaning into Madison as she tells some ridiculous story. The guys on the team are slowly filtering over, one by one, to say hi, grab a selfie, or just hover with that easy, athletic charm.

Blood pumps in my veins–I won't deny it. Why can they talk to her and I can't? Because I don't want them talking to her. Making her laugh. Making her smile. I want her sitting with me. Touching my hand. Kissing my mouth. Sucking my–

I clamp my jaw shut, forcing the thought back down.

"Dude," Reid says, dropping into the empty spot next to me. "Just go talk to her."

I glance at him. "What?"

"Go talk to her. Everyone knows you have a crush on her, and I don't blame you. She's hot and really fun. I like her."

"I don't need your permission to talk to a woman, Wilder," I snap, though my voice is quieter than I want it to be.

He rolls his eyes. "Stop being a pussy and go, because there's only one reason you haven't found another chick to spend the night with and she's sitting over there with my girlfriend."

He's not wrong. I *am* being a pussy. And if Ingrid wasn't here, I'd be balls deep in one of the girls hanging out in the main bar, chasing the high from the win a little bit longer.

I stare back at her, the way her hair falls over her shoulder, the way she tilts her head, caught mid-laugh. I know what I want. Wanting her is the easiest thing in the world. It's an urge I've had since I hit puberty. And if this was just about sex, it would be a no brainer. I could get in her pants, make her feel good, and walk away without another thought. But that's not where my head's at. The

timing, the expectations, the unspoken rules we're dancing around–
it's confusing.

And yet, the longer I stay here, frozen, the longer I watch other guys inching toward her, the more I realize that hesitation isn't going to make it any easier. I inhale, pushing the adrenaline and nerves down into my chest. My eyes flick to Reid, who smirks knowingly, and then back to her. Tonight is chaotic, loud, messy, and perfect.

And then everything kicks up a notch.

One of Ingrid's songs comes on and everyone notices. Heads turn. Some people clap, some whistle. Me? My stomach drops. This could be weird. Embarrassing. But not for her. She's too fucking classy for that. She grins, hops up from the table, and without hesitation pulls the other girls with her. Shelby, Twyler, Nadia–they squeal like teenagers as Ingrid drags them onto the dance floor.

And just like that, the room shifts. The energy spikes. She doesn't just *own* the moment–she *is* the moment. Wearing a midriff bearing black sweater and a thigh-skimming plaid school-girl skirt, and a pair of thigh-high boots that have my cock at a perpetual half-mast. She throws her arms up, hips swaying, mouth open on a laugh, singing her own lyrics like they belong to the entire room. The crowd eats it up. Guys slip in around her, trying to join the circle, sliding closer than they should.

My blood heats.

It's not the dancing. It's them making her laugh. Making her smile in ways that I want to claim. Before I've fully decided to move, I'm on my feet, threading through bodies, ignoring the slaps on the back and lures to get into other conversations. The closer I get, the tighter the knot in my chest pulls. Some asshole tries to put his hands on her hips and I shove past, knocking into his shoulder hard enough he stumbles.

"What the fuck, dude," Mitch, one of the younger defensemen, snaps at me.

I don't care. My fingers are already at her waist, sliding against the hem of that short skirt. I spin her, and she collides into me, all heat and soft curves slamming against my chest.

She's tall in those heels, almost eye level. Close enough to kiss. Close enough to feel her breath on my mouth. I like it.

The song fades into a new one, but I barely hear it. My hands tighten on her waist, and I bend to her ear.

"Before this goes any further, I need you to understand something about me." My voice is low, rough. "I'm a player. I spend my nights on sorority row hooking up, moving from one girl to the next. I've got every puck bunny on campus on speed dial. I don't do relationships. I'm focused on my future. I have six weeks of school left, exams, and a contract waiting for me in Florida. I left you that message before your concert hoping that you'd give me a call and I could fulfill a fantasy."

She looks up at me, not with anger or even rejection, but with this sharp, curious spark, like she's dissecting me the way she does a song. "And?"

"And," I swallow, pulling her tighter against me, "I didn't take my shot that night, not the way I planned, because you're different than I expected. Fun. Smart. Talented." A shudder rolls down my spine and settles in my balls. "Sexy as fuck. And I think if I get a taste of you, a real taste, it won't be enough."

The confession hangs heavy, drowning out the music and the crowd.

Her brows lift, amused, deliberate. "So you're saying you'll ruin me?"

"Other way around. You'll ruin me." I release a humorless laugh. "I don't get ruined, Angel. I'm the guy who keeps things casual, easy, forgettable. A quick night of fun for everyone. But the way you've been looking at me? The way you've got me waiting on the next text, the next contact? It's driving me fucking crazy. And just when I think I'll never see you again, you show up in my team colors, wearing short skirts and painted red lips. Yeah, what I have in mind isn't casual." My pulse is hammering so loud I can feel it in my ears. "So before we do this, you need to know the truth. I'm selfish. I'm entitled. And if I get you, I don't think I'll be able to go back to pretending I don't want you again tomorrow."

Her lips curl slow, dangerous, deliberate. Like she knows exactly how much power she has and how much of it I just handed her. "You make it sound like a warning."

"It is."

She leans closer, so close her tits press against my chest, so close the lights flash in her eyes like fire.

"Good thing I'm not easily scared off." Ingrid tilts her head, eyes glittering. "If I was one of those girls–the phi whatever or the puck bunny–what would you do right now?"

I don't hesitate. "I'd have my mouth on you, not giving a fuck if anyone could see. I'd slide my fingers between your legs to see if you're good and wet."

Her cheeks turn pink and she swallows thickly. "A-and?"

I splay my hand across her lower back, pulling her an inch closer. "I'd get you somewhere quiet, alone. Spread you out where I can see you and lick your pussy until you cried my name out, begging me to stop, unable to take more."

Beneath that black sweater I see the hard peaks of her nipples, tightening with every filthy word. The room has vanished around us, even though I know every single person is watching. Any question about who Ingrid came to see at the game is slowly being answered.

Her lips part, like she's trying to catch her breath. I know I've pushed too far saying it out loud, half the damn team and their girl-friends are probably lip-reading, but I don't care.

Her hand brushes mine, just barely, but it's enough to light me up.

"You talk a big game, Parks," she whispers, low enough only I can hear.

I grin, leaning in so my mouth grazes her ear. "Sweetheart, that's the difference between me and those other guys littered across your past–I don't just talk. I back up my words with actions."

Her nails dig into my palm, and my pulse nearly snaps my veins open.

And just like that, the game's changed.

But before I can make my next move, the music dims and Reese Cockblocker Cain, claps his hands over his head, calling for attention, and the music cuts. The noise dies down quick. When the captain speaks, everyone listens. He hops up on the stage where the DJ is set up and raises his beer like it's a trophy.

"This season," he says, voice carrying, "has been the best damn ride of my life. You all know how bad last year stung. Losing that championship–I felt like I'd let every single one of you down." He pauses, grin tugging at the corner of his mouth. "But turns out, sometimes you gotta lose everything to figure out what really matters."

The guys clap and hoot, and Reese holds up a hand for quiet. "Most of all, I need to thank the one person who made it happen. Twyler, you helped me get my head out of my ass and reminded me what fighting for something important actually looks like." The cheers rise again, whistles and stomping feet, Twyler's blue eyes are huge as the spotlight hits her. She's not one for big gestures or attention. Reese barrels on anyway, raising his voice. "And I gotta give it up for the rest of you, too. Axel–our brick wall. You've carried us when we couldn't get the puck in the net." The crowd laughs, Axel bows like a showman. "Reid—always there to take the hits, and the main reason I still have all my teeth. That's love, man. And Jefferson…" Reese looks right at me, grinning wide. "You've been the best friend and wing-man I could ask for, and I know your career's just starting. Florida's not ready for you, bro."

The room erupts again, noise crashing over us. The mood shifts softer, warmer, less like a party and more like a family gathering. And while every eye is locked on Reese, I lean down, lips brushing Ingrid's ear.

"Come with me."

She blinks at me, startled, but the hum of approval around us keeps everyone's attention fixed on the captain while he continues to go through the team's roster, thanking everyone for their efforts. I lace my fingers through hers, tugging gently, and she doesn't resist.

We slip off the edge of the crowd, weaving between bodies, unnoticed as Axel shouts another joke. Past the buffet, past the bar, and into the quieter stretch of the hotel's hallway. My pulse is a steady drum in my ears as I tug her into a tucked-away alcove between the elevators and the coat check, a former payphone bank, shadows curling around us like a secret.

Finally, alone.

The second we're out of sight, I pin her to the wall, my hands braced on either side of her head. Her breath hitches, and then my mouth is on hers, hungry and hot, like I've been holding myself back for too long. She tastes like champagne and heat, and when her lips part for me, I nearly lose it.

Her hands slide up my chest, fisting in the collar of my shirt, pulling me closer. Crowding her space, I want her to feel my full body, every line and how much I want her. My fingers skim down her sides, over her hips, before locking around her waist and dragging her tight against my erection. She gasps into my mouth, and it only makes me kiss her harder, deeper. I'm starving and she's the only thing that can feed me.

"Fuck you feel so good, Angel," I tell her, watching as her back arches off the wall, that tight body pressing closer into mine. I let my hand travel lower, fingers dipping under that teasing skirt. I cup her ass, grinding her up along my erection, wanting the friction. She moans, soft but desperate, and the sound shoots straight through me.

There's no space between us now, just heat and want and the frantic slide of our mouths. Every kiss feels like it's tearing me apart and putting me back together again.

"Angel," I rasp against her mouth.

"God, Jefferson," she whispers, kissing me like she's starved, like she's been waiting all night for this exact second.

I grab her thigh and hitch it up higher against my hip, my palm sliding back under her skirt. She's warm. So fucking warm. My fingers trail up the inside of her leg, and she shivers, breaking the kiss just long enough to breathe, to tilt her head back against the wall.

"I've been dying to touch you," I say, my voice rougher than I mean it to be. "All night. Knowing you were watching me on the ice..." My lips trace down her jaw, hot and open, until I find the spot under her ear that makes her tremble. "You have no idea what you're doing to me."

Her hips shift, pressing against mine, like she's daring me to prove it.

"I think I do," she whispers, dragging her nails down my chest, lower, until she brushes right over where my cock is threatening to split my pants. The pressure makes me groan into her throat.

I can't stop. My hand slides higher, dragging her skirt up with it, my thumb grazing the edge of her panties. She arches into me, breath stuttering, eyes dark and blown wide when I pull back just enough to look at her.

"Tell me to stop," I manage, even though every part of me is screaming to go further, faster. But she doesn't. She shakes her head, lips curving in this sweet little smile that seals my fate.

"Don't," she says. "Don't you dare stop."

I've always been good at following directions.

She gasps, clutching at the front of my button down shirt like she's trying to hold herself steady, but I press in closer, caging her against the wall with my hips so she knows she doesn't have to. I've got her.

My fingers glide over her slick heat, teasing the soft folds, and I bite back a groan because it kills me that we're not going to have sex tonight. Not here. Not yet. But that doesn't mean I can't give her something. Doesn't mean I can't take this chance and show her how much I want her.

"You feel that?" I murmur against her lips, my thumb circling slow, firm pressure against her slippery clit. "So wet. That's all for me, isn't it?"

She whimpers, a sound that shoots straight to my cock, and nods like she can't even find her voice. Her hips move on their own, chasing the rhythm of my hand, grinding down against me with this desperate little urgency that makes me dizzy.

I kiss her harder, swallowing every broken breath, every sound she gives me. My free hand fists in her hair, tugging her head back so I can taste the soft line of her throat, then her jaw, before I claim her mouth again.

I don't care that there's a party raging down the hall. I don't care if someone notices we're missing. All I care about is this: the way she's coming apart under my hand, the way her thighs tighten and shake when I slide a finger inside her painfully tight pussy, the way she moans into my mouth like she's giving herself over to me completely.

"Fuck, you're tight."

"Maybe it's your massive fingers," she replies, exhaling the words.

I move slowly at first, stretching her out, then ask, "You want more?"

She nods, eyes fluttering shut. I push in another and watch her face as she takes me in. "So good, Angel, you're doing so good."

I feel like a man possessed, wanting nothing more than to make her feel incredible. I know I probably won't get another chance like this, not for a long time. So I'm going to make damn sure she remembers tonight.

12

I ngrid

I'M PUTTY in his hands.

Like completely lost to the sensation of this big, hulking, magic-fingered man.

Every nerve ending is on fire. Every brush of his fingers against me makes me forget the world outside, forget the music and the crowd and all the impossible logistics of what we're doing.

I'm Ingrid Flockton, the biggest pop star in the world, and I'm getting fingered in a hotel alcove by a college hockey player. Yes, somewhere in my functional mind, I know this is wrong. It's crazy. Dangerous in a million different ways.

But in the part of my brain that seeks pleasure? It's the best moment of my life.

I ride him. Ride his hand, his thigh, his fingers pumping in and out. He's rough. Not clumsy–God no. *No.* There's skill in his movements. Strong. Sure. My hips buck without thinking. My chest presses against him, my hair tangling against my cheeks. I cry out at every brush over my clit, hot and sensitive–*desperate*, trembling, needing.

He says dirty things to me. Muttering how I'm tight. How good I'm taking him. How he can't wait to feel me clench around his cock. He tells me he jerks off thinking about me. How he can't wait to taste and feel my tits.

There's no poetry there. No flashy lyrics or tender, sweet words. No. His tongue is filthy, and I want it in my mouth.

I can feel the tension in his body, the taut muscles beneath my palms. His other hand snakes up my back, gripping, anchoring me to him so I couldn't run even if I wanted to.

"I'm close," I tell him, my voice breaking under the intensity. Because if he stops, I think I may die. My eyes flick to his, searching, and I see that same stubborn, raw determination that I saw on the ice. It's unbelievably sexy and hot.

"Come for me, Angel."

He keeps calling me that and I don't know why, nothing about this moment is angelic–although it may fall into the divine. Whatever it means, I don't care. I can't stop chasing his touch. My body is entirely his, trembling and pliant, craving the next stroke, the next push, the next spark of contact that will rocket me into oblivion.

I push up, clamping my teeth around his bottom lip in a mixture of protest and need, and crumble apart, shattering into a million glimmers of starlight. Every nerve ending seems to explode simultaneously, every shiver and gasp magnified, drawn out and infinite.

I cling to him, eyes squeezed shut, letting the sensation wash over me. His lips find mine, hot and insistent, tasting, claiming, holding me through it. I can feel his cock straining against my thigh, hard and heavy, and I want it. I want him. But right now, I just need this–*need him* to keep me together while I fall apart.

When it finally ebbs, my body still quivering, I feel the heavy press of his hand against the small of my back, steadying me. I lean into him, forehead against his chest, inhaling the scent of his skin, the heat radiating from his body, the strength in his arms.

I let out a shaky laugh. "It's your night to celebrate and it feels like I'm the one who got the prize."

He tugs me a little closer, lips brushing the top of my head. "Trust me, if I got to feel you come on my fingers, I'd win every game for the rest of my life." He pulls out and I mourn the loss of the fullness, but he's not finished. "If anyone's ever made you feel like you weren't the best part of their day, give me their number. I'll fuck him up–and then find you and make you come again."

I shiver at his words, a flush creeping across my chest, and my hands clutch at his shirt as if I can anchor myself to him. For one stolen moment, the world outside this alcove doesn't exist. There's only him, only me, only the pounding of my heart and the echo of what just happened.

And even though I know it's insane, maybe even stupid, I can't bring myself to care. Because I've never felt this seen. This wanted. This *alive*.

One thing I do know for sure: whatever control I thought I had in this situation is slowly slipping away.

THE NEXT DAY, we're on the bus by dawn, heading for the next city. I'm sitting in my chair while Steven, my massage therapist, works wonders on my sore calves.

"Why are your muscles so tense?" he asks, running his thumb along the back of my leg.

"Because she wanted to look cute last night, she wore heels." Madison drops into the chair across from mine, phone in hand.

"I did look cute." Do I have regrets that those heels made me tall enough for Jefferson's hands to reach me better? No. Will I pay for it on stage for the next week? Definitely.

"Ready for your daily dose of chaos?" Madison asks.

I flop my head back and groan. "Do I have a choice?"

"Nope. Listen to this one." She clears her throat like a news anchor. "*Stage Lights, Stadium Ice: Is Ingrid Falling for a Frozen Four Star?*"

I roll my eyes. "Very creative. Ten points for rhyme."

Madison grins and scrolls. "*'Pop Princess + Hockey Hunk? Fans Think They've Cracked Ingrid's Love Life.'*"

"Ugh." I press my hands on my face. "That one even sounds like bad fanfiction."

"Oh wait, here's my personal favorite." She reads it slowly, savoring every word. "*Frozen Four Favorite Scoring More Than Goals? Ingrid Fans Demand Answers.'*"

"They didn't actually write that."

"They did. And it gets better." She holds up the screen. "*'Backstage Pass... or Boyfriend? Rumors Tie Ingrid to Hockey Heartthrob.'*"

Steve snickers under his breath. Traitor.

"I *danced* with him, Madison. That's it."

She smirks. "Yeah, sure. Just dancing. Totally explains this one–" She scrolls again and reads, sing-song: "*'Ingrid's Mystery Man Revealed? Sources Link Her to Wittmore Enforcer Jefferson Parks.'*"

I snatch her phone. "Give me that."

She holds it just out of reach, cackling. "Oh no, honey. We're not done. '*Caught Off-Ice: Ingrid Flockton Dances With Frozen Four Winner at Victory Party.'*"

I bury my face in my hands. "I hate everyone."

Madison pats my knee with mock sympathy. "Correction: you hate everyone who isn't six-foot-four, blond, and currently headed to the NHL."

I peek at her through my fingers, my cheeks burning. "You're the worst."

"And you're trending." Which leads her to ask the big question. "So, what's really going on with Jefferson Parks?"

"Jefferson who?" I play dumb, like my body doesn't light on fire just hearing his name.

"The hockey player that everyone saw you canoodling with last night."

"I don't even know what the word canoodling means." I blink. "But fine. We've been talking. It's no big deal."

She holds up the phone again, and there's a grainy image of me and Jefferson on the dance floor. If only they knew what he was saying to me. "The media thinks it's a big deal."

"Me, dancing with a guy at a party, is a big deal? What? Can I not be seen with any men and it just be a casual thing?" I snap back, though the edge in my voice comes more from exhaustion than actual anger. After Jefferson gave me the most epic orgasm of my life, we went back into the victory party like nothing had happened, celebrated for a few more hours, and then went our separate ways.

I haven't heard from him, which is fine. Normal, right?

Please. I have no idea what 'normal' looks like.

"It's not that you can't," Madison says gently. "But you've cultivated a specific persona. When you're seen with a man, the fans and the media speculate. You know they're invested in your love life."

Invested. These people have no clue what's going on in my life. Most of them would be ecstatic for me to get back with Jake. That's because they have no idea how awful he was to me. But have I told anyone? No. I keep my mouth shut and let my music do the talking.

"Fine. Then let's put out a statement, tell everyone he's a friend of a friend. Appease the fans. Done."

"And what is really going on? You'll start seeing him on the sly? Sneaking around again?" That question hits like a punch and she knows it. She shakes her head, patient but firm. "This guy isn't from your world. He doesn't get your life and what you go through."

"And you think the guys I've dated before–the musicians, the trust fund babies, the artists–got me?" My laugh is sharp, bitter. God, my dating history is littered with the worst, most entitled, immature men. "Jake didn't get me. He destroyed me. And we both know it."

Madison's face softens. "I'm just saying, focus on your work. If this thing is meant to be, it'll happen. But your schedule is insane right now. Don't let some hot guy with muscles distract you."

I hesitate, then smile despite myself. "He is hot, right?" I can't help it–the memory of his big hands feels branded across my skin.

"Super hot," Madison admits.

"Blazing," Steven chimes in. No surprise. He has a thing for blonds.

"Look, Ing," Madison says, "I get the attraction. Just, please, don't let another guy pull you away from your goals."

The thing about break-ups, particularly the one with Jake, is that it lit a fire under me creatively. I wrote two dozen songs, put out the best-selling album of my life, and this tour has been one sold-out night after the other. Breakups are good for me, financially. Falling in love? Well, that's less of a positive track record.

Whatever statement Madison and the PR team cobble together doesn't matter. By the time we roll into the next concert, the fans have already woven little pieces of Jefferson into their costumes and signs. The number 23 surrounded by Flock Wings has been painted onto posters. Gold and black badger mascots wave from the pit. And the wild part? They don't seem angry. They seem... happy for me.

The vibration in the arena is higher than ever, or maybe it's just me. Maybe it's the texts I exchanged with Jefferson right before walking out on stage.

Jparks23: *Figure it out yet?*

I'd smiled so big that Roxy, my makeup artist, had to touch up my lipstick. I don't care, the game is back on.

IngFlock: *What about "Mellow"?*

Jparks23: *Good one, but nope. You're bad at this game. You should quit.*

IngFlock: *Never. I'll crack the code.*

Jparks23: *Good luck tonight.*

IngFlock: *What are you doing tonight?*

Jparks23: *Playing video games, eating some of Nadia's Kolaches, and replaying how sexy your face looked last night when you fell apart on my fingers.*

The words still hum through me as I step under the stage lights, the crowd's roar crashing over me like a wave. Jefferson has a dirty mouth. He's bold and not afraid to say what he's thinking.

It's different, and for a woman who cycles through the same days and nights, the same heartache and pain, it's enticing, enthralling. It should have just been a one-off, but sitting here texting with him? I think I may want more.

"Wʜᴀᴛ ᴛʜᴇ ʜᴇʟʟ ᴡᴀs ᴛʜᴀᴛ?" I barely hear Madison as she accosts me the second I'm off stage. The fans are losing it in the arena, their screams and shouts bouncing off the rafters. Me? I'm not finished yet. This is the part of the show no one sees. I'm immediately surrounded by people. Costumers, makeup, hair, and physical therapists. I'm sweaty, vocally spent, and about to crash. I'm handed a smoothie filled with enough calories, vitamins, and electrolytes to keep me from passing out after a three-hour-long workout.

Glancing over at my friend, I know that Madison's question isn't an admonishment. No way. I know what happened on that stage. It may have been the best show of my life.

"That was epic. Fucking incredible."

Doctor's orders keep me from responding. I rest my vocals for two hours after each show. And truthfully, I have no way to answer the question. I was just filled with new energy. A desire to bring it all onto the stage. I kept thinking about Jefferson and the team, how they owned that game.

I want to own my game, too.

Back at the hotel, I limp straight to the recovery room. The trainers are already waiting with a professional level set up. There's an ice bath, a massage table, and a doctor ready to tape and check the blisters on my feet. Glamorous, right? This is the part no one sees on stage.

My phone buzzes right as I lower myself into the tub, a hiss escaping through my teeth. The trainer holds up the phone, and Jefferson's name lights up the screen.

Like a teenage girl, I yelp, wave for it, and accept the video call.

His handsome face appears on the screen, those sharp cheekbones carving up the screen. "Hey–wait, where are you?"

"Ice bath." I punctuate this with an exhale. "Post show recovery."

"Wow, that's hardcore. We have the same thing at the arena."

"Told you I was tough," I reply, trying not to flinch when the cold water bites at my skin.

"Never doubted it, Angel."

I'm smiling, even though my teeth are chattering. "So, what's up?"

"So this statement about us..."

My stomach drops. "Oh god, you saw it." I press my hand over my face. "I just told Madison to smooth things over. Hopefully it didn't cross any lines."

He chuckles, low and unbothered. "I guess there are worse things than being called the '*The handsome enforcer that led his team to a Frozen Four Victory.*'"

"Wait, read it to me."

Jefferson's lips quirk as he scrolls through his phone. "You ready?"

"Hit me."

"'Is Ingrid Flockton Off the Market? Frozen Four Sparks New Romance Rumors,'" he begins. "'Speculation has run wild since international pop star Ingrid Flockton made a surprise appearance at the Frozen Four in Chicago last weekend. Fans weren't sure if she was there for a friend, family, or something more. Those questions heated up when Flockton was spotted at Wittmore's Victory Party, where she hit the dance floor with Jefferson Parks, better known as *the handsome enforcer that led his team to a Frozen Four Victory.*'" He emphasises the last line and gives me a wink that threatens to warm me up in the cold bath. He continues. "'Seeing them together, you couldn't miss the sparks,' a source at the party shared. 'They weren't hiding it— they looked like they were in their own world.' So... are they an item? Did Parks take home more than the trophy?'"

I wrinkle my nose. "Oh jeez. Is the rest of the team mad you were singled out like that?"

He shakes his head. "Not mad. Jealous probably. They're all petty bitches."

"That is not what we sent in," I say quickly, cheeks burning even though he can't see me. "So don't get a big head. They embellish everything for clicks."

"You sure?" His voice turns cocky, that grin growing wider in my imagination. "Because every time I talk to you, my head gets bigger." His eyes darken. "At least the one in my pants."

I nearly slip in the tub. "You did not just say that."

"I think I did."

I groan, but the sound melts into laughter before I can stop it.

"Time," Carlos calls. I'd forgotten he was here.

"Thank god. Hold on." I set the phone face down and let Carlos help me out of the tub. Cold water rushes down my body. My skin is pink, but I feel invigorated, and a moment later I'm wrapped in a warm robe and led to my suite. Once I'm alone, I open the video again.

"Better?" he asks.

"Yes." There's a covered plate, and I carry it over to a cozy chair. Propping my phone on my water bottle, I open the lid, revealing my dinner. The next thing he says surprises me.

"You were incredible tonight."

I look up from my salmon and rice bowl in surprise. "You watched?"

"I don't think I've missed a show since the tour started."

It hits me again. He's a fan. Which makes it hard to know what is real and what isn't.

Ingrid, my inner voice speaks up, *that orgasm was one million percent real.*

But that's the thing about Jefferson, every encounter, every text, phone call, dance on a crowded floor; he's genuine. Talkative. Sweet. Raw. And yeah, undeniably sexy.

So slipping into conversation with him is easy.

We talk about everything. I tell him about the show–the way it's blocked and choreographed, how every step has to look effortless while hiding the fact that I'm counting beats in my head. I explain how I choose the songs for the set list, the push and pull of tempo, how the ballads have to be placed just right to give both me and the crowd a breather. I even let him in on the endless debates about costumes, how many backup outfits I carry in case something rips or malfunctions.

He listens like every word matters. Then, with a little prompting, he tells me about Wittmore–about how it's important for him to get his grades based on merit, not by just being another college athlete, about the exams and final projects he has left and the way hockey bleeds into every corner of campus life. At some point, he leans away from the camera, bangs on his wall, and yells for Axel to turn down the music. The sudden flash of irritation makes me laugh.

But then the shift of his body catches me off guard. The camera tips just enough to reveal the pale slope of his shoulders, the cut of muscle across his chest. He's shirtless, sprawled against the headboard of his bed, the glow of his lamp painting his skin in warm tones. The sight steals the air from my lungs.

Any lingering chill from my bath vanishes as heat licks through me, slow and insistent. My robe suddenly feels too heavy, too warm. I tug at the collar, my fingers brushing the hollow of my throat as I force myself to keep talking like nothing's changed, like I'm not imagining what it would feel like to be the one lying against him instead of watching through a screen.

"When can I see you again?" he asks, after I've yawned for the third time. The way he says it is like he already knows the answer, but needs to hear it anyway.

I sigh. "Not for a while. I've got two straight weeks down south. Charlotte, then three nights in Atlanta, another four in Florida…"

He groans, shoving his hand through his hair, giving me a peek of his rounded bicep, black ink branded into the smooth skin. "Guess I'll just have to keep calling and texting."

"I guess I'll keep answering," I tease back.

He licks his bottom lip and my mouth parts. The heat between us is charged, even through the screen. Maybe because of it. I feel as if he's standing right in front of me. And the ache blooming in my chest feels dangerous–like wanting more is the first step toward heartbreak. Staring back into those blue eyes, I have to decide if Jefferson Parks is worth the risk.

13

J efferson

It's Friday night, almost a week after winning the Frozen Four, and the high still hasn't stopped buzzing in my veins. I'm not the only one riding it. The guys decided to throw a party at The Manor. It's our last hurrah before exams, before scattering to the crush of work and graduation. Why not? Our Wittmore days are running out, and it feels like everyone's determined to wring every last ounce of glory out of the win.

I've got a cold beer sweating in my hand and three puck bunnies orbiting like satellites. Usually, that would be my idea of a good night filled with easy smiles, soft hands, girls who know the game and what I'm good for. But tonight? They've got questions.

"Ingrid Flockton," Chantel says, her eyes glittering with gossip. "Did you really meet her? What's she like?"

The truth is on the tip of my tongue: smart, sexy, beautiful, fun.

Fuck. Too much for words. But I lock it down, sip my beer, and give them the line. "A lot like what you see in the media."

Alicia leans in, her eyeliner thick and angled. "How did you end up dancing with her?"

We returned from Chicago not just Frozen Four champions, but also with the buzz of having partied with Ingrid. I've heard the girls tell the same story over and over: they met her at the Badger Den. Became friendly. It developed from there.

That would have been enough to appease the masses, but the two of us being spotted on the dance floor escalated the gossip another few notches. Not only that, the pom-pom beanie was one of Reid's designs for the team. After she was seen in it at the game, it, and every other piece of his merch in the team shop, sold out in an hour.

This woman is electric.

I look back down at Alicia. "The same way I end up with any woman," I smirk, though it feels hollow. "I took a chance."

Ruby lays her hand flat on my chest, nails sharp through my shirt. "Did you kiss her? If I kiss you, does that mean I've had one degree of separation between me and Ingrid Flockton?"

"Funny." My gaze dips to her lips. Soft pink, familiar. I've had them wrapped around my cock before, more than once. Normally, the memory would stir me up. Tonight? I close my eyes, and it's not Ruby's mouth I picture. It's *hers.* Red lips that taste like sunshine. Lavender hair brushing my cheek. And a laugh that makes my stomach lurch like I've just dropped down the first hill of a roller coaster.

The beer goes flat in my mouth. I need out. I need air.

"Excuse me, ladies," I give them my heartbreaker smile, but I'm already backing up, sliding past them before one can grab me again.

Pushing through the closest door, I find myself on the porch–only it's not empty. Wrong turn. It's Shelby's room. She's perched on Reid's lap, and they're making out like the world's ending.

I freeze, then lean against the doorframe, watching. Not sure why–probably just to remind myself what it looks like when some-one's all in. Their relationship is still new, they haven't had time to become tired of one another. And it's well known that Reid was Shelby's first. She's still getting a taste of sex and love. I guess that's why I stand still and track Shelby's hand in Reid's red hair, and he's holding her like he'd fight off an army just to keep kissing her.

Reid breaks first, noticing me. "What the fuck, man?"

I shrug, lifting the bottle in my hand like it explains everything. "Didn't want to interrupt."

He's already annoyed, adjusting himself as Shelby slides off his lap, cheeks pink. "Do you need something? Are you okay?"

"I needed a breather."

"From who?" Reid asks, shooting daggers at me. I don't blame him. I'm cockblocking him hard.

"The puck bunnies." I rake a hand down my face. "Is it me, or are they worse since we won the playoffs?"

Shelby snorts.

"What?" I ask.

"They're always awful," she says matter-of-factly. "You just usually enjoy it."

Reid barks a laugh, eyes narrowing. "Seriously, man, you're usually balls deep by now, with another one on deck. What's the deal?"

My shrug is stiff, defensive. I feel stupid even standing here. Should've just gone to my room. They're both watching me, waiting. Pressure builds until I shove a hand through my hair. "I'm just not into it."

Shelby's grin is slow, knowing. "Because you're thinking about someone else."

Our eyes meet. Fuck. She knows. These girls *always* know.

Reid sees the look pass between us, and he groans, already standing. "Alright. I'm going outside for some air. You two can have your girl talk in here."

He drops one last kiss on Shelby–surely hard enough to aggravate the boner still straining his jeans–before he slips out the door that leads outside, muttering about how he's going to pay me back for this one day, under his breath.

The door clicks shut, leaving me with Shelby's sly little smirk and the truth she's already pieced together.

"We don't have to do this," I say quickly, wondering how this turned so fast. "I will happily go out there and have a three-way and forget this ever happened." I look around the room, anywhere but at her. Shelby still has clothes in here: dresses hung off the bike rack, her work clothes air-drying on hooks originally for plants. She spends most nights upstairs in Reid's room now, but she never moved her things out. A peace offering to Axel, I guess. He can't handle the idea of his best friend banging his little sister every night.

"Sit," she says, patting the spot Reid just vacated. I don't want to, but girls like Shelby make me nervous. She's got that innocent, girl-next-door vibe that has never been my thing, which means I can't sweet-talk my way out of this.

I sit and run my hands down my thighs.

"You've got it bad."

I frown. "What?"

She flicks her gaze up at me, sharp and knowing. "Don't play dumb. I've seen that look before. Same one Reid had when he was trying to pretend he was okay with me going back to Texas."

Within twenty-four hours, he'd followed her home to get her back.

"I don't know her, Shelby. I just met her and she's cool, and yes, gorgeous, but she's not even here. She never will be. So what's the point?"

Well. That was a lot of truth vomited out all at once.

"Tell me something..." She sits up, tucking her legs under her, smirking like she's already won. "Did you sleep with her?"

"Where? At her apartment? At the victory party?" I play it off like it wasn't the second and third time we'd been together. Like there hadn't been another opportunity. "I work fast, Rakestraw, but not that fast."

She makes a face like she doesn't believe that. Fair. I *do* work that fast. When I want to.

"So you had the opportunity to cross her name off your list and you didn't do it." She tilts her head. "Why?"

"It didn't feel right."

Her eyebrow lifts. "Jefferson Parks. Wittmore's resident player had a chance to bang Ingrid Flockton and didn't because 'it didn't feel right'?"

"She's just–" I cut myself off, shaking my head. "Forget it."

Shelby studies me, and I don't like it. "Not what? Not just hot? Not just famous? Not just a name you wanted to check off your list?"

I glance at her, jaw tight. "She's not a game."

That earns me a grin, wide and smug. "Oh my God. You actually like her."

I grab a pillow and hurl it at her, but she just catches it and hugs it to her chest, laughing.

"You're screwed, Jefferson," she teases. "Totally, completely screwed."

"Yeah," I slump back against the couch, "tell me something I don't know."

"Fine, I will." Shelby leans forward, elbows on her knees, eyes cutting right through me. "Ingrid isn't the kind of girl you screw around with. She's been hurt in the past. She puts on a brave face, but she's lonely, Jefferson. She's been through heartbreak. She plays it off like it's just music, just the tour, just the spotlight–but the way she opened her home to me and the other girls? That's not normal. That's someone who's craving connection."

I rub a hand over my face, exhaling slowly.

"If this is something you want," Shelby continues, steady and sure, "be serious about it. It may not work out in the long run, but if you treat her like you've treated the other girls at Wittmore? You'll lose her–and you'll hurt her. And she doesn't deserve that."

Her words settle like lead in my chest. The worst part? She's right. I've made a career out of chasing the fun, the easy, the temporary. But Ingrid? She feels like something else. Something slippery, like it could easily slide through my fingers. But most of all, she feels like something that could wreck me if I screw it up.

REID RETURNS and gives me a hard stare that screams, "Get the fuck out." I take the cue and head upstairs, the noise from the party trailing after me, and close myself in my room. It's quieter up here, though the bass still thuds through the floorboards. I grab my phone, flop back onto the bed, and before I can overthink it, I hit her number.

She answers on the third ring, voice low–sleepy–face coming into view. "Hey."

"Hi."

I smile without meaning to. Just hearing her knocks something loose in my chest.

"Did I wake you?"

"Not really." She shifts, and I see the thin strap of her tank top falling off her shoulder. "I was working on some new music."

Of course she was. I picture her on that bus, guitar across her lap, headphones in, scribbling lyrics that'll end up in people's veins one day.

"Can I hear it?"

She laughs a little, soft. "Maybe when it's finished."

"I can't wait." And that's the thing. I can't. The idea of her keeping pieces of herself tucked away while I'm out here starving for them makes me restless. "I want to see you again."

There's a pause, and I watch her shifting again, brushing hair from her face, biting down on that puffy bottom lip. "I'd like to see you too, but–"

"Yeah, we're busy," I cut in, trying not to sound disappointed. "I know." We just look at each other, through the phone, through the silence. The urge to be with her intensifies.

"I mean," I push on, "I could probably get away next weekend…"

That wakes her up. I can see it on her face when she sits straighter. My eyes dart down to the teasing dip of her cleavage, the darkened outline of her nipples as they press against the cotton. My fingers twitch. "You'd come to Atlanta?"

"Why not?" I grin. "I could drag Reid with me, or Axel. For once, we don't have hockey practice or games. We could hang out and wait for you to finish your show, and then you and I..."

I don't finish the sentence. No way to say what I mean without laying it all bare. The things I want to say, the things I want to *do*–they sit heavy on my tongue. Jesus. This girl has me fucking tied in knots.

"Let me see what I can work out," she says finally.

"Don't go to any trouble. We'll figure it out. Road trip, right?"

"Sounds good."

In the background of her side of the call, I hear faint movement, maybe the hum of the road under the bus tires. Then she notices the noise bleeding into mine. "Is that Axel again?"

I roll my eyes, glancing toward the window where the house lights flare with shadows. "Eh, the guys are throwing a party."

"Why aren't you down there?"

"Guess talking to you seemed like the better way to go." I stretch out, propping up on my elbow, making it clear I'm in no rush to leave. "I mean, you're alone, I'm alone...we could make this interesting."

"Smooth," she says dryly.

My eyebrow arches. "You travel for a living, and it's well documented that you've been in relationships. Don't tell me you've never had phone sex."

"Fair," she admits, though her voice softens like she's not sure she should give me that. "But something tells me you have other, real-life opportunities to hook up at the moment."

I can hear the faint thump of bass as the rhythm changes and the squeals of girls when their favorite song comes on. She knows they're here. Knows they're available.

"I'm not interested in them," I say with more intent than I plan.

Her brows lift, skeptical. "No?"

I remember what Shelby said, how if I'm going to make a play for Ingrid, I need to be serious. So why the hell am I beating around the bush? "I got a taste of you, Angel. I'm not going to be satisfied until I get more."

Her lips part, just slightly, her chest rising as though the air has been stolen right out of her. "Is that how this works? Jefferson Parks always gets what he wants?"

"Pretty much."

The flush runs up her throat, blooming across her cheeks. It's impossible not to picture it spreading lower, down her collarbone, over the pale swell of her breasts, painting every inch of her in that same delicate pink. The image makes my mouth dry and my pulse hammer.

She catches the way I'm looking at her and gives me that grin—wicked, teasing, like she's the one with control here. She is. We both know it. "Good thing I've made a career out of not giving guys what they want."

My laugh comes out low, rougher than I mean it to. "Guess I'll just have to convince you I'm not like the other guys."

Her eyes narrow, amused, sparking with challenge. "Good luck with that, Parks."

And damn if the way she says my name doesn't make me want her even more.

THE SEASON IS OVER, and we've got the trophy, the rings, the bragging rights. I'm certain that I should be coasting on a high, not sitting outside Coach Bryant's office with Reese, both of us staring at the door like it's about to eat us alive.

"Any clue what this is about?" I ask, leaning back in the chair with my legs sprawled out.

"Nope," Reese says, twirling my championship cap in his hands. "But if it's bad, it's your fault."

I snort, but when Coach calls us in, neither of us is laughing.

The office has looked the same since I got here freshman year: plaques, photos, the faint smell of coffee that's been sitting too long in the pot. Bryant gestures to the chairs across from his desk. We sit.

He studies us a moment, then clears his throat. "I'm sure you're wondering why I've called you in here, and no, you're not in trouble."

He's joking and we both know it, but old behaviors die hard.

"I've been a member of the board of a non-profit designed to identify and cultivate young athletes coming from high-risk environments. Over the years, I've linked many of the young men up with local hockey programs."

"You mean like the foster care program that Reid was in."

"Exactly." His chair creaks underneath him. "This year few young men are in a position to transfer from a junior college program into something bigger, and I've offered them a spot on the team next year."

Reese's brows go up. "Okay, sure, anyone we know?"

"Probably not." Coach leans back in his chair, like he's bracing himself. "These boys come from a specific high-risk community." He finally decides to stop beating around the bush. "They were part of the Serendee community before it was shut down."

Reese blinks. "You mean the cult?"

Bryant's mouth tightens. "I'd rather not use that word. But yes."

Cult is *exactly* the right word. Everyone in Wittmore knows about Serendee–at least the surface version. Started by a Wittmore environmental science major twenty years back. They called it a "sustainable utopia." Living off the land. Growing their own food and butchering their own meat. Sewing their own clothes. Blah blah blah.

But underneath? Whole different story. Tim Wray, the founder, was a fucking creep. He had them all hooked into this breeding program-slash-free labor ring. Guns. Drugs. Sex trafficking. The whole thing was unbelievable. His own kid blew the whistle a few years ago. After that, the Feds raided the compound.

It was pretty much shut down by the time I got here, but the legend was still being passed down, not to mention the documentaries Twyler forced us to watch. The members dressed in plain, old-timey clothes, with blank stares. The women covered up head to toe. You'd catch them walking down Main Street, going in and out of their "recruitment office."

"So you think they're ready for D1?" I ask because none of that adds up to ice rinks and slap shots.

He nods. "These boys are good. Really good. Good enough to carry on the legacy you built."

I exchange a look with Reese and ask, "Why bring us in? We're not even gonna be here next year."

"I know that, dumb ass," Bryant snaps, though there's a twitch of a smile under the gruffness. "I need a few guys with nothing on the line to take some time with them on the ice, maybe show them around campus and help them get comfortable. Welcome them in. Ease them through it. I'll have a few of the rising seniors there, too."

Reese adjusts the brim of his hat. "Sure, Coach. We'd be happy to."

Coach's eyes soften. "They've been through a lot. But you two know as well as anyone–hockey can be a great unifier."

Reese nods. I do too, though my mind is stuck on those old images of blank-eyed kids in hand-stitched clothes. A new batch of teammates, coming from that? It's weird. Unexpected. But maybe Coach is right. Maybe hockey really can fix anything.

THE PACKAGE IS DELIVERED by courier the next evening. He bangs on the door hard enough to rattle the hinges, and Reese is the one who answers it, wiping his hands on a dish towel.

"It's for you, J."

The house is full–the seven of us congregated for dinner. The music Reid picked is humming low under the buzz of conversation. It feels like everyone's trying to soak up these last weeks before everything changes. Tonight we made dinner together, us guys and the girls, crammed elbow to elbow in the kitchen. They cooked, we cleaned, a rhythm we've fallen into without thinking.

Reese holds the door open as I cross the room, Axel feeling up Nadia in the middle of the room. My shirt sticks to me where I swipe my wet hands down the front of it.

"Hey, man," I say, taking the little electronic box the courier thrusts out and scrawling my signature across the screen. "Thanks."

"No problem." He pivots, already heading back down the steps.

"What is it?" Axel asks, releasing Nadia, as I shut the door with my foot.

"Not sure–" I start, but then my eye snags on the stamped and embossed wings in the corner of the package. A sharp jolt kicks through me. "What the fuc…"

I barely have the thing open and the badges in my hand before the room goes apocalyptic.

"She sent us passes?" Shelby blurts, wobbling like her knees just gave out. Her cheeks go pale; she looks seconds from fainting.

I nod, dumbly, as Nadia swoops in, snatching the stack of lanyards right out of my fingers with a gasp.

"What else is in there?" Twyler's voice cuts in, pitched so high it almost cracks.

"Tickets, box seats, backstage passes–" I unfold another sheet of paper, my throat dry, and then look up at the wide-eyed faces staring back. "Directions for getting on her private plane."

"She's flying us down?" Reid demands, his jaw slack. "Dude, what did you do?"

I shake my head, heat crawling up the back of my neck. "Nothing. We've just been talking."

I told her I wanted to see her, and fuck, she made it happen.

They exchange a look, an unspoken chorus of disbelief passing between them.

"Seriously." I raise my hands. "Swear on it."

I know what they think–that I've got her dickmatized or whatever word they'll toss around later. Normally, I'd let them speculate, grin and lean into the legend. But not this time. For once, I'm playing it slow, trying not to burn it down before it even starts. And maybe–it feels insane to even think it–maybe it's actually working.

She wants to see me.

Axel squints, tugging at the hoop in his eyebrow, his voice flat with suspicion. "So you mean, for once, you *didn't* sleep with a woman, and she rewards you with all this?"

"I guess so. I mean, I did–" I cut myself off, swallowing the memory. No way I'm telling them about the fingerbang during the victory party.

Reese smirks, but no one notices because the girls don't give a shit, already falling into a discussion about Shelby getting off work, and Nadia figuring out her outfit and what she can wrangle Twyler into that isn't black jeans and a hoodie.

And me? I just stand there in the middle of it all, pulse hammering, trying to act chill when the truth is I've never felt more unsteady.

Because this–*her*–feels bigger than anything I've let myself want before. And if it all goes south, I don't know if I'll recover. But I started this. I left her that note, and for some crazy reason, she responded. I've never been afraid to take the chance–to shoot my shot–and I'm sure as hell not going to pull back now.

14

____

I ngrid

The next week moves painfully slow, and I do what I do best–throw myself into work.

It's not just the concerts, I work my way into some studio time to lay down the new songs I've been working on. We update the choreography to make sure the show stays fresh. I make a stop at the Children's Hospital to sign autographs and hand out merch. That day is exhausting, and at the end of it, I talk to Jefferson for three hours, just for a slice of goodness in an otherwise tough day.

Our calls have started carrying a new weight–the intensity of our attraction to one another palpable through the line. I'm pretty sure we both get off the call frustrated, pent-up sexual tension bubbling at the surface. He's kind, though. Understanding I can't put something like that into the ether. It could ruin me, and in return, ruin *us*.

Whatever we are.

They're flying down tonight, and I'd made sure they had a suite of rooms at the same hotel–it's easier than shuttling them back and forth. Or that's what I tell myself. I want him close. Even if I don't get to see him as much as I want to, I want him nearby.

It's late when their plane gets in, and I don't expect to see him. My night's been nothing but vocal warmups, emails, and a hot shower I never got around to taking.

So when Marv buzzes the suite and asks if I'm available for a visitor, I almost say no.

Almost.

The way he pauses, just a beat too long, makes my stomach twist.

"It's him, isn't it?" I ask.

Marv is like a big brother on steroids. Fiercely protective. Highly suspicious. The wall you have to get through to get to me. When he says, "Yep," without a lecture, I know he approves.

"Send him up," I say, even though my pulse is hammering and I have no business letting him see me like this.

The second the line goes dead, I bolt for the mirror. Casual mess– that's what's staring back at me. Ponytail that's half-falling out, leggings that have seen better days, and a plain t-shirt that screams *I gave up hours ago.* My eyeliner is smudged from rubbing my eyes too much. This is not the outfit you wear when six-foot-five of dangerous temptation shows up at your hotel door.

A knock.

Too soon. Way too soon.

I swallow hard, try to pat down my hair, and open the door.

There he is. Jefferson Parks. Dimple in his cheek, blond hair that feathers back from his annoyingly perfect, chiseled face, with eyes like polished steel cutting straight through me. He fills the doorway in a way that makes the whole suite feel small.

And then the nerves I've been carrying all week, the what-ifs, the should-I-even-do-this, evaporate.

Because he doesn't hesitate. Not even a beat.

The door shuts behind him, and before I can think, before I can breathe, his mouth is on mine.

It's hard, almost desperate, like he's been holding back since the second he scrawled that stupid note and taped it to his locker. Jesus, he's good at this. I feel the kiss everywhere. In my blood. Rushing through my veins. Deep in my lower belly. His hands are on me instantly, bracketing my face, thumbs grazing my jaw, claiming the right to touch me. He tilts my head back and kisses me like there was never a question of whether I'd let him in.

Or maybe, if he waited for permission, I'd say no, so he's taking the risk.

My fingers fist in his shirt before I even realize I've moved, tugging him closer, grounding myself in the sheer size of him. Six-foot-five of hockey enforcer muscle caging me in, chest solid against mine, heat radiating off him like he's been carrying this burn around for weeks.

Whatever this is–it's fire, it's gasoline, blazing hot and out of control.

I can't get enough.

The taste of him is heat and mint, sharp and addictive, his lips dragging across mine with a hunger that pulls me under before I can think about resurfacing. He kisses like he plays–fast, dangerous, like every second is sudden death overtime. No hesitation. No breaks. Just full tilt until the buzzer.

My back hits the wall with a soft thud, and I don't care. I don't care that my hair's a mess, that I'm in leggings and a t-shirt, that I swore to myself I'd be careful with him. I don't care that I can already hear Madison's warnings screaming in my head. None of it matters.

What matters is the way his breath shudders when I kiss him back, the sound that escapes him when my lips part and his tongue slides against mine, deep and claiming. He makes a low, rough noise in his chest, one that vibrates straight through me, leaving my knees weak.

I'm lost. Completely, stupidly lost. And the worst part is that I don't want to be found.

When we finally pull apart, finally take a breath, he drops his forehead to mine and says, "Holy fuck, Angel, I've been wanting to do that for weeks."

It's not just his words that spin me. It's the thick line of his erection straining down his leg as he presses into me, the heat of his body soaking into mine. He makes no effort to hide it, confident and at ease with his body and his wants. Hard muscle flexes under my palms, solid and unyielding, and all I can think is how badly I want to peel that shirt away. To see his skin, to taste every inch, to memorize him the way I've memorized lyrics.

"Where's everyone else?" I manage, though my voice is wrecked, shaky from the kiss. His big hands are still clamped to my waist, fingers digging like he's scared I might vanish.

"Don't know, don't care," he states, his tone as firm as the steel-gray of his eyes. They flash with a glimmer of something feral.

That's all it takes. A heartbeat later, I'm climbing him like he's the only safe place in the world, my legs wrapping around his waist. He catches me without hesitation, like it's second nature, his mouth crashing back to mine.

The kiss turns wild, messy, his tongue stroking against mine with a hunger that leaves me trembling. He's everywhere–his hands gripping my thighs, his chest pressed tight to mine, his breath ragged in my ear when he tears away just long enough to whisper, "You drive me fucking insane."

I bite his jaw, desperate for more. He jerks me higher, grinding against me in a rhythm that makes my head fall back. A sound tears from my throat, unfiltered, and his answering groan vibrates straight through my body.

We're on the edge of something here, something that could ruin both of us if we let it go too far. And I don't care. Not when he kisses me like I'm oxygen. Not when his body feels like the only thing tethering me to the ground. I fist the back of his shaggy blond hair, tugging hard enough to make him groan, and the sound goes straight between my legs. Every grind of his hips drags heat through me, every press of his body stoking the ache.

I swore I'd be more careful the next time: with my heart and body. With my soul.

But those thoughts are lost when my shirt rides up, his hands spreading across my bare waist, hot and callused, moving like he's memorizing me. I arch into him, desperate, my chest pressed to his, nipples hard against cotton. His eyes burn down into mine, like he's asking for permission and taking it all in the same second.

"Jefferson…" My voice is breathless, a warning, a prayer.

"I know," he says, forehead pressed to mine, hips rolling once more before he stills. His restraint is a thin thread, trembling between us. "I know, but I can't stop touching you."

Neither can I.

His hands trace slowly over my sides, the tips of his fingers drawing tiny circles that leave sparks in their wake.

"Can I touch you?" he asks, voice raw. "Can I make you fall apart again?"

The ask is hotter than anything that's ever happened to me. The way he hands control back over to me, like he knows how much I need it.

I nod, and he eases me across the room until my backside hits the desk. His hands are gentle but insistent, sliding beneath the waist-band of my leggings. He doesn't rush; he takes his time exposing one leg and then the other. His mouth hovers near my ear, whispering encouragement, teasing little moans, and each one twists something deep inside me.

He lifts me up on the desk, wedging himself between my knees. "Let's see how wet you are for me."

When he bends before me, I can feel his presence is completely different from before. He's no longer feral, he's grounded, patient, intent. My panties come off, a slow drag that feels excruciating. His hands split me apart, pushing my thighs and exposing myself to him. The way he looks at me, my skin crackles and flares, it's like a man seeing the universe for the first time.

"Goddamn, Ingrid."

"What?" I ask, rising up, horrified.

He runs a finger down my slit. "Prettiest fucking pussy I've ever seen."

The declaration is insane, and coming from another man I may have laughed in his face. But Jefferson Parks looks like a starving man in front of a buffet.

He spreads me apart with his fingers and then licks.

I fall back on my hands, letting him meet me in the most exquisite way. Slow, deliberate strokes, circling, tracing, teasing every sensitive nerve. I cry out softly, and he hums against me, like he's tasting the sound, drinking it in.

His fingers join in, gentle but insistent, coaxing me higher and higher. He watches every expression, every twitch of my body, every hitch in my breathing, adjusting and responding to my reactions. My chest rises and falls–my breath something foreign and slightly humiliating. My nipples peak, every nerve ending on fire. I'm lost in the sensation, in the deliberate, attentive rhythm of his mouth and hands.

"Oh, God," I gasp, clutching his shoulders as he continues, careful and patient, every motion designed to drive me closer. My thighs tremble, my nails dig into his back, and his name falls from my lips like a prayer.

"Almost there, Angel?" he murmurs, a smirk on his pretty lips. "You ready to come for me?" His eyebrow lifts. "Soak my face."

That's all it takes. I shatter, wave after wave crashing over me, my body shuddering in his hands. He doesn't stop; he rides it with me, pushing my legs wider, covering my pussy with his flat, wide, tongue. Guiding me, letting me collapse against him as I quiver.

When it finally ebbs, he lifts his head, breath warm against my skin. His long fingers linger at my hips, thumbs brushing over my spine. "You okay?" he asks softly, voice low, raw with emotion.

I nod, still shaking, leaning into him. "If you call surviving an earthquake okay."

I'm still gaining my wits when he slides my panties back up my legs. He helps me off the desk and I step close to him, the heat between us unrelenting. My hands trail upward, slipping under his shirt, over the hard ridges of his abs, feeling every flex of muscle. He shudders beneath my touch, a ripple of power passing between us that makes my pulse spike.

I pull back just slightly, my eyes locking with his. A spark passes there–something daring, something urgent–and I know exactly what I want. I slide my hands down his chest and grip his shoulders, guiding him backward until he hits the nearest chair. The motion is decisive, instinctual, as if I've already claimed him.

His eyes widen for a moment, surprise flashing across his face, before darkening with approval, raw desire mirrored back at me. I don't give him a chance to speak. My fingers rip the shirt over his head, tossing it aside like it was never there, and I press my mouth to his bare skin, tasting the heat, inhaling the strength, claiming him just as fiercely as he claimed me.

His chest tastes of salt and heat, his heartbeat hammering against my lips. I trail kisses across the lines of muscle, over his collarbone, down the center of his chest. He groans, low and wrecked, when my teeth scrape lightly against his nipple.

By the time I'm sinking to my knees in front of him, his breath is coming fast, his hands gripping the armrests of the chair like he needs the anchor. My fingers fumble with his belt, tugging it loose, popping the button of his jeans.

"Angel–" His voice cracks on the nickname. His hand dives into my hair, not pulling me away, not pulling me closer–just holding, shaking with restraint as his abdomen dips. "This isn't what I came for."

I glance up at him through my lashes, my palms pressing against his thighs as I lean in closer, crowding the space between us. "You've been very patient with me," I tell him. "And very giving. Let me do the same for you."

His jaw flexes, his gray eyes burning like storm clouds about to split open. His hips twitch, his breath hissing out between clenched teeth. He looks ruined already, and I haven't even touched him where he aches.

And God–there's nothing more intoxicating than knowing I can bring him there.

Reaching into his pants, I swallow at the size of him. He's big. I knew this, just from the overall size of him. From the way I've felt his want pressed against me every time we kiss. But when I free him, it takes a minute to process.

He's thick and heavy in my hand, the heat of him searing against my palm. I stroke him slowly at first, savoring the way his chest heaves, the way his head tips back and a groan tears from his throat. His restraint is unraveling, thread by thread, and I want to watch every piece snap.

I lower my mouth, brushing my lips over the flushed tip, tasting salt and skin. His thighs tense beneath my hands. "Jesus," he grits out, his voice raw. His grip in my hair tightens like he's fighting himself, like one wrong move will shatter his control.

I part my lips and take him in, inch by inch, until he's filling my mouth, stretching my lips. His breath stutters, breaks, and then his other hand finds the back of my head. Not forcing, not demanding– just firm, like he needs the connection.

I set the pace, slow and unhurried, sliding my mouth down, hollowing my cheeks, swirling my tongue around the sensitive ridge. He swears, low and guttural, hips jerking despite himself. Every time I pull back, I stroke him with my hand, wet and glistening, before sinking down again.

His body bows forward, muscles straining, as if he's being undone from the inside out. His voice drops into rough, desperate murmurs– my name, pleas, curses.

"Your mouth, I knew it was something special, but *fuck*."

His hips rise off the chair, fucking into my throat.

I love the dirty little things he says, the things that make me want to take my clothes off. To feel him inside. Every sound makes me ache, makes me want to push further, to ruin us both.

When I hum around him, his head snaps back, a strangled sound ripping from his throat. "Angel–fuck–I'm not–" He breaks off, chest heaving, hands clutching me tighter. "I can't hold it–"

I don't let him. I don't give him the space to pull back. I want this, want to feel his undoing.

And then he does.

His whole body goes rigid, breath shuddering, and he spills into my mouth, heat flooding down my throat. His groan is broken, almost pained, and it echoes in my bones. I swallow, taking all of him, holding his gaze as I do.

When it's over, he collapses against the chair, chest heaving, sweat slicking his temples. His grip loosens in my hair, his hand sliding down to cup the back of my neck, thumb brushing against my skin like he can't stop touching me.

I sit back on my knees, wiping the corner of my mouth, lips swollen, breath still ragged.

His gray eyes burn into me, wrecked and tender all at once. "Much more of that and I'm pretty sure you're going to kill me," he whispers.

And the way he says it, it sounds like he wouldn't mind it happening.

15

—————

J efferson

THE CONCERT IS UNREAL. We're up in the box and I can't stop grinning. Off-season means I can finally breathe–no coaches, no early mornings, no curfews. My friends are with me, along with a few well-known celebrities Ingrid must have also given tickets to. But I'll be real. The memory of Ingrid on her knees, her pretty lips circling my cock, and the way she swallowed me down, doesn't hurt, either.

"I think Vanessa Kirby is checking you out."

I cut my eyes at Nadia, and not over at the brunette who is well known for striding down runways and dating professional athletes. We'd had some brief introductions when we first got in the box, and then huddled in our own groups.

"So." I take a sip of my beer.

"So it's been weeks since I've seen you with a woman, and you don't care that a supermodel is eye fucking you from across the room? A supermodel known for her lingerie catalogue work?" Nadia tends to make it her business to be in everyone else's. "Something you need to tell us, Parks?"

She knows. They *all* know, but I haven't spoken the words out loud. How can I? We still haven't defined this. Even after having my tongue in her pussy and talking to her almost every night. It's been so long since I've been in a relationship, I don't even know how to go about it. And what kind of relationship would we even be able to have?

I thrust my hand in my hair. "There's nothing to tell, but you'll be first on the list if there is."

Her smirk tells me she's enjoying every minute of my discomfort, but thankfully Axel reels her in to wrap his arms around her. The second she's gone, Shelby is on me.

"Not you, too," I grumble.

"You really do know every song," Shelby teases, knocking her shoulder into mine.

"I never denied I was a fan." But even I know this goes beyond a basic interest. I've started watching her concert streams nightly, noticing the little details that she puts so much time and energy into.

How she changes her set list depending on the city. The way she builds into it with costumes, staging, even the lighting–turning three hours into a story no one else could tell. I catch the secret looks she throws to her bandmates, the inside jokes with her dancers, the way she makes an arena of thousands feel like they're crammed into the front row of a tiny club.

It's more than music. It's art, discipline, obsession. And the more I watch, the more I realize it's the same kind of dedication I feel on the ice. Only she's got the world's spotlight, and I'm just the guy checking bodies into glass.

The result of all of Ingrid's hard work is the crowd. The Flock, as they call themselves, is infectious. They're a living thing, pulsing under the lights like a single organism. The sound moves through me, low and steady, like a second heartbeat.

She finishes up the last song and vanishes under the stage. When she emerges again, the dancers are gone, and it's just her in a floaty blue dress with tiny sequins catching every flash of light. Guitar strapped over her shoulder like she was born with it. My chest goes tight. She owns them–all of them–but it feels like she owns me most of all.

And instantly, I'm back to last night.

Her lips on me, mine on her. Her mouth warm and soft. It wasn't just heat pulsing between us–it was raw, stupid need. And when it was over, when we were both catching our breath, I didn't feel that usual rush to leave. I hated it, actually. Hated pulling my clothes back on. Hated the thought of closing the door behind me. For the first time ever, I wanted to stay.

That memory is still thrumming in my bones when the first chords hit. My ears snap to attention.

Past Midnight.

A deep track. Not something she's played in years. The crowd reacts–surprise ripples like a wave. But I already know it's not for them. It's for me.

And then she sings:

"Used to hate the silence when the night dragged on,
Lonely hours stretching till the break of dawn.
But now the dark is golden when the screen lights up,
Every stolen minute, I can't get enough."

THE AIR LEAVES MY LUNGS.

She's singing it to me. To us.

If I had any doubt, the way her eyes flick up to the box burns it all away. The arena vanishes. It's just her voice, threading straight into me. Like she's cracked open my chest and branded me with it.

I don't even notice when the song ends. Or the one after. I just sit there, vibrating, waiting for the next glance. The next proof that I'm not alone with these feelings.

"Damn," I hear whispered next to me. I glance over at where

Nadia and Shelby share a covert glance, like they can see my heart threatening to jump out of my chest.

Damn.

Long after Ingrid left the stage, the Flock is still buzzing with the kind of post-concert adrenaline that feels like it'll never fade. Shelby and Nadia link arms, swaying as they belt out one of Ingrid's hits off-key, like they just stumbled out of the bar instead of a sold-out arena. Twyler is much more into emo music, so this isn't really her vibe, but her hand is linked with Reese's, and she seems really happy. The hallway smells faintly of popcorn and beer, and their laughter bounces off the concrete walls, sharp and careless.

I hang back, a few steps behind, soaking it in. The night's perfect, better than I imagined. My ears are still ringing from the set, from *her* voice. The girls are giddy, alive, and for once, I'm not focused on finding a girl to spend the night with. I've *got* the girl, and I'm being carried on the high of being with her.

A few feet away from the stairs, we hit the checkpoint.

Two uniformed security guards stand stiff in front of the exit, radios buzzing low. Their faces are wrong–serious, closed-off, not the relaxed kind of watchfulness I've seen all night. One glances at me, then away too quickly. Another shifts his weight, murmurs something into his walkie-talkie. The girls keep singing, oblivious. But the hairs on the back of my neck prickle. The easy warmth drains from the air.

"Sorry but there's no entry," one says, giving a stern look.

"But we have passes," Twyler says, holding up the special wristband that Ingrid sent us.

"I understand," he says, "but due to a situation the entire area is under lockdown."

My gut goes cold and in a heartbeat, I'm stone sober, fists clenched, staring at the door I can't get to.

I fire off a text.

Jparks23: *You okay? They won't let us back.*

No reply.

Shelby says something-her voice high, confused-but I can't hear her over the pounding in my ears. Reid pulls her into his side, steadying her while more cops appear. Radios crackle, the words *"threat... lower level..."* filtering through the static. Nobody tells us a damn thing.

Then some guy in black, a handler or assistant, whatever, appears out of nowhere and orders the officers to evacuate the area.

"Anything?" Nadia asks, when I check my phone for the hundredth time.

"No."

"The only thing I see online is that the concert was great," Axel says. "Oh wait, here's something. 'Large police presence at the Intown Arena following Ingrid Flockton show." His eyes skim down the screen. "But no details."

"I'm sure she's fine," Reese says with authority. He's always the leader-a captain through and through-but I see the wrinkle in his forehead. He's nervous too.

Me? I don't think it's nerves. It's outright panic. Ingrid has intense fans. She's spoken to me about the parasocial relationship that happens with someone at her level of fame. Hell, we've even felt it a little bit ourselves being high level hockey players, but nothing compared to the way her fans love her. They get her symbols tattooed on their bodies. They write her long letters saying that her songs changed their lives. And some get darker-scarier.

Is this one of those times?

Did someone get to her?

We exit the arena without any update, and she's all I can think of on the car ride back to the hotel. The back seat of the limo is silent other than the girls' scrolling their phones looking for any piece of information. It's just rumors at this point, which is only ratcheting up my anxiety even more. By the time we get there, it's deep into the night. Marv waits at the hotel doors, arms crossed, carved from stone. I'm shocked to see him.

I open my mouth to ask about her, but he's already jerked his chin. "Come with me."

I'm not intimidated by many people. I'm a big guy–I've been big since puberty, now I spent six days a week dropping two-fifty pound defenseman. But Marv? He's terrifying. The way he looks at me makes me think I'm either in trouble or something really bad has happened.

"Is she okay?" I blurt as he swipes a badge over the keypad. He doesn't answer. Doesn't even look at me. "Seriously, man, I'm freaking out here."

We ride the elevator in silence. My stomach twists tighter with every floor. Marv finally says, "There was a threat. Someone breached her dressing room–somehow they got past security and left a box. We had to call the bomb squad in to do a sweep."

"Fuck. Was it anything dangerous?"

"Not sure. There were a few online threats, but unfortunately that's not unusual. The box turned out to be a gift that some poor fan spent a lot of time on, but is now destroyed. The big question is how they got in."

"Will the police follow up on it?"

He nods. "Them and Ingrid's full security team. We treat every potential threat as if it's real."

Thank God for that.

The doors slide open to the penthouse.

I step inside, heart in my throat. Madison paces the floor, flanked by staff whose names I don't know. They look shaken.

And then I see her.

Curled on the couch in sweats, damp purple hair hanging over her shoulder, eyes heavy, but alive.

Relief crashes into me so hard I have to catch myself on the wall.

She lifts her head, gives me the softest smile, and it undoes me. Madison clocks the look on my face, then waves everyone out. One by one, the suite empties until it's just us.

I cross the room, fists still balled tight as I take in every single thing about her, cataloging her body for the smallest damage. My voice comes out rough.

"Angel. Tell me you're okay?"

Ingrid tries for a smile, but I see the crack in it. "I'm fine. Really. Things like this happen sometimes. Security handled it."

Her casual tone doesn't land. Not when I can still hear the muffled voices in the next room. For the last two hours she was out of my reach, and all I could imagine was someone slipping past the walls meant to keep her safe. Someone taking her away.

I close the gap between us, taking her hand and pulling her away from the couch. It's hard enough that she blinks, but I need to feel her. The words scrape out of my throat, raw, "Don't tell me it's nothing. You have no idea how fucking scared I was. I thought–"

"You thought what?"

I shake my head, refusing to put that fear into words. Instead I lead with my body—the one thing I'm sure of and that never fails me. I pull her into me, into my arms, and I bury my face in her neck, breathing her in. The rest of the world may still be moving, but none of it matters. Only her. "You're mine," I whisper, voice breaking with it. "And no one touches what's mine."

She leans back just enough to search my face. "Yours?"

"Fuck yes," I say firmly, the words slipping out before I can second-guess them.

It lands between us like a thunderclap. We've been dancing around it for weeks, pretending it didn't matter what we were. Playing it cool, like the games were enough. But tonight stripped all of that away. I almost lost her before I even had her. That thought makes me reckless.

"I want you, Ingrid," I tell her, the truth laid bare in my chest. "I've wanted more since the first night I met you. Tonight just made it crystal clear. I don't want almost. I don't want halfway. I want you."

Her breath catches, lashes trembling. Then she nods. "All I thought, when security surrounded me, was if I'd get back to you."

That's all the permission I need. My mouth is on hers, rough with relief, with the crash of adrenaline still roaring through me. She kisses me back like she needs it just as badly, like she felt the same fear. Her fingers clutch at my shirt, pulling me closer until there's no space left between us.

By the time we stumble into the adjoining bedroom, I'm half mad with possessive need. The need to remind myself she's here, she's safe, that *she's mine*. The door slams behind us, and I press her back against it, mouths fused, hands tangled in her hair. Her little gasp makes my control snap.

"Ingrid," I groan against her throat, tasting her skin. "You do something to me. Something I can't explain."

She tilts her head, inviting me deeper. "Show me."

I lift her in my arms, carrying her toward the bed like there's nothing else in the world. The city, the threats, the chaos outside–it all falls away. It's just her. And me. And the raw, undeniable truth that this woman belongs to me.

I lay her down gently on the massive bed, wrinkling the pristine white sheets, then immediately cage her in with my body, braced over her.

"The concert was incredible," I tell her, nipping at her bottom lip, "you're fucking incredible." Our lips crash again, but this time slower, deeper. I kiss her like I'll never run out of time. As much as I want her hard and fast, I've waited a lifetime for this moment. I'm going to savor every single second.

Her hands trail down my chest, fingers splaying against my shirt, tugging at the hem until I strip it off and toss it aside. Her eyes roam over me, hungry, and I swear I could combust just from that look.

"It's like your muscles have muscles," she says, skimming her fingers over the V that carves along my hips and dip below my waistband. Her touch sends a jolt straight to my cock, the throb making it hard to think.

I press my mouth to her neck, her pulse thundering beneath my lips. "You like my body, Angel?" I rasp, nipping lightly at her skin. "You can have it. Do whatever you want to me."

Her nails dig into my shoulders, her hips arching against me. She's so hot and horny, and fuck if I'm not right there with her. I lift her shirt, revealing a lacy lavender bra. Her nipples press at the sheer satin, and I rub a thumb over the peak. She moans and the sound rips a groan from me in return.

I pull the fabric aside, freeing her tit so I can see her–taste her–sucking the tip between my lips. She purrs, hips rising, and I do the same to the other, yanking the lace aside, staring down at her gorgeous body.

"Jesus Christ," I mutter, running my hand down her side. Ingrid isn't a tiny girl. She's a woman with curves and hips and full, incredible tits. Her back arches, and I reach behind her, unhooking the scrap of lace with practiced ease, and tossing it aside. "Fuck, you're beautiful."

I take a deep breath, trying to slow down just enough to savor it. Cupping her tits I add, "One day I'm going to fuck these." I exhale. "But not today."

Sliding my hand over the curve of her hip, slipping my thumb beneath the fabric of her sweats. Every movement is intentional, deliberate. I'm not rushing this and I'm sure as hell not going to be careless. I need her to feel exactly how much this means.

Pushing the sweats down, my fingers trace the delicate edge of her lace underwear, she gasps, hips jerking. I pause, holding her gaze, waiting..

"Please," she whispers.

I strip her down, every inch of revealed skin making my control unravel further. She's laid out beneath me, flushed and perfect, and I can't stop telling her how beautiful she is, how much I need her. I don't know if she's got a praise kink, but when I touch her between her legs she's slippery wet, just from sucking on her tits and telling her how good she is for me.

I rise up, pushing off my jeans, grabbing a condom out of the back pocket. I don't come back right away, instead I fist my cock and watch her. Studying those smooth hips as they rise and fall, rutting into the air. Her colorful hair is splayed across the white pillowcase, fanning out like a halo. Her skin is flushed, some from my mouth, from the scratch of my beard, but mostly from want.

Ingrid Flockton wants me. I'm not going to fuck this up.

"You going to do anything with that?" she asks, eyeing my erection. I give it a long stroke, feeling it all the way deep in my balls.

"Just trying to make sure I don't come in one pump."

She looks like she doesn't believe that, but I'm damn near the edge. I climb back on the bed, ripping the condom with my teeth. Propped on her elbows she runs her thumb over the tip, spreading pre-cum across the head. I nearly fumble, dropping the condom and taking her right there, but our eyes meet and I swallow, "You're playing with fire."

"Good," she falls back, spreading her thighs. "I want to get burned."

Shifting over her, her hand flattens against my shoulder and I notch between her legs. There's this moment where the working parts of my brain vanishes, lust taking control, and I fight with it, wanting to remember everything, because there's this little voice in the back of my head whispering, "This is it, man. This is the last first time."

It should freak me out, but instead it spurs me on, and when I finally push into her, the world stops. Her hand slides down my back, nails digging in, her mouth opens on a cry, and I bury my face against her neck, my jaw clenched tight.

"You gotta let me in, Angel."

She exhales, muscles releasing, and I ease the rest of the way in.

"Good?" I ask.

"So good."

Rocking into her, I can't decide where to look. Her sexy little mouth, the shifting bounce of her tits. The way I fit into her perfectly. I take it all in, absorb every last moment, because it's never been this good.

Ever.

The rhythm builds between us, tension snapping tighter with every thrust, but I don't give in too soon. I hold her there–keep her right at the edge–making her feel every second, every ounce of my claim. Her moans fill the room, raw and desperate, my name spilling from her lips like it's the only word she knows.

"Come on me," I grit out, nerves frayed, the need to see her unravel clawing at my chest. "I want to feel you come while I'm fucking you."

I duck my head, flattening my tongue over her nipple, teasing and claiming at the same time. Her hips arch up in answer, body trembling, pulling the trigger I've been holding tight. And then she breaks–shattering against me, clutching at me like I'm the only thing tethering her to earth.

Her release rips through both of us, and I keep driving into her, owning every cry, every pulse of her body as mine. I don't last much longer, rocking into her with a final, pulsing thrust.

That feeling, the way our bodies sweat and slide together, it's a vow, seared straight into my bones.

She's mine.

16

I ngrid

He spends the night.

He spends it next to me, and I'm consumed by him. By the hard lines of muscle. By the length of his thick, dark eyelashes. By the mouth that both says and does dirty, filthy things to me, and yeah, his cock–God–his cock, as he so crassly calls it... I didn't know could be so magnificent.

It's magnificent. I said it.

His magnificent penis made me feel things I didn't know were possible.

Twice.

When morning drags itself into the room, he stirs first, pulling me back against the warmth of his chest. His lips brush the top of my head before finding my cheek, then lower, catching the corner of my mouth.

"Any regrets?" he murmurs, voice rough with sleep.

"Nope," I whisper back, shifting against him. "Well... maybe that it took us so long to do that."

He grins into my skin. "Nah. Just made it better."

Then his mouth is on my throat, slow and hot, and my body reacts instantly. He's already hard again, pressed thick and insistent against my hip. I should tell him no. I have another show tonight, a routine to follow. Teas to drink, vitamins to take, yoga to help stretch my limbs. Nothing, not even the sexiest hockey player alive, should drag me off schedule. I pay too many people to keep me focused.

Except...

The ache building between my thighs drowns out the sensible voice in my head. I roll onto him, pushing his broad shoulders into the mattress. His grin spreads wider when I swing a leg over his hips and settle down, straddling him. His hands grip my waist, steadying me as I drag my pussy over his length.

"You're trouble," he says, steel-gray eyes locked on me like he's daring me not to finish what I started.

"Yeah," I breathe, lining him up. "But, I'm pretty sure you love it."

"Condom," he grunts, hand failing for the bedside table.

There's nothing but discarded wrappers.

"I'm on the pill," I tell him, forcing my brain to work–to be responsible.

"We were tested before the playoffs. I'm clean." We stare at one another for a long moment. It's risky and dumb, but holy hell I want to feel him in me again. His hand reaches up to cup my face, "I haven't slept with anyone since before then."

What he's saying is unspoken. *Since he met me.*

"I trust you," I tell him, although it seems crazy. The decision is made more by my body than my mind, and I sink down in one long, slow stroke, and the stretch makes me gasp, makes his jaw go tight beneath me. My palms flatten on his chest, feeling every flex of muscle beneath my hands as I start to move.

"Fuck, Angel," he groans, his hips rising to meet mine, filling me deeper.

The rhythm builds fast, needy, my body greedy for every inch of him. He grips my ass, pulling apart my cheeks, dipping his long fingers into the valley. The teasing urges me to go harder, faster, until I'm grinding down on him, chasing the high that sparks low in my belly. He rises up, his mouth finds my breast, teeth grazing before he sucks my nipple deep, pulling a broken moan from my throat.

I ride him harder, my nails digging into his shoulders. The friction, the fullness–it's too much. My thighs tremble, the orgasm hits sharp and blinding, ripping through me as I cry out his name.

He doesn't stop, doesn't give me time to catch my breath before flipping us, pressing me into the mattress with his weight. He pounds into me, deep and relentless, his lips at my ear.

"Again," he growls. "Give me another."

And God help me, I do, the tremors starting again, spurned on by the possessive commands, the hard feel of him deep inside of me, the knowledge that his man may be all I've ever wanted.

From the look in his eye, I think I'm all he's ever wanted too.

LATER THAT AFTERNOON, I sit cross-legged in the makeup chair, cradling my mug of tea while the artist works her brush across my lids, layering them with shimmering silver. The routine should calm me, it usually does, but Madison's voice keeps threading through, steady and businesslike as she runs down the latest update from the arena.

"They've tightened security for tonight. Extra checkpoints, more staff in the pit, and backstage access is on complete lockdown."

I nod, sipping my tea, pretending the warmth loosens the knot in my stomach. "Any idea who was behind it?"

"They're tracking the IP for the online threats," Madison says, glancing down at her phone. "And following up with the delivery company that brought the box in." She goes on, explaining that they found out earlier today that the box was delivered by a company–that's how they got through security. Somehow it was slipped in with packages by an approved vendor. The action seemed more like seeing if they could penetrate our defenses. "It could be a troll, could be something more. The police are on it."

There had been a press conference earlier by the Atlanta Police Department, assuring everyone that the venue was safe and that tonight's show would go on as planned. I spoke at length about it with Marv, making sure that not only was it really safe for me, but for everyone else. The fans, the arena staff, my team. The last thing I want is for anyone to get hurt.

I've been assured everything is under control.

My phone buzzes on the counter beside me. I don't even reach for it. It's been going off all day: friends, family, people checking in to make sure I'm okay. I appreciate it, I really do, but my nerves are already pulled tight, and I can't spare the energy to reassure everyone else. Not right now.

The makeup artist tilts my chin, dusting glitter into the crease of my eyelid, when Madison's voice shifts, softer, slyer. "So…"

I blink, my lashes brushing the brush. "So what?"

"So. He spent the night."

A smile sneaks across my mouth before I can stop it. "He did."

"And he didn't seem like he was in a rush to leave this morning."

That grin deepens, helpless. I can see him in my head again, the rumpled blond hair, steel-gray eyes still heavy with sleep, his body warm and solid against mine. I exhale a little laugh. "I would've stayed in bed with him all day if I could've."

Madison narrows her eyes like she's pressing me for details. "That good?"

"Incredible," I admit, my voice low, almost reverent.

She leans in, conspiratorial. "I'm listening."

Madison has been with me through the highs and lows, the heartache and euphoria. Sharing some goodness after the last few months of Jake induced pain, seems fair.

I set the mug down, curling my fingers together in my lap. The words come out in pieces, colored by memory. "He was… sweet. But strong. The kind of strong that doesn't just overwhelm you, it holds you up. He asked if I had regrets before I even had the chance to think them, and when I said no, he smiled like he already knew. He kissed me like I mattered." My throat tightens, heat spreading in my chest. "He worried about me. About everything."

Madison's brows lift, and her mouth curves into a knowing smirk.

I duck my head, though I can't wipe the silly smile off my face.

"I saw his friends checked out," she says casually, flipping through her notes.

"They had to get back," I reply, still caught up in the glow of remembering. "But he's staying one more day."

And just saying it out loud makes my pulse quicken. I can't stop thinking about the way he felt inside of me, but it's more than that. I'm not used to this–someone choosing me when they don't have to. Making the sacrifice instead of forcing me to choose. Most men I've been with have made me feel like my career was a third person in the relationship, this jealous ghost they couldn't compete with. Like I had to make myself smaller, dim my own spotlight, just to make them feel big enough. I learned early on that it's dangerous, being too much. Too successful. Too visible. Too *me*.

But Jefferson didn't flinch. Not after the concert when our night was almost ruined. Or when I let myself go with him completely. Not even in the light of day, after he had me, when the reality of who I am–what I am–was right there between us. He didn't treat me like a prize to be won or a trophy to show off. He just...held me, kissed me, made me laugh. He made me feel like Ingrid the person, not Ingrid the name on a sold-out tour poster.

And that terrifies me. Because the better it is, the harder it is to believe it's real.

I smooth my hands down my stage outfit, catching my reflection in the mirror. Shimmering eyes, perfect hair, lips painted just so. A pop star, through and through. But under the glitter, there's still the girl who's been left behind more times than she's been chosen. The girl who's learned that love often comes with conditions–*if only you weren't so busy, if only you weren't so famous, if only you weren't so much.*

Madison nudges me gently out of my head, or more like she's reading it. "So...you're sure he's not after something?"

"Yeah," I say, soft but certain. "I don't think he is. What could a drafted pro hockey player possibly need from me?"

The truth is, the road ahead won't be easy. We're both chasing demanding careers, pulled in a dozen directions we don't get to control. That's always been the breaking point for me—men who couldn't handle being second to the thing I love most, who wanted me to shrink just enough so they could feel taller. Jefferson will have to decide if he's strong enough to stand next to me without asking me to make myself small. I guess I'll have to decide that too. For now, I want to believe we can figure it out.

"The girls say he's a notorious fuckboy." Madison's tone is light, but the jab lands sharp. "You could just be another notch on his headboard."

"You're right, I could be," I admit, forcing myself not to flinch. "But I can't live in that headspace, Mads. I like him. He likes me. He's shown up for me in ways he didn't have to, and I believe that means something."

After Jake, I wasn't sure if I could let myself believe that wanting someone doesn't automatically mean losing everything else I've built. That maybe, just maybe, I don't have to choose between being loved and being enough.

Jefferson isn't Jake.

I have to remember that.

THE ROAR of the crowd is deafening, and I walk off the stage buzzing, that jittery after-high that comes from after a show. Jefferson waits for me just off stage, leaning against a speaker, his thick arms crossed over his chest, grinning at me.

I don't even think. Not about who can see me, not about what it looks like. I run straight into his arms. He catches me effortlessly, lifting me up and spinning me around. I squeal, half laughing, half delirious from the adrenaline.

"You were amazing," he whispers in my ear, his voice warm and rough, the kind that makes me melt no matter how many times I hear it.

"You weren't bored?" I ask, pulling back to search his face. "Coming two nights in a row?"

He presses a kiss to my mouth. "Nothing about you bores me."

Swoon. Literal swoon. My knees would've buckled if he wasn't already holding me up.

"Well, the next part is boring," I tease as he lowers me to the ground. "I have to peel this costume off and scrub a pound of makeup off my face."

"I like it," he says, keeping me close. His big hand trails slowly down my back. "Warrior mode. It reminds me of the locker room. Post-game. Especially after a win."

I grin, catching that glint in his eyes. "I can see that. The energy's elevated. My team killed it tonight. The show went off flawlessly–for the audience, at least. We always see the little crises, the mix-ups, the missteps. But as long as we smooth it over and make it the best night of their lives, then we've done our job."

"Fuck," he says, dropping his mouth to mine again. "You're smart and sexy."

By the time we make it to the dressing area, I'm starting to come down. Jefferson makes himself at home, sprawling on the couch, long legs stretched out, scrolling on his phone like he's completely at ease in my world. It doesn't hurt that he looks like a fashion model, his face angled lines of perfection. Meanwhile, my team gets to work on me–pulling pins from my hair, carefully noting missing sequins, peeling off my lashes. Bit by bit, Ingrid Flockton fades away, until I'm just Ingrid again.

I'm in a new outfit when the door opens and Marv steps inside. His face is blank, *too* blank, and instantly my stomach tightens. He leans down to whisper something to Madison. Her brows flick up, and a ripple of unease runs through me.

"What?" I blurt. My voice is sharper than I intend. "What's wrong?"

"Nothing's wrong," Madison says too quickly. "There's just someone outside who would like to come back."

That's not unusual. After almost every show, there's someone–celebs, local personalities, politicians. I'm used to smiling, shaking hands, playing the gracious host. But the energy between Marv and Madison is off. Too still. Too careful.

"Why are you being weird?" I press, my chest starting to buzz with that telltale anxiety.

Madison sighs, her eyes flicking to Jefferson on the couch. He hasn't noticed, still focused on whatever's on his screen. Finally, she meets my gaze.

"It's Jake," she says softly, "he's here and he wants to see you."

17

I ngrid

MADISON LOOKS at me like she's trying to decide if I heard her or not. Fair, I think I'm in shock, because for a moment my tongue feels heavy in my mouth. I stumble over my words.

"Jake is here?" My head spins. "Why here? Why now?"

"He's filming something in the city and I guess production had a box?"

That answer is bullshit. Pure, 100% bullshit. He's here because I have someone else in my life and for the first time I'm the one moving on first.

The expression on Madison's face tells me she's thinking the same thing.

Marv gives me a careful look, like he's weighing my reaction. "I can tell him to leave if you want."

"No." I shake my head too quickly, forcing in a steady breath. "It's fine. Just…"

My eyes drift toward Jefferson. He's across the room, half in conversation with one of the trainers, but already his gaze has found me. The shift in the air between Marv and me hasn't gone unnoticed. His gray eyes narrow slightly, a crease of concern forming as he studies me.

I cross the room, trying to gather my scattered thoughts. Jefferson meets me halfway, his hand brushing over my arm as though anchoring me.

"What's going on?" he asks softly, dipping his head closer so no one else hears. "Another threat?"

I shake my head. "No, nothing like that. Everything's fine. There's someone who wants to see me."

He tilts his head, brow furrowed. "Yeah? Who?"

I force the words out. "My ex."

For a beat, Jefferson studies me. Then the tension drains from his shoulders, his jaw loosening. He exhales slowly, a puff of relief. "Oh." A faint smile ghosts over his lips. "Okay."

I blink at him. "You don't care?"

His hand slides up, gentle but sure, tucking a loose strand of hair behind my ear. The brush of his knuckles against my cheek is so tender it nearly undoes me. "I only care about what you care about, Angel," he says. "If you want to see him, that's fine by me."

Something in my chest swells, warm and fluttery, filling every corner until it's hard to breathe. It's almost unbearable, the way he looks at me like I'm the only thing that matters. Jefferson Parks, the man everyone swears is nothing but a cocky playboy, is proving, again, that he's one of the good ones.

I swallow hard. "I think it's just easier to do it this way." My smile is shaky, more grimace than grin. "Just rip the bandaid off."

The faint crease of worry returns to Jefferson's brow, but I've already straightened, pulling in a deep breath, trying to steady the nerves rattling under my skin.

Marv re-enters, Jake a few steps behind him. As much as I hate it, my body reacts before my brain does and I brace myself. It's instinct. I haven't seen him face-to-face since the night I walked out of his apartment in LA. Humiliated. Heartbroken. Determined never to look back.

And now here he is, walking toward me with that stupid, fake, easy grin he always uses when he's uncomfortable. His dark hair's an inch too long, curly and wild. He's slim, wiry–shorter than me if I'm in heels, which is exactly why, when we were together, I never wore them. Flats only. I'd shrunk myself to make him feel taller, bigger, enough.

Jake's pivoting into acting after his music career, his sound always skewing more alt-rock than my brand of pop storytelling. We'd been a clash of opposites, the kind of fire that either catches and burns hot or fizzles out.

We didn't just fizzle. The man doused us with a bucket of cold water.

I wait for the sting to come back, the bitterness, the anger, but it's not there. Just a dull echo, like a song that's faded from the charts.

"Ing," he says, loping toward me. Yes, the man lopes. It's annoying as fuck. "How are you?"

Not *the show was incredible. Good work. You were great.* Of course not. Getting a compliment from him was like pulling teeth. Jake never liked this version of me. Glitter, sequins, stadium tours. He thought I was wasting myself, selling out. He never quite said the words, but it was always in his eyes.

"Great, actually." My voice comes out brighter than I feel. "We're finally on the last leg of the tour. Just a couple more weeks." I hesitate, then throw him a crumb. "Madison said you're here working on a movie?"

"Just a little indie film." He props himself against a chair like he owns the room. "I thought maybe we could grab some dinner. Either out somewhere or back at your hotel if you're tired from the show."

"Dinner," I repeat, flat.

"Yeah. A chance for us to catch up." His head tilts knowingly, the move rehearsed. "Talk over a few things."

"There's nothing to talk about, Jake." My arms fold across my chest before I can stop them. Defensive. Guarded.

"You're really still mad," he accuses, his grin twisting into an incredulous smirk.

I take a deep breath, fighting the familiar pull of his orbit. He's baiting me–he always baits me. Makes me feel small, guilty, like I've overreacted. That's how he's reeled me back in, over and over. But before I can snap back, movement at the corner of my vision cuts through the tension.

Jefferson.

He's crossing the room with that loose, easy stride, all six-foot-five of him, those broad shoulders and long legs filling the space. He doesn't look rushed, doesn't look threatened–just calm, casual. But when his hand settles warm and steady at the small of my back, the message is clear.

Mine.

Jake's eyes flick to the gesture, narrowing just enough to betray the hit to his ego.

The two men couldn't be more different. Physically, they might as well belong to separate worlds–Jefferson with his athletic body made of thick muscle and an imposing frame that commands every room he enters. But the contrast runs deeper than appearance. Jefferson carries an ease, a steady confidence that Jake could only dream of. One he'd kill to possess.

Jefferson leans down, brushing his lips near my temple, his voice pitched low enough for me but not so low Jake can't hear. "Everything okay here, Angel?"

The word–*Angel*–lands like a sparkler in my chest.

"Yeah," I say, lifting my chin, heat crawling into my cheeks. "Everything's fine."

The room feels suddenly smaller, the air dense with different energies colliding. Madison is pretending to scroll on her phone, but there's no doubt she's eating up every single second of this. Marv hovers in the corner, alert as always, while the hum of voices from crew members moving equipment filters in faintly from the hall. All of it blurs behind the pulse pounding in my ears.

I step closer to Jefferson, like my body knows where it belongs before my mind does. "Jefferson, this is Jake. Jake, Jefferson."

The men shake hands. Jefferson doesn't overplay it–no flexing, no posturing–just a firm, steady grip that makes Jake shift on his feet. I lean into Jefferson's side, his presence a solid wall at my back, grounding me.

"Did I hear someone mention dinner?" Jefferson asks, voice casual, as though this isn't a standoff between past and present. His hand settles at my waist, heat radiating through the sequined fabric of my costume.

"That was me." Jake grins easily. "I thought Ingrid and I could catch up while we're both in town. You're welcome to join us."

A laugh bubbles in the back of my throat, a touch of hysteria and disbelief. Thankfully Jefferson maintains his wits and looks down at me, brushing the pad of his thumb over my cheek. "I know you're starving, but you probably need to get off your feet and recover." Then, with a glance at Jake, he adds, "Maybe another time?"

The silence stretches just long enough for me to savor the way Jake blinks, caught off guard by the consideration of this man touching me–*with* me. Thinking of my needs over his own. His confidence falters, brown eyes flickering with calculation. "You know, I've got an early call time tomorrow and should probably head back, anyway. There are a few pages of lines I need to memorize too."

Of course. A subtle reminder that he's an actor now, important enough to brush off dinner with his ex. Whatever keeps him from losing more ground.

"That makes sense," I say, keeping my tone polite, neutral. Inside, though, I feel lighter, as if I've just dodged a trap I didn't realize was waiting to spring shut.

"Nice to meet you," Jefferson says. He means it in that smooth, civil way that's somehow still edged with finality, like a handshake closing a door.

"Right. You too." Jake tries for one last connection, his gaze flicking toward me, searching for any crack in my resolve. But before I can react, Jefferson's hand slides under my chin, tilting my face up until all I see is the intensity in his eyes and the promise inside them.

Then his mouth is on mine. Firm. Sure. Unapologetic.

The dressing room vanishes–the racks of costumes, the whir of curling irons, Madison's muffled words as she escorts Jake quietly out the door. The only thing that exists is the man kissing me, his lips parting mine, the taste of him banishing every ghost Jake might have stirred up.

It might have started as a show, a deliberate claim in front of my past, but the second my body melts into his, the kiss shifts into something else–something real. Something that makes my chest ache and my knees weak.

And when he finally pulls back, my breath shaky against his cheek, I know the only hunger left in me has nothing to do with dinner. It's for him. Always him.

18

Jefferson

THE SCENE after the concert isn't mentioned on the way back to the hotel, and once we're up in her suite, Ingrid falls into her post-show routine. I'm learning quickly that it's non-negotiable. Ice bath first–her teeth chattering as the timer runs down. Then massage, every knot in her shoulders and back worked out by a pair of hands that aren't mine, and it kills me to sit there watching her melt under someone else's touch. After that, it's blister checks, bruise assessment, all the little repairs that come from performing a three-hour, high-intensity set on stage.

While the physical therapists poke and prod, I eat. It feels strange at first–me stuffing down steak and potatoes while she's being tended to like a prize fighter–but she insisted.

"That's what it is," she said, chugging down fluids. "The show is my game, this is my recovery." And she's right. It's the same discipline, just dressed in sequins instead of pads.

As I wait for her upstairs in the suite, I'm still not ready to let go of the Jake thing. I know all about her ex. Semi-famous musician with a cult following of girls who quote his lyrics like scripture. He and Ingrid were on and off for years, tossing lines about each other into their songs, playing coy with the press. It was a circus, the kind I've been happy to avoid with puck bunnies and quick hookups that never made it past the next morning. The last breakup? Tabloid gold. They stayed quiet, but the whispers said she'd been gutted. Her latest album only added fuel to the fire, with her anger seemingly threaded into betrayal, heartbreak sharpened into anthems.

That's what sticks in my head now. Not jealousy, but this ugly feeling in my gut. Did he hurt her? Did he think he could break her and try to walk back into her life again? Because she looked shaken to see him tonight. Not wistful or longing, but shaken, like an enemy slithering into her territory. I want to know why.

I want to make sure I never make her look that way.

My fingers clench around the knife in my hand, and I toss it on the cleaned plate.

The sound of the bathroom door opening pulls me out of the spiral. She's fresh-faced now, makeup gone, hair damp from a shower, a little tank and shorts hugging her body. Her heels are wrapped with bandages, and she's moving slower than she did on stage.

She slides into bed beside me, tired but beautiful, and I can't stop myself. I crawl across the sheets, take her foot in my hands, and press my mouth to the injured spots one by one. Tiny, reverent kisses where the skin is raw. She watches me with wide, soft eyes, chest rising and falling like she can't quite catch her breath.

"Want to talk about it?" I ask, my voice low.

Her lashes flutter. "You mean the foot fetish you're revealing to me right now?"

"I don't have a foot fetish. I have an Ingrid Flockton fetish." I take a gentle bite out of her ankle and she squirms. "Is this your way of avoiding the topic?"

She sighs. "No. You're right. We should probably talk about him."

I nod but clarify, "Understand something: I don't give a shit about your exes. My body count is too high to even attempt to calculate, and I'm not even going to pretend to justify the last four years. You're a grown woman—a sexy, strong, powerhouse of a woman," I rub my thumb over the arch of her foot, "and living, fucking, stumbling through relationships is part of it. You deserve that as much as anyone else, despite the spotlight, despite the pressure." I take a deep breath, forcing the weight of what I mean into the space between us. "But what I do care about is why that asshole got you tied up in knots tonight."

Her eyes flick away, teeth catching her bottom lip. She hesitates, like maybe she'd rather swallow the words than let them out.

"Be honest with me," I press, voice gentle but firm. "I can take it, and I'll keep your secrets."

For a long beat, all I hear is her breath. Then finally, she sighs, curling her knees up toward her chest, arms wrapped tight around them. It's a defensive posture, one I've never seen her take before and I realize that this part of Ingrid is even more sacred than the one she shared with me last night.

"Jake and I..." She shakes her head, staring at some invisible spot on the wall. "We were fire. The kind that either burns hot or leaves nothing but ashes. Guess which one we got."

I stay quiet, letting her pick her way through it.

"In the beginning, I never thought he'd be into a girl like me," she says softly. "Not 'Ingrid Flockton the pop star,' but he was interested, and *interesting.* Not just another guy in a boy band our PR agents wanted to tie together for publicity. He wanted to talk about poetry and art, about philosophy and craft. He showed me a life I hadn't experienced yet. We'd sit on his shitty balcony in Silver Lake, drinking cheap whiskey out of mugs, and he'd play chords on his guitar until the sun came up. He used to write lyrics on the backs of receipts and napkins and leave them in my pockets, like little love notes. I'd write the next line, develop a bridge, and sneak it back under his pillow. We felt like a yin-and-yang, two opposite forces, bound as one." She looks away. "I thought that meant something. I thought it meant he believed in me even if he couldn't say it out loud."

Her voice drops lower. "But the more my career grew, the more he dug into his 'principals.'" She uses air quotes. "He'd sneer at rehearsals, call my songs 'bubblegum bullshit.' If I wore sequins, he'd call me attention seeking. If I sold out a stadium, he'd say I was pandering. And I started... I don't know, folding myself smaller." Her blue eyes meet mine. "Like literally smaller. I'd wear flats so I wouldn't tower over him. Holding back in interviews so I didn't sound too proud. Take separate exits so the press wouldn't see us together. I let him make me less, just so he wouldn't feel threatened."

The muscle in my jaw ticks. I want to find the prick and put him through the boards, make him choke on his own pathetic insecurity.

She draws in another breath, shaky this time. "The night it ended he accused me of choosing fame over him, again, but this time it was about going on this tour. The shows had sold out in *minutes*. The servers crashed. It was a complete nightmare, but also incredibly rewarding. I had a big idea, and I was determined to do anything to see it through. His reaction was an epic meltdown and he claimed I belonged to the machine, not to him. Then he threw one of my Grammys—" she cuts herself off, wincing. "Anyway. I walked out, and I swore I wouldn't look back. But he has this way of showing up when I least expect it and getting under my skin, even now. Like tonight."

Her arms tighten around herself, and all I see is the girl who once believed she had to dim her light just to keep a man. I shift closer, uncurling her from that ball, wrapping my arms around her so she can't retreat into herself. "Angel," I say, pressing my lips to her temple, "don't you ever make yourself small for me. Or for anyone. I want the whole damn you–the sequins, the glitter, the big-ass stages, the voice that owns the world. If he couldn't handle that, that's on him. Not you."

Her eyes shine when she finally looks up at me. "You really mean that?"

"More than I've ever meant anything," I say, my thumb brushing over her cheek. "And if he ever tries to make you feel less again, I'll remind you who the fuck you are."

"Why do you call me that?" she asks, tilting her head back.

I frown. "Call you what?"

"Angel." She runs her hand down my forearm. "Everyone else thinks of it like a flock of birds–whatever. The fans think they own the wings. They made it into a brand. But you say it different. Why?"

Now it's my turn to feel exposed, even if it doesn't compare to what she just shared. "Junior year I took this art history class–"

Her brows jump, and she cranes her neck to look at me like she misheard. "Stop. You took an art history class?"

I roll my eyes. "It was mandatory. I thought I'd sleep through it and beg one of the girls in the class to partner up with me on the project, but it was actually pretty interesting. One thing we studied was the use of angels in art." I pause, watching her lips part slightly, her breath catching like she already knows where I'm going. "They were never just soft and pretty, Ingrid. Not the way people think. They were rare. Messengers. Warnings. Gifts. They carried power, sometimes terrifying power, and they were a glimpse of something divine–something untouchable. Not meant for ordinary people to hold on to."

Her lashes lower, and I feel her pulse quicken against my chest.

"That's what you are to me," I say quietly, like it's the only truth I've ever been sure of. "You're not just a voice or a stage presence. You're not a costume or a headline. You're more than glitter and songs people scream back to you. You're this rare, powerful, impossible thing I can't believe I get to touch."

My hand slides up her spine, anchoring her closer. "And I don't want to share you with the rest of the fandom," I admit, my voice dropping to a growl. "I don't want you to just be their wings, their flock, their story to consume. I want you for myself."

Her eyes glisten, and her fingers curl tighter around my arm. "That's different from how anyone's ever said it to me before."

"Good," I murmur, tipping her chin up with my thumb. "Because I don't see you the way they do. I never fucking will."

The words hang there, heavy, final. Her chest rises and falls like she's holding her breath, like she's terrified of breaking the moment. My pulse pounds so hard I can feel it in my throat. What the hell is this woman doing to me?

Then she leans into me, her lips brushing mine, tentative but searching. I don't hesitate. I kiss her back, slow and deliberate, a claiming she can feel in every drag of my mouth over hers. She tastes faintly of mint and sugar, her tongue brushing mine like she's testing, teasing, but I deepen the kiss until she's melting into me.

Her hands slide up, threading into my hair, tugging me closer. I groan against her mouth and cup her jaw, angling her just how I want. Every wall between us—the fame, the distance, the bullshit—crumbles in a single, desperate collision.

She whispers against my lips, "Jefferson..." It's soft, raw, like she doesn't know if she's allowed to want this.

"I know this is a lot. It's fast," I breathe back, my forehead pressed to hers. "But if you let me, if you want it, I'll prove to you that I'm not him, that what we can have together is better."

The hesitation in her eyes flickers, then disappears when I slide my hand down her side, over the curve of her hip, anchoring her to me. She nods, barely, but it's enough.

I lift her easily, her legs wrapping around my waist as though her body's been waiting for this. She gasps when her back hits the mattress, but her fingers never stop clinging to me, pulling me down with her.

The kiss turns frantic, years of hunger and denial spilling out. My hands roam over her waist, her ribs, the hem of her tank top. She arches her tits into me, whispering, "Please."

I pull back just enough to see her flushed face, her hair spread out wild on the pillow. "Angel," I say again, reverent this time, like a vow. "You have no idea what you're doing to me."

Her answering smile is shaky but sure. "Then show me."

I do—pressing my mouth to the curve of her throat, tasting her pulse, kissing down her collarbone while my hand slides beneath the thin cotton of her tank, splaying over warm skin. Her sharp inhale fuels me. My body's on fire, but I force myself to move slowly, to savor every sound, every shiver.

By the time I peel away her shirt, laying my eyes on her amazing tits, tearing off those sexy, thin, shorts, baring her pussy to me, there's no doubt left–no spotlight, no exes, no past. Just Ingrid, trembling and radiant beneath me, and me, getting to claim what I've wanted from the moment she first looked at me like I was more than a hockey player sliding into her DMs.

Her lips part on a sharp inhale as I press my mouth against her clit, kissing the bundles of nerves with light, feathery kisses. I love the sounds she makes, how hard they get me. I strip down, basking in the way she looks at my body. My cock bobs between us as her fingers trail over my abs making every rep, every added pound to the barbell, worth it just to see her appreciate it.

She's the first woman I've been with where I haven't used a condom and everything about it is fucking amazing. I climb over her body and press into her, slow and careful at first, letting her feel every inch of me. Her nails scrape down my back, a strangled sound escaping her throat that nearly undoes me.

"Jefferson," she gasps, clutching at me like I'm the only solid thing she has left.

"Shh." I press my forehead to hers, kissing her again, swallowing that sound. "I've got you. Every second, I've got you."

She's tight around me, almost unbearably so, and I fight the urge to drive deep too soon. Instead I rock slowly, savoring the way her body opens for me, the way her legs hook tighter around my waist. She moves with me, tentative at first, then bolder, rolling her hips until we're finding a rhythm that has her head falling back against the pillow, her breath catching.

"God, you feel–" Her words break on a moan. "Fuck, babe. *Harder.*"

Her demand wrecks me. I capture her mouth again, thrusting deeper this time, punching into her until we're both lost in something neither of us can come back from. Her cries are muffled against my lips, her body trembling beneath me, every muscle straining like she's right on the edge.

"What they get and I get are different," I growl against her skin, nipping her jaw, her throat. "You're not a brand. Not a fucking mascot. Not something to be hidden. You're mine, understand?"

"Yes." The word rips out of her, desperate, like a confession. "Yours."

Her surrender unleashes me and as much as I hate it, I pull out, flipping her over until she's on her hands and knees. I hold her in place with both hands on her hips and then slot myself between her legs, feeling her slippery heat, and drive into her with a raw hunger I've never felt with anyone else.

"Oh," she gasps, backing into me. "God, that feels good."

Every thrust wrings another gasp from her lips, another broken cry that tells me she's losing herself in this just as much as I am.

She arches suddenly, a shudder tearing through her, her walls clenching tight around me. Her cry is sharp, guttural, shaking her whole body. Watching her, eyes locked on her spine, feeling her unravel beneath me is the most brutal, beautiful thing I've ever seen.

"Fuck–" I grit out, barely holding on. Her orgasm drags me down with her, my body surging once, twice, before I spill inside her with a groan that vibrates against her chest. I bury my face against her back, breathing her in, holding her like if I let go, I'll lose the best thing that's ever happened to me.

For a long moment, neither of us moves. Just the sound of our ragged breaths filling the room.

Finally, I lift my head and pull out, easing her down to her side, where I take in her flushed cheeks and swollen lips. Her eyes are wide and glassy. And she's smiling–small, disbelieving, but real.

I press a kiss to the corner of her mouth, softer this time. Reverent.

She runs a hand over my jaw, thumb tracing my bottom lip like she's memorizing me. "Thank you," she says. "For letting me be me."

The words hit me harder than anything else tonight.

And I know, as I settle beside her and pull her into my chest, that nothing about this is casual. Not a hookup. This–*her*–is the only thing that's ever felt like it mattered.

19

I ngrid

THREE DAYS LATER, it still feels like a fever dream, like maybe I made him up–this six-foot-five hockey player with abs made of steel, with the uncanny ability to give me many, many, amazing orgasms. We barely slept that night, caught between getting to know each other and getting one another off–like we wanted to memorize every part of one another before having to part.

I should be sad and missing him. And I do miss him, but I'm also caught up in the energy of it all. It's no secret that I fall hard, but also, the world doesn't stop spinning just because I've fallen into Jefferson Parks.

I took the plane from Atlanta to Miami, the bus loads of equipment arriving a day later. I needed a full day to recharge and get a night without Jefferson distracting me from sleep. What makes it even better is that Miami has become home base for me, with my parents living there most of the year. My mother loves the water. My father is devoted to golf. After a good sleep in my own bed, I feel a million times more rested the day of the first concert. I've had my morning smoothie and am stretching on a yoga mat on the back patio. Madison is in a similar position across from me, but is glued to her phone. I recognize the look, the pursed lips and furrowed brow. That look never means anything good.

"What is it?" I ask, bracing myself.

She turns the screen around. A headline glares back at me:

"Love Triangle? Ingrid Flockton's Ex Jake Seen Backstage–But What About the Hockey Hunk?"

The article is full of candid photos, including one of Jake exiting through the back door. There's another of Jefferson in the wings during my encore, a wide grin on his adorable, sexy face.

Heat crawls up my neck. "Another one? Don't they have something better to talk about?"

"Of course not. You're the story, Ing. Always have been." Madison places the phone on the floor in front of her, eyes still skimming the article, and pretends to stretch. "The question is–who leaked it in the first place?"

"A fan probably. They miss nothing."

"I don't know." She thumbs down the screen and reads, "*Backstage Power Play: Ingrid's Ex Jake Merchant and New Flame Jefferson Parks Face Off.*"

I shake my head. "A hockey pun?"

"Do you think it was Jake?" she asks, turning her phone over and actually focusing on what we're doing.

"Are you crazy?" I snort. "Jake hates press more than I do, and getting caught coming in and out of my dressing room isn't his style."

Even worse, being caught at one of my shows.

Her gaze flicks to me, sharp. "Then maybe it was Jefferson."

The suggestion makes my stomach drop, but almost immediately, I shake it off. "No. He'd never."

"You've known him, what, a few weeks? You don't know what a guy like him is capable of."

I bite back my retort, because fighting with Madison the morning before a show is the last thing I need. She's been my right hand for years, my anchor. I trust her. I do. But something in her tone makes me uneasy, like she wants me to doubt him.

And the thing is—she's not wrong. I haven't known Jefferson for long. Not really. A handful of weeks. A blur of late-night calls, stolen hours, one perfect weekend tangled up in his arms. That's not much to build a foundation on. She's right about that.

But what I *do* know feels solid. He's not angling for camera time. He's not dropping my name in interviews or trying to squeeze himself into a spotlight he doesn't need. Hockey already gave him more attention than most people could handle. If Jefferson wanted fame, he could've had it years ago.

When I think about him—the quiet way he waits for me after shows, the way he listens when I unravel the chaos of my day, the way he looked at me when he thought I might've been in danger—I know he's not here for the publicity. He's here for *me*.

That thought is both scary and comforting all at once.

"Jake knew the risk of this going public when he showed up at the concert. It's not my problem." I lean to the side, feeling my quads stretch. "We both know there's nothing we can do to stop gossip, and if it's not hurting anyone, then it doesn't matter."

I straighten, meeting Madison's gaze, my voice steady. "For once, I'm focusing on my own happiness—and I'm not letting anyone make me second-guess that."

A breeze blows off the water, lifting strands of hair from my face as I press deeper into a stretch on the yoga mat. My muscles burn in that good way, the kind that makes me feel present instead of scattered.

Madison's phone buzzes. She glances at the screen, mouth tightening. "I need to take this."

I finish the sequence on my own, trying not to watch her retreat inside. When my lungs are steady again, I roll up my mat and pad across the stone toward the French doors.

Just before I step in, voices stop me.

"I heard from the police. Their tech team got more details on the box found backstage," Marv says, voice low and measured. "Turns out it was the sister of the delivery person. She convinced him to bring it in with the rest of the catering."

"So, just a crazy fan," Madison replies, clipped, like she's already put the whole thing behind her.

"We're still working on the online threats, but it seems like it was a coincidence."

The wind shifts, carrying salt air and the distant hum of a boat engine. My shoulders stay tight, the relief never coming. All of this is part of the job, a part I hate, but one that comes with the territory.

Then Marv says something that makes me freeze. "The background check came through."

Her tone sharpens with curiosity. "Oh, anything worth noting?"

"Overall the group is pretty clean. A skirmish at a frat house a few years ago, and a drunken disorderly on Rakestraw that was dropped. The girl, Nadia, is involved in a case with the police, but she's the victim in that."

"And Jefferson?"

What the heck?

"An underage drinking charge three years ago. Nothing big."

"The media won't see it that way. They'll have a field day."

My heart pounds, confusion twisting in my chest along with something dirtier–betrayal.

"He seems like a good kid," Marv says. "And he makes her happy."

"Well, it's our job to keep her safe," Madison answers, defensive. "And I had to check."

Like hell, I want to shout, but don't, because there's instant conflict. In one way, she's right. Someone did need to follow up. I was just too in my head to realize it. My usual circles are people who wear their sins in headlines and gossip columns, every misstep immortalized in print. Jefferson and his friends don't live in that kind of spotlight, at least not yet.

Still, I think, waiting for the sound of their retreating footsteps, someone should have told me.

THE NEXT MORNING, the sunlight hits the patio just right, glinting off the pool behind the house. I step out, stretching, and find Mom already in her favorite wicker chair–the one that overlooks the garden–coffee cup in hand, with her legs crossed. A faint breeze ruffling her chestnut hair.

"Mornin', sweetheart." Her southern lilt has never completely faded, even after decades of living in other parts of the country, and it always makes me think of home; safe, steady, grounded.

"Good morning." I circle the table. "Where's Dad?"

"Already at the office."

'The office' is code for golf.

"Ah, of course." Neither of us mind. My father loves fresh air and exercise. I pull out a chair and sit across from her. My mother, Ruth Flockton, is tall, lean, elegant without trying, and there's a sharp intelligence in the set of her jaw and the tilt of her eyes. That look had come in handy when she'd been a real estate agent when I was growing up, and later over the negotiating tables with record labels. She's the central reason why many of my investments are in property ownership, and why I have complete ownership over my masters.

She never wanted to be a mom-ager, but she managed every detail of my life anyway: my business, my money, my estate–always a few steps ahead to keep me safe. Now that I'm old enough to make decisions for myself, she's pulled back a little and mostly handles my charitable works. Primarily the Flockton Foundation.

"The show looked great last night," she says, tilting her head as she sips her coffee. "You've got a lot of energy for someone on the final leg of a world tour."

"I'm glad it looks that way, because I'm beat."

"Maybe it has something to do with the new young man you've been seen with?"

"Have you been reading the tabloids?" I arch an eyebrow. I lift the carafe and pour myself a hot cup of coffee. "If you want to know about my love life, Mom, just ask."

Her lips quirk up. "I'm asking."

I laugh softly and give her a measured version of the story, careful where I stop and start. "His name is Jefferson Parks. He's a college student and hockey player although he's graduating in a few weeks and has already signed with a team for next season. He's... interesting. Funny, smart, steady in a way that's surprising. Not flashy for no reason, not chasing attention. Makes me feel..." I search for the words and come up with, "...normal. Grounded."

She studies me closely, sipping her coffee. "You're not usually into jocks."

"I'm not, but I figure my track record with musicians and actors hasn't been so great."

"You're too hard on yourself."

I let the words hang in the air, then admit, "Old habits are hard to break."

Mom leans back, eyes narrowing just a little. "How does Madison feel about him?"

It irks me that there's an implication that my best friend should get a voice in this, but I get it. I shrug, leaning forward and resting my elbows on my knees. "She likes him, I think, but she's always worried when I start dating someone new."

Mom smiles faintly. "She's just protective, sweetheart. Maybe she's seen too many people hurt you before."

I stare at the glinting water, fingers tracing the edge of my coffee cup. "Maybe. I just don't like that we're at odds on this. I want her to be happy that I'm happy, not–"

"–not second-guessing every man you meet?" Mom finishes for me, eyes softening. "I get it. That's her role in life as your friend and assistant."

The lines in this life have a way of getting crossed. It's important to surround yourself with people you trust, which means friends and family get on the payroll, but they aren't just employees. They're my people. My truth tellers.

I nod slowly, letting it settle. "Yeah. I know." The look in her eyes tells me she understands without me finishing.

Mom pats my hand. "The fact that you're smiling this morning–that's enough for me."

And for a moment, looking at her, listening to the faint hum of the pool and the birds in the yard, it really is. Mom leans back in her chair, tilting her head as if weighing something carefully. "The Spring Gala's coming up in three weeks," she says. "Everything is running smoothly, and I think it may be our biggest year yet."

"Thank you, Mom, you do a great job organizing it."

The Flock Foundation isn't just for one thing. It's a way to help multiple charities as needs are presented. Some are for individuals having hardships or illness. Other times we donate large amounts of funds or items during natural disasters like tornadoes or floods.

"You know," my mom continues, "it could be the perfect opportunity to bring a date."

There's no mistaking what she's insinuating. I blink, caught off guard. Stepping out like that is a big commitment. Being seen together at an event like that–it's practically a public announcement. Bigger than going ChattySnap official. And three weeks isn't far off, especially with Jefferson's graduation just a week before.

I shift in my chair, fingers tightening around my mug. "I'll think about it," I say finally, soft but deliberate. "I'd like to, but you know it's more than just showing up with a date. What it means and what people will think."

"Since when did I raise you to care about what other people think?" Mom's southern twang rises up, her eyes sharp but gentle. "You don't owe anyone an explanation. You get to decide when, and if, that world gets to see the parts of you. If it makes you happy, I'll be happy."

I nod, staring out at the pool again, imagining the flash of cameras, the whispers in the room. Showing up with Jefferson in person would squash every rumor about Jake or anyone else, once and for all. But it would also mean it's real. Official. And the truth is, I'm not sure I'm ready to decide if it is–*if* we are.

Mom smirks, reaching for her coffee again. "I think he'd look good in a tux."

"No doubt." I laugh softly, the sound thinner than I intend. "I'll consider it," I say, and leave it at that.

She's right, but also wrong. Jefferson Parks wouldn't just look good in a tux, he'd look deadly.

"How was your exam?" I ask, tucking my knees up to my chest on the bed. He's shirtless, hair damp from the shower, and leaning back against his headboard. That's all I can see of him on the video. It's enough. He should be asleep, but he waited up for me. That knowledge alone makes my chest ache.

"All done," he says, flashing that boyish grin that slays me every damn time. "Just one paper left, and I'm officially out of here."

"That sounds amazing." My smile is instant, impossible to hold back. "I'm proud of you."

He grins wider. I grin back. We're two stupid grinning fools staring at each other through a screen, like neither of us has any idea how to play it cool.

His gaze dips, soft but knowing. "How are your blisters?"

"They'd be better if you were here to kiss them."

The words slip out before I can stop them, flirty and dumb, but when his grin goes wolfish, my stomach curls.

"Flirty little thing," he teases.

"It's dumb," I say quickly, laughing to cover the flush creeping up my neck.

"No," he cuts me off, shaking his head. "It's perfect. You're perfect."

My throat tightens. It makes no sense that just a few words from him leave me drenched between my legs, but here I am, clutching my pillow like it'll keep me from combusting.

"I miss you," he says suddenly. His voice softens, but the weight of the words slams into me. "I miss your face and your mouth–and that pretty pussy that takes me so good."

"Jefferson." I laugh, scandalized. "You're filthy."

"I'm honest," he corrects, his tone as unbothered as it is devastating.

And he is. That's what's so refreshing about him. Him and the guys he runs with. They're solidly who they are–loud, brash, funny, *horny*–and there's no pretending, no polished mask of celebrity. It makes it so easy for me to be my true self in return.

Still, Madison's voice gnaws at the back of my mind. "Madison thinks we're going too fast," I confess, tucking a strand of hair behind my ear. "She says I don't know you well enough."

His brow furrows, but his voice stays steady. "Angel, that's not even close to true. But what do you want to know? I'm an open book."

I tilt my head at him. "An open book, huh? Tell me everything. Dazzle me."

He shrugs one broad shoulder taking up half the screen. "The first time I picked up a hockey stick? Six. The year I learned to ride a bike? Eight. I did better on skates than wheels. First kiss? Twelve. Carla Goodwin." His lips twist. "First time I had sex–not with Carla Goodwin, by the way: I came in three minutes flat. To one of your songs."

I groan, covering my face with both hands. "Don't remind me. I'm still trying to figure out which one."

He laughs, low and smug. "And I'm still not telling."

"Was it *Blue Skies, Full Hearts*?" I peek at him through my fingers.

"Nope." The smirk tugging at his mouth makes me want to both kiss and strangle him.

I drop my hands, squinting at him. "*Hate to Love*?"

His lips twitch. Nothing.

"*Cupid's Bow*?"

Still nothing. The bastard just watches me, eyes glinting with amusement.

I huff, hugging the pillow to my chest. "This is actual torture. Why do I even care?"

He leans closer to the camera, voice soft but sure. "Because you want to know everything about me. And you should. I want to know everything about you too."

The air between us shifts, heavier now, his grin fading into something deeper. I speak before thinking. "I want to see where you live."

His lip quirks. "You want to come to The Manor?"

I nod. "I want to know that part of your life."

His expression flickers between surprise and something darker–want, maybe. "Can you even fit me into your schedule?"

I think on it. "It'll take a miracle, but if I rearrange a few things, I've got three days off before the final shows in New York. I can come then." I pause. "If you want me to."

"I want you to," he says with zero hesitation.

Relief, and something headier, sweeps through me. "I'll talk to my team and make it happen."

"Good."

We're grinning at each other again like idiots, a thousand miles apart but tethered tight. His hand rests on his firm chest, fingers tapping a restless rhythm. "Now," he says, his voice lowering, "let me see you."

I blink. "See me?"

His smile sharpens, equal parts sweet and wicked. "Show me what you're wearing."

I glance down at the oversized hoodie I threw on after my shower. "This glamorous ensemble?" I deadpan, tugging at the fabric. "Very tour chic."

"Take it off," he says, quiet but firm.

Heat floods me. "Bossy."

"I know what I want."

I hesitate, glancing toward the locked door of my suite. My skin buzzes, my pulse quickening. Slowly, deliberately, I tug the hoodie over my head and drop it on the floor. My tank clings to the bare skin underneath.

Jefferson's jaw flexes. "Fuck, Angel." He drags a hand down his face, then back through his damp hair. "Do you know how much I think about you like this? Laid out in your hotel bed, soft and messy, just waiting for me to get my hands on you?"

My thighs press together instinctively. "Tell me," I whisper. "What would you do if you were here?"

"I'd start slow," he says, his voice a gravelly promise. "Mouth on those bruises, your blisters, every sore spot from grinding it out on stage. And then I'd work my way up until you're spread open under me, wet and desperate, begging for my cock. And I wouldn't stop until you're screaming my name so loud they'd hear it down the fucking hallway."

A breath shudders out of me. "Jesus, Jefferson."

He leans closer to the camera, eyes locked on me like I'm the only thing in his world. "Touch yourself for me, Angel. I need to see how bad you miss me."

My hand trembles as it slips beneath the waistband of my shorts. The things this man can get me to do. "You're insufferable."

"I'm dying for you," he counters, his hand fumbling just below the screen. His jaw tightens when he's got a grip on his shaft. I know that clench. I love it, it means he's desperately trying to stay in control. "Now let me watch."

I bite my lip, the distance between us both unbearable and intoxicating. My fingers slide lower, circling my clit the way that feels so good, the way he taught me with his tongue. His groan rattles through the speaker, dark and hungry.

"Fuck...that's it. Nice and slow. Let me see your pussy."

My hips lift off the mattress as I rub tighter circles. Heat sparks everywhere his words touch me. He strokes himself in time with me, broad shoulders flexing, his lips parting on ragged breaths. I want his weight, his sweat, his mouth–but right now I'll take this, the raw need on his face, the way he looks like he'll crawl through the screen just to get to me.

"More," he urges, his voice low, rough. "Push those shorts down. Let me see what's mine."

I shove the fabric out of the way, baring myself to the phone, heart racing. His eyes darken, pupils swallowing color.

"Lick your fingers, taste yourself." I do as he says, sliding my fingers between my lips. "Beautiful," he growls. "Fucking perfect. I swear to God, Ingrid, you're the sexiest thing I've ever seen."

"I doubt that," I whisper back, slipping two fingers inside, the wet sound filling the silence between our gasps.

He shifts his own camera, giving me a view of his cock as he fists it harder, his shoulders hunching forward like he's chasing me, chasing the sound of my moans. The words stop, both of us too deep to communicate. My body arches, shuddering as I cry out his name, the climax tearing through me, leaving me breathless.

Through the screen, Jefferson curses, his body tightening, his head falling back as he spills over his hand, thick spurts of cum pooling onto his abdomen. His groans tangle with mine until it feels like we're in the same room, the same bed, the same skin.

"Jesus Christ," he mutters.

"Yeah," I reply, unable to speak any further. I'm nothing short of undone. Ruined. Flushed and panting, the sheets damp beneath me. But I don't feel lonely. For the first time in forever, I feel truly satiated. And I don't just mean from the orgasm, but from *all* of it–his voice, his hunger, the way he sees me like no one else ever has.

20

───────

J efferson

"Where's the bottle of cleaner?" I'm rummaging under the kitchen sink, head first. "I know we have one. It's yellow. Smells like lemons?" Straightening, I look over at the living room where Reid, Axel, Shelby, and Nadia stare back. "Are we out? Fuck, don't tell me we're out."

"What's happening here?" Axel asks from the couch, one eyebrow raised.

"I think this is what Jefferson looks like when he likes a girl," Nadia replies, grinning.

"Shut up," I snap, pointing at her with the rag. "And get your feet off the coffee table. I just wiped that off."

Ingrid is coming to town. No, Ingrid is coming here. To the Manor. To a house where four hockey players have lived for the past three years. I know it smells like hockey pads and stale beer. I know it, even if I can no longer smell it. I got desensitized long ago.

Madison's coming with her–it was the only way to get everyone on board. With the final shows coming up, it's too risky for her to be out alone, even though I've made it pretty clear she's not likely to leave my bed, much less the house, while she's here. I've got plans and most of them involve us being naked.

Still, I've got this nervous energy, which apparently, in the off-season presents itself in stress cleaning like a maniac.

Shelby comes over, calm as always, walks into the laundry room and comes back with a caddy of cleaners. Ah, the laundry room. Of course. She plucks the rag out of my hands. "Chill. I'll do the kitchen. You–go sit down and maybe drink a beer before you combust."

"You don't have to clean, Shelby. I can do it."

"Jefferson, Ingrid Flockton is coming to our house." She snorts like I'm the crazy one. "Do you honestly think I'm going to let you be the one responsible for making this place presentable?"

Shelby's turned into a bit of a house mom since she moved in two months ago. Axel told her not to baby us, but it's what she likes to do. And she's right. I'm acting like a lunatic.

I grab a beer from the refrigerator, twist off the top, and sink into the couch cushions. Reid, Axel, and Nadia are all staring at me.

"What?" I ask gruffly.

"Is this really happening?" Reid finally says.

"Is what happening?"

"You. Having a serious relationship. Or at the very least a more-than-a-one-night-standship?"

I rake my hand through my hair, frustration buzzing under my skin. "Fuck if I know."

Because honestly–maybe this was a bad idea. Am I even ready for this? I'm about to head into the NHL. She's a megastar. Sure, we like each other. Sure, our bodies are ridiculously in tune. And god, yes, I want nothing more than to get my hands on her the second she steps through that door.

But having her here? In this house I share with three guys and... sort of one girl? That's what feels insane. That makes it real. There's no hotel sheets. No concert as a buffer. Just me, her, and my life.

"Leave him alone," Shelby says, spraying some kind of foam all over the island. "This is new for him."

"Thanks, Shel," I give her a grin before turning back to the others and glaring at them.

Nadia lifts her chin, dark eyes sharp. "Look, I know better than anyone that it's a big deal for athletes, and hockey players in particular, to be complete sluts and non-committal." Her gaze slides deliberately to Axel, who smirks without shame. He'd been a legendary player long before she tamed him. "But what's the big deal? Do you just want to keep sleeping around forever?"

I shake my head because that's not it. I haven't hooked up with anyone else since Ingrid and I met. I don't want anyone else. Not in the slightest. "I'm just not into the idea," I mutter, taking a swig from my beer. The carbonation burns down my throat but does nothing to settle the nerves coiling in my gut.

Reid leans forward, elbows on his knees, grinning like an asshole. "He's afraid settling down will make him boring or something."

Bastard. That's what I get for confiding in him.

"Is that really it?" Nadia asks, eyes narrowing at me like she's trying to peel me open.

"No," I shoot back too fast. But then I sigh, shoulders sagging. "Yeah. Kind of."

"What kind of bullshit is that?" Axel finally speaks, shaking his head.

I scrub a hand down my face, trying to find words for the thing that's always sat in the back of my mind. "My parents have been together for almost thirty years. Thirty. Obviously something made them fall in love, but now? They've got nothing in common. Zero things. My mom's this wild, free-spirited artist–oil paints everywhere, canvases stacked in the garage, paint under her nails. And my dad? He runs his own tech company. The guy speaks in code and algorithms. They don't fight, they don't even dislike each other, they just... don't connect. Not anymore." I glance down at the bottle in my hand, rolling it between my palms. "The thought of settling down with someone forever, then growing apart until you're just two people in the same house, bored out of your minds? That freaks me the fuck out."

Reid leans back, shaking his head like I'm the dumbest guy alive. "You're overthinking it, man. You don't go into a relationship planning for it to crash and burn. You go in because you want it, because it feels good right now. That's it. Then you see where it goes from there."

"Spoken like a guy who's a serial monogamist and whose most recent relationship is two months old," I shoot back.

Reid's grin only widens. "Two months, six months, two years—doesn't matter, dude. At least I'm not too scared to try. You'd rather sit on the bench than risk taking the shot."

"You did not just hockey metaphor me."

Axel snorts, but Reid has zero fucks to give, and just shrugs. "Coach rubbed off on me."

Nadia crosses her legs, looking thoughtful. "Jefferson, you're acting like love is this math equation you can screw up if the numbers don't match. People change. Interests change. That doesn't mean the relationship has to die." She tips her head toward Axel, who's lounging with one arm draped along the back of the couch. "Especially when the sex is good." Her eyes meet mine. "It's good, isn't it? Ingrid Flockton is amazing in bed, isn't she."

"You're a lunatic," I tell her, but fuck yes, she's good in bed. And out of bed. And everywhere all at once.

"She's right," Axel says, combing his fingers through his hair. "You're building this whole hypothetical future in your head when the truth is, it's simple: if you want her, you make it work. Period. You don't worry about what might happen twenty years down the road."

"Yeah, but what if it doesn't–" I start, but Shelby cuts me off, her voice sharp from across the kitchen.

"What if, what if, what if. Jesus, Jefferson. What if the plane crashes on the way here? What if you tear your ACL in practice tomorrow? You can 'what if' yourself to death. Or," she slams a rag onto the counter for emphasis, "you can actually enjoy the fact that someone incredible wants to spend time with you."

I stare at her, jaw tight. They're all ganging up on me, and worse, they're not wrong. I've always told myself I love the thrill of the chase. The competition of locking down a hot chick with one look. Chasing Ingrid had been amazing, but keeping her? That could be even better.

"See how the weekend goes," Shelby continues, bracing her hip against the counter. "If she's still interested in you once she sees you here–in your natural habitat–that's the real test. Because she may take one look at that disaster of a room upstairs and run like hell."

"Shit." My stomach drops. My room. Total trainwreck. I shoot up from the couch. "I need to take care of that."

"He's so whipped," Axel says under his breath.

"Shut it," I say, dunking his head as I pass, heading for the stairs.

"Change your sheets!" Shelbly shouts.

"And clean the bathroom!" Nadia adds, wrinkling her nose. "Seriously, you guys are pigs."

The last thing I see before disappearing onto the second floor is Axel tugging Nadia into his side, grinning down at her with zero shame. "But I'm your pig," he says, pressing a kiss to her temple. Then he glances up at me. "If a disaster like me can make it work, Parks, maybe you and your angel have a shot too."

Angel? I stop. "You've been eavesdropping on me?"

"Paperthin walls, brother," he winks, making it clear he's heard me and Ingrid in the middle of some of our late night calls.

I'll have to kick his ass later, but if he's right, maybe I won't. Maybe I am getting ahead of myself. This entire weekend could be a disaster and whatever future Ingrid and I have together will be over before it really starts. Or, I step into my room and start ripping off the sheets, maybe it's exactly what I need to prove to myself that I'm not afraid of something real.

THE HOUSE IS UNNATURALLY QUIET. Clean. Shelby really went all in–lemon scent in the air instead of the usual stench of stale beer and gym bags. I'd kicked everyone out hours ago and told them they could come back later. Maybe. Depending on how this went.

Ingrid steps just inside the door, glancing around. "This is…"

My chest seizes. "What?"

Her lips twitch. "Not what I expected."

Panic spikes, and I start rambling before I can stop myself. "College housing is, you know, kind of take what you can get. The Manor's the biggest house in the area. It's called Shotgun because it was part of the old mill that used to be here. Most of the houses are shotgun-style, long and narrow, but this one was the owner's place. At some point the hockey players got an in and we've kept it that way for years…"

I trail off when she looks up at me, eyes sparkling with barely-contained laughter.

"I'm rambling," I mutter.

"It's cute," she says softly.

"You're cute." The words slip out before I can reel them back.

It takes everything in me not to scoop her up right there, haul her upstairs, and strip her bare.

"Where is everyone?" she asks instead, her mind not as deep in the gutter as mine.

"At the Badger Den, I think." I shrug, trying to act casual when my pulse is anything but. "Fishbowl margarita night."

"What does that even mean?"

I laugh. "I forget you're not savvy to the ridiculousness of college. Basically it's a giant margarita, the size of a fishbowl. It's a shitton of tequila and a promise of a terrible hangover."

She grins, that wicked little tilt of her mouth I know too well. "You know what I could go for right now?"

I arch a brow hopefully.

Her fingers curl into my shirt, tugging me closer. "The Jefferson Parks Special."

"You don't mean my cock, do you?" I laugh under my breath, already caving. How the hell could I ever say no to her–to whatever she wants? I'd give her everything. "If that's what you want, Angel, that's what you'll get."

Twenty minutes later, we're weaving through the crowd at the Badger Den, Ingrid tucked against my side as I push us toward the back table. The place smells like fried food and cheap beer, the floors sticky, the music too loud, but when she slides her hand into mine, I feel ten feet tall walking her in.

There's a ripple of excitement as people recognize us–*her*. I'm used to the looks from men and women when I come into the bar. Being a hockey player at Wittmore comes with instant recognition, but the energy this time is different. It's both quiet and loud.

"You sure this is okay?" I ask her, the sense of protectiveness surging in my veins. "Should we call Marv?"

I've gotten used to her bodyguard's quiet, but intimidating presence. Ingrid's fingers squeeze mine. "He's around here somewhere, and this is nothing. I can handle it." She tilts her head. "The real question is, can you?"

People try to slyly take photographs, but honestly I don't care. I drop my mouth to her ear. "I want everyone to know you're with me, Angel. And if anyone tries to overstep, they'll have to deal with me and my friends." I just want her to know that she can relax a little and have fun. We'll keep her safe.

At the table, everyone greets her with the kind of enthusiasm usually reserved for championship wins. Hugs, hellos, the girls pulling her into quick side squeezes before launching into compliments about her outfit and chatter about where they got their own. They ask about Madison, who is getting to town late, due to dealing with some last minute tour logistics. The guys, less subtle, shove a frosty pint into my hand from the pitcher already sweating on the table.

"What happened to holing up and staying in all weekend?" Reese asks.

"She realized Parks in bed for an entire weekend wasn't worth the hype," Axel snarks back.

"Shut it." I snap. "She just wanted to experience college life a little."

The guys seem, well, happy for me, which is weird. I haven't done anything but show up with a girl to a shitty bar. When the girls settle back in at the table, I drag her chair right up next to mine, feeling her warm leg against mine. Josie, the waitress, brings a fresh round of fishbowls to the table. Ingrid's eyes widen at the huge glass.

"Pace yourself," Reid warns.

Nadia takes a sip out of her straw, draining her glass, and leans forward, blunt as ever. "So did Jake really show up backstage after your concert?"

The table goes quiet, all eyes on her.

Ingrid doesn't flinch. She just takes a sip of her own drink, eyes steady. "He did. It was pretty awkward," she admits. "For him, more than me."

"Did he see you?" she asks me.

"We met," I answer gruffly, thinking about how if I see him again, I'm going to have a hard time restraining myself.

"He totally showed up because you're dating someone new," Twyler says. "Never underestimate a man wanting what another man has."

"Where'd you get that? In a horoscope?" I ask.

She leans into Reese's side. "Wise words told to me by your captain."

"Fuck, tell me he pissed on your leg after that?" Axel howls. "He did, didn't he?"

"No." Twyler grins. "But he did give me his hoodie emblazoned with his name."

"I like that." Ingrid grins, twirling her straw in her hands. "I may put it in a song."

"Go for it," Reese says, tipping back his beer. "I give you permission."

I slip an arm around the back of her chair, protective, even though she doesn't need me to be.

The conversation moves on to graduation in two weeks and

summer plans. Ingrid and I stay close, thighs pressed together under the table, her laugh slipping into my shoulder every time the guys say something dumb. And fuck if the guys weren't right. It's nice–better than nice–having someone here who's mine, instead of prowling for something quick and empty.

At some point, she leans back, lips shiny from the greasy burger she inhaled, eyes soft as they catch mine. "Thank you for showing me this," she says, almost shy. "I never had a life like this. Mine was always work and carefully orchestrated play."

"You're welcome," I murmur, leaning in to kiss her cheek. She smells like beer and fries and her expensive perfume, and I want to bottle the moment forever.

"That's what I want this weekend to be about," she adds. "Seeing your world."

"Anyone up for darts?" Reid asks, sliding out of the booth. "There's a free board."

"Yes, please!" she says, rising up to follow him to the dart board in the corner. "You coming?"

"Let me finish this," I say, pointing to my uneaten dinner. I'd been too focused on fun, focused on her to eat. "Go have fun."

She flashes me a smile over her shoulder before disappearing into the little crowd near the dart board, and the table feels quieter without her beside me.

Reese lingers back, shoulders loose but eyes steady–Captain through and through. Stoic, calm. A leader at heart and the first out of all of us to fall hard.

"I like her for you," Reese says, finishing his fries with a shrug like it's no big deal.

"Thanks for your approval," I retort, smirking, but it means something and he knows it.

"I heard the guys were giving you shit for being hesitant to commit, but don't listen to them," he says, leaning in a little. "You know I was afraid of falling into family footsteps. I was afraid I'd lose Twyler over hockey the way my dad and mom got divorced. So afraid I almost fucked things up big time. Axel ran like hell away from his oppressive and controlling father and found someone who accepts him for who he is. Shelby, too. And Reid? He was looking so hard for a stable family system that he almost settled for the wrong girl."

He tips the pitcher, filling my glass and his until the last drops of beer slide out in a thin stream.

"Ingrid may not be the one," Reese continues, "but she may be the one that shows you this is something you want. Fucking around, chasing sorority girls and puck bunnies is fun as hell, but nothing–" he holds my eyes, his voice firm, "and I mean *nothing* comes close to falling in love with your best friend." He coughs into his fist. "*Girl*friend, that is."

"That's some kind of speech, Cap."

"Well, we're running out of time, and I need to get them in while I can." His grin is faint and a strange seriousness settles between us.

I lift my glass toward him. "Thanks. For everything. For being my best friend. For being an awesome team leader. I'm going to miss you."

"Eh," he says, grinning wider now, "I'll see you on the ice. Don't cry when I kick your ass."

It'll be crazy playing against one another, but I also can't wait. The road ahead is exciting, and I can't wait to get to it.

Across the room, I see Ingrid start toward the back hall where the bathrooms are located. I swallow the last of my beer and then cross the room. It's dim back here, quieter, with the bass from the speakers thumping faintly through the walls. When she pushes open the bathroom door, I grab her wrist and tug her into the shadowed corner, pressing her back to the paneling.

Her brows lift, amused. "What's this?"

I cage her in with my arms, leaning down until my lips hover over hers. "Part of college is getting drunk and making out in dark corners."

Her laugh is a whisper against my mouth before I kiss her, hungry and messy, like I've been waiting all night to taste her. She hooks her fingers in my shirt, pulling me closer, and I let one hand slide into her hair, the other gripping her hip. She tastes like beer and salt, her mouth opening under mine like she was made for this. The world fades–no crowd, no noise, no spotlight–just her, pressed to the wall, kissing me like she doesn't care if anyone walks by.

And maybe that's the real point. This isn't staged, or polished, or carefully controlled. It's raw, unfiltered. Ours.

"You want to finish this here or head back home?" I ask her. If she's down for a dirty fuck in the alley behind the Den, who am I to stop her?

Her hand slides down the front of my pants and she squeezes my erection, "Jefferson, please take me home."

21

———————

I ngrid

THE WALK across campus feels endless, every shadowed corner another temptation. Jefferson can't keep his hands off me, and I don't want him to. Every time we pause, his palm slides under my shirt, fingers teasing skin, or he presses his hard, insistent cock into my stomach until I'm gasping, desperate. By the time we cut across the quad, I'm clinging to him, dizzy from lust.

"What would you do in a normal situation like this?" I ask, trying to catch my breath as we start up a path toward the center of campus. "With a girl who isn't famous. With no gossip sites waiting to post photos of us in a compromising situation."

He slows, thinking on it. Like this man is *seriously* thinking about it. Then he looks at me with that crooked grin that makes me melt. "Follow me."

We veer off diagonally down a short hill. At the bottom stands a modern-looking building, all glass and steel.

"Welcome to Wittmore's student center," he says, pushing open the door like he owns the place.

Inside, the building is quiet, humming with the faint buzz of vending machines and overhead lights. "It's open twenty-four hours." He points to the shuttered food court. "That's where everyone goes between classes. The coffee shop," he gestures toward a separate little alcove, "where Reese shoved his tongue down Twyler's throat for the first time."

I laugh, imagining always-in-control Reese in a scene like that.

"There's a movie theater, the store where you can get books and sweatshirts and keychains..." Jefferson takes my hand and leads me down a long flight of stairs, then a hallway lined with locked doors. He stops in front of one, glances back at me.

"What's this?"

"Room 110."

"What's room 110?"

He punches in an access code on a keypad. The lock clicks, and he pushes the door open.

"The athletic tutoring and study room," he says. Then his grin goes wicked. "But the more popular use is for a quickie."

I blink at him. "On campus?"

"Yep." He pulls me inside and shuts the door with a solid click. "During the day, night, whenever the urge strikes." He steps closer, his voice dropping. "Obviously."

"That's insane."

"That's college, Angel. Especially when you're one of the chosen ones." He winks. "A D1, varsity athlete."

Before I can roll my eyes at him, his mouth is on mine, hot and urgent, licking my lips open for access. His hands frame my face, then trail down, tugging at my shirt, already greedy for skin.

"Jefferson–" I try to breathe, but he swallows my words, kissing me deeper, hungrier.

In the next moment, he lifts me, setting me down on the desk at the center of the room. The surface creaks under the sudden weight.

His body slots between my thighs, his cock hard against me, and I whimper at the pressure.

"I can't keep my hands off of you, Ingrid," he groans, dragging his mouth down my neck, teeth scraping at the soft skin. "You have no idea how badly I want you."

His hands are everywhere, squeezing my tits through my shirt, kneading my thigh, slipping higher, higher. He pulls my top up, baring me, and yanks my bra down until my nipples are pebbled in the cool air. His head dips, tongue flicking, lips closing over me.

The moan that escapes me is shameless. My fingers twist in his hair, holding him there as he sucks and bites, lavishing attention on each breast until my back arches off the desk.

"You taste better than I dreamed," he mutters, glancing up, mouth wet, eyes wild.

"You've dreamed about this?" My voice trembles.

"Every damn night since we met." He smirks, then lowers his mouth again, trailing kisses down my stomach until I can barely think straight.

"Tell me to stop," he challenges, voice rough.

"Don't you fucking dare."

That's all he needs. My jeans are around my ankles before I realize he's undone them, panties following in one swift tug. The cold air hits me for half a second before his warm mouth replaces it, lips sealing over me, tongue lashing my clit.

I cry out, gripping the desk edge until my knuckles ache.

He groans against me, like he's the one unraveling, and the vibrations send a shiver up my spine. His fingers join his mouth, sliding inside, curling just right. I buck against him, shameless, the wet sounds of his tongue and the rasp of his breath filling the room.

"I love your pussy, you know that?" He spreads my folds, then flicks his tongue inside.

"I'm getting the idea," I breathe, close to falling apart.

One more hot kiss, and I'm gone, spiraling apart on the desk of room 110, with Jefferson Parks between my thighs, giving me the kind of memory I know will burn in my veins forever.

I'm still trembling when he pulls back, wiping his mouth with the back of his hand, pupils blown wide. He looks wrecked, and I love it.

But I don't want to just be another girl in Room 110. I want to be the one he remembers–the one who gives him something he's never had before.

"Jefferson..." My voice is still ragged from the orgasm, but I press my palms to his chest, stopping him before he can lean in to kiss me.

"What?" His brows knit like he's worried I'll bolt.

"I don't want this to be just another hookup spot for you. Another story you can tell." His mouth opens, but I shake my head, cutting him off. "I want it to be ours. Something different. Something you haven't done with anyone else."

He searches my face, and I can see it, he gets it. That need in me to stake a claim. To matter. Then I smile, sliding my hand down his chest, over his stomach, stopping just at the waistband of his jeans. "You told me once what you wanted to do with me."

He freezes. "What did I say? Because there's a never-ending list of things I want to do with you."

I lean closer, whispering against his ear. "That you wanted to fuck my tits."

The sound he makes is half-growl, half-groan, his cock straining hard against the denim. His hands grip my hips, like he's holding himself back.

"Angel..." He says it like a prayer, like I've undone him. I push off the desk and pull my panties back on before perching on one of the hard desk chairs, face level with his waist. He stands before me and tugs his jeans down until his cock springs free, thick and heavy, flushed with need. My mouth waters just looking at him.

He's already panting, running a hand through his hair, the other running down my neck. "You don't have to–"

"I want to," I cut in. My fingers curl around him, stroking him once, watching his head tip back. Then I squeeze my breasts together with my hands, thumbs running over my nipples.

"Fuck, Ingrid." His voice is guttural, his hips jerking on instinct. His hands take over, lifting my tits in his big, wide palms. I've never been a small girl. Always tall for my age, developed early. The way this man touches me makes me forget every insecurity I ever had.

I duck my head and take his cock in my mouth, getting him slippery and wet, before releasing him. The weight of him, hot and slick, sliding over my skin makes me throb all over again. I glance up at him through my lashes. "Like this?"

He looks down, eyes dark and hungry, watching himself disappear and reappear between the swell of my breasts. "Exactly like that," he grits out between thrusts.

I start to move, rocking my body in rhythm, squeezing tighter to give him more friction. He fists my hair, guiding me, his cock dragging over my skin, the tip smearing precum across my chest.

"Angel, baby, fuck," he groans.

I flick my tongue out, catching him every time he thrusts forward, giving little sucks that make him shudder. The sound of his breath, the low curses spilling from his lips, it's everything.

This isn't just sex. It's bigger, it's the way we meet each other's needs. I've never had this with anyone before.

I press my tits tighter, working him harder, faster, until he's trembling, hips jerking with no control. His hands pinch, and it hurts in a good way, my nipples raw from the stroke of his thumbs.

"Fuck–" His voice cracks as he looks down at me, desperation in every line of his body. "I'm not gonna last."

"Good," I whisper, flicking my tongue over his head again. "I don't want you to."

With a broken groan, he comes, spilling hot and messy over my chest and throat, his whole body shaking as he holds my head to him.

I keep him tight between me until he finally collapses back against the desk, spent and gasping. I look up at him, wiped out and undone. "Promise me something."

"Anything."

"I'm the last girl you bring in here, understand"

He leans down and holds my eye, saying, "Deal," and then seals it with one last, blistering kiss.

THE NEXT MORNING, Jefferson insists on making the first stop of the day the campus coffee shop. He orders for both of us without even asking, rattling it off like he's done it a hundred times.

When the wide-eyed barista, who definitely recognizes me, hands me a caramel oat milk latte, I raise a brow. "You pay attention."

"I'm observant," he replies, smug as hell. "I overheard the rant about whole milk with Madison when I stayed over in Atlanta. I wasn't risking it."

He looks so annoyingly pleased with himself that I stick my tongue out at him. Which, of course, just makes him lean down and kiss me quickly, right there in line. Too fast for anyone to grab a photo, thank God, but enough that I'm buzzing by the time we leave.

"Madison texted this morning. She said she and the girls are going for brunch."

She texted other stuff too, like a million questions about my night and how things were with Jefferson. How photos had popped up online, but we looked happy, and the overall reaction was good. "Overall reaction" is code for, my fans are excited for me. My haters? Well, they hate everything.

I told her to stop scrolling and take a break.

Jefferson has big plans for the day and is taking me to the arena to show me the rink. I get it–there's nothing I love more than showing off the stage right before a concert. It feels like a second home–something you want to share with a person you care about.

And caring about Jefferson Parks seems to be easier and easier to do.

By the time we make it there, I've got caffeine warming my veins. It's just him and me. No crowd. No flashing cameras. Just quiet ice.

Jefferson pulls two pairs of skates out of his bag with ease, tossing me a pair that looks practically brand new. "These should fit. Twyler bought them when she was working with the team. Wore them twice before she gave up and stuck with her sneakers."

I laugh, plopping onto the bench to tug them on. "Perfect. Let's hope I don't break an ankle."

God, Madison, and everyone else associated with the tour would kill me.

"You won't," he says firmly, crouching down to help tighten the laces on one boot. His big hands make quick work of the knots, and for some reason, that simple act, him kneeling at my feet, making sure my skates are secure, sends a wave of heat straight through me. "I won't let you."

He puts on his own skates with incredible speed, and when we step onto the ice, it's like stepping into another world. The place smells faintly of cold metal and rubber, the boards echo every scrape of the blades, and the ice looks impossibly smooth, like glass. I immediately cling to the wall, my legs threatening mutiny.

Jefferson's laugh is so loud it echoes through the rafters.

"Not funny!" I scold.

"It's hilarious," he counters, easily gliding to me and prying my death grip off the boards. "Come on, Angel. Trust me."

"I do trust you," I grumble, wobbling as he pulls me toward the middle, "but my body isn't so sure."

He grins, cocky as ever, pulling me flush against him so I can feel the strength of his chest beneath my hands. "That's okay. You can fall into me."

The way he says it makes my stomach flutter, and suddenly I'm more worried about melting through the ice than actually falling. Last night was amazing. Hanging out at the bar with his friends, the naughty things we did in room 110. After that, we went back to the Manor and he showed me his room—*his bed*—and it was perfection.

Now, he skates backward with infuriating ease, dragging me forward with him. For someone who spends their nights doing dance routines and choreography, I'm stiff as a board, walking more than gliding, but soon I'm laughing too hard to care. It's ridiculous, and fun, and the first time in forever I don't feel like I'm performing for anyone but myself.

"You're actually not terrible," he admits after a few wobbly laps. "Why am I not surprised?"

"What does that mean?" I ask.

"It means that everything you attempt to do is a step higher than everyone else." His smirk softens, eyes flicking down to my mouth. He spins me carefully, catching me by the hips before I can slip. "You're special."

My cheeks heat despite the cold. "You're ridiculous."

"Maybe," he shrugs, tugging me into a slow circle, his breath misting in the air. "But I think I'm falling ridiculously hard for you."

The sincerity in his voice knocks the wind out of me. For a heartbeat, it feels like we're the only two people in the world–me in my borrowed skates, him holding me steady on the ice that's his second home.

Of course, that's when the door bangs open.

"Parks!" A gruff voice echoes across the rink. "What the hell are you—"

Jefferson stiffens, mutters, "Shit."

An older man stomps onto the ice in battered skates, hands planted on his hips. "You can't just–" Then he sees me, and everything about his face changes. His jaw drops. "Holy hell. You're Ingrid Flockton."

"You know who Ingrid Flockton is?" he asks, shocked.

"I have a thirteen-year-old daughter, Parks, of course I know who the biggest pop star on Earth is." He says it like Jefferson is the biggest dumbass on earth. His gaze darts back to me, and he thrusts out his hand. "I'm Syd Bryant, coach here at Wittmore." Then he lowers his voice. "Are you seriously here with this knucklehead?"

"Nice to meet you," I shake his hand and then wobble a bit. Jefferson doesn't move an inch, holding onto me tight while I cling to him like a baby deer on ice. "And yes, I'm here with Jefferson."

Coach Bryant shakes his head, incredulous at the pairing. "My daughter is a huge fan. Knows every one of your songs. I don't usually do this, but... would you mind...?"

He fumbles for his phone, looking almost sheepish.

Jefferson mutters under his breath, "Unbelievable," but doesn't move his arm from around my waist as I nod.

"Of course," I say, smiling.

He shoves the phone at Jefferson, who has to release me for a moment to take the picture. I manage not to fall as we grin at the camera.

"Thank you." He slides the phone back in his pocket. "You just made me father of the year."

"I'm sure it's more than the photo," I tell him, earning me another grin.

"You two have fun," he says, but shoots Jefferson a look. "Don't you fuck this up, hear me?"

"Yes, sir."

Coach Bryant skates off the ice, and Jefferson shakes his head. "Only you could turn my coach catching me breaking the rules into a fan meet-and-greet."

I grin back at him, heart still racing from the glide of his hands on my waist. "You're welcome." I'm still laughing when the thought nudges at me. It's probably the worst time to bring it up–skating around like we're in some cheesy rom-com montage–but the words spill out anyway. "Actually, there's something I wanted to ask you."

Jefferson tilts his head. "Yeah?"

"There's a fundraiser in a few weeks. For my foundation. I go every year—it's kind of a family affair. Black tie, big auction, lots of champagne and awkward speeches." I skate a half-circle around him and stop, nerves creeping in. "I wanted to know if you'd go with me."

His eyebrow lifts. "You want to see me in a tux, huh?"

I roll my eyes, heat crawling up my cheeks. "That wasn't the primary reason I was asking. But sure, Parks, walking in with some eye candy never hurts."

He chuckles and skates toward me, wrapping his hand around my back as he glides me back until we brush the boards. His arms bracket my head, caging me in with that ridiculous mix of cocky and tender only he can pull off.

"I think it would be fun," I continue, heart thudding so hard I can hear it in my ears. "You could meet some of my family and friends, but... it would be public. Lots of cameras. It would be viewed as a statement." I swallow. "If you're ready for that."

For a moment, his expression softens, the humor melting into something deeper. He leans in, his breath warm against my cheek. "Ingrid, I'd wear a damn tux every night if it meant I got to stand next to you. Escorting you for a good cause? That's not work–it's an honor."

The world tilts a little, the way it always does when he says things that cut straight past my defenses. I rest my hands on his chest, steadying myself on solid muscle and steady heartbeat. "Careful, Parks. You keep talking like that and I might start believing you."

His lips graze the corner of my mouth, teasing. "That's the idea."

WHEN WE STEP out of the arena, the quiet, sweet bubble we'd built on the ice pops.

"Ingrid! Over here!"

"Give us a smile, Ingrid!"

"Jefferson! What's it like dating the most famous pop star in the world?"

"Selfie? Please, just one selfie—"

They're everywhere–press, fans, cameras, phones held high. It's a wall of noise and flashing lights, the air thick with the sharp tang of perfume, coffee, and winter air trapped under too many bodies.

The crush closes in fast, microphones thrust forward, cell phones shoving into my face. A pen nearly jabs my cheek. Someone yanks on my sleeve. A camera flash blinds me white.

My heart races, panic rising in my throat. I can barely breathe.

And then Jefferson moves.

His whole body shifts, hard and deliberate. He plants himself in front of me, broad shoulders cutting a path like a shield, arms coming back until he's wrapped me fully against him. A fortress of muscle and heat. He doesn't flinch when someone shouts his name, doesn't even look at the flashing bulbs. He just keeps his focus on me.

"I've got you," he murmurs, low and steady, a sound meant only for me.

The crowd doesn't stop. "Jefferson! Are you her new boyfriend?"

"Is this for real or just publicity?"

"Ingrid, what about Jake?"

"Back up!" Jefferson snaps, voice rough and commanding, the tone of a man used to being in charge. He tucks me tighter into his side, one hand firm on my hip as if he could haul me straight out of here if he had to. "Give her space."

But they don't. They never do.

The flashes keep coming. The questions grow sharper, louder, messier. Everyone's shouting over one another–*"Ingrid, is it true you're quitting the tour?" "Jefferson, are you sleeping together?" "Ingrid, look over here!"*

Hands wave, cameras jab forward, bodies crush closer. My chest tightens. I can't breathe. The only thing keeping me from unraveling completely is the steady weight of Jefferson's arm, the way his big frame shields mine, like he's daring them to try to get through him.

Then it happens.

A man lunges, hand snagging my shirt. There's a sharp *rip* of fabric, the neckline tearing down my shoulder. My scream catches in my throat.

Jefferson *snaps*.

One second, his arm is wrapped around me, the next he's exploding forward, shoving the guy so hard he crashes to the ground. His camera cracks against the pavement, the plastic splintering. All around us, the crowd gasps, stumbling back. Jefferson's voice booms over the chaos, raw and furious: "Anyone else want to fuck with me and my girl?"

For a beat, everything stills–just Jefferson, chest heaving, towering over the swarm, eyes blazing like he'll take on every single one of them if they so much as breathe wrong in my direction.

The tension is disrupted by the sound of wheels screeching to a stop at the curb, horn blaring. The crowd startles, scattering back like pigeons, because whoever's behind the wheel clearly has zero concern about mowing them down.

The window cranks open, and Coach Bryant leans out, face red and furious. "Get in the car!"

Jefferson doesn't hesitate. His big hand closes around mine, and he yanks me with him, cutting a path through the stragglers. The door groans as he shoves me up into the cab, then crams himself in after, shoulders so broad he takes up half the space.

The photographers find their nerve again and rush forward, but Coach slams his foot on the gas. Gravel spits. The truck fishtails once before lurching forward, and the mob disappears behind us.

"Thanks, Coach," Jefferson says, his arm still locked around me, holding me tight against his side like I might shatter.

I can't stop shaking. My teeth chatter even though I clamp my jaw shut. I focus on breathing in, breathing out, trying not to tip into full-body tremors.

"What can I do?" Jefferson asks quietly, head bent to mine. "What do you need, Angel?"

"I'm fine," I whisper. It sounds unconvincing, even to me. I feel both men exchange a look over my head, the silence weighted.

"They came out of nowhere," Coach mutters, knuckles white on the steering wheel. "No one was there when I got to the arena this morning."

"Same," Jefferson says, voice tight. "Someone must've followed us. Posted about it online."

"It wasn't me." Coach's eyes flick to the rearview mirror, pinning me with a firm look. "I haven't even told Britt I met you yet."

"It's fine," I say, forcing the words past the lump in my throat, trying to steady the tremble in my voice. "It happens."

"Not at my arena," Coach grumbles. His jaw ticks, anger simmering under the words. "I called security. They'll have them cleared out fast." Then his tone softens, just slightly. "Where do you want me to drop you two?"

Jefferson tilts his head down, steel-gray eyes searching mine. "Want me to call Marv? Get you back to the hotel?"

I shake my head instantly. "No. I want to go back with you. To the Manor."

His grip tightens on me, protective and possessive all at once. I lean into him as the truck turns toward the Manor, the safe bubble of Jefferson's world closing around me again, holding onto it for as long as I can.

22

———

J efferson

I GIVE Coach a wave of thanks and get her inside. The house is blessedly quiet. I notice she's still trembling, and my gut twists. I don't know if it's from the mob or from *me*. From what I did back there.

Because yeah, I've shoved guys around before. Dropped gloves, thrown fists. It's what hockey demands–what's expected. But the way I went at that guy when he grabbed her? That wasn't hockey. That was raw, ugly fury. And if she saw it–really saw it–then maybe she's shaking because she realizes what I can do.

"Ingrid," I start, searching for the words. I'm not sorry. I'm fucking not, but also... "Tell me what you need."

"I'm fine. I told you that."

I look down at her. She's shivering, face pale. Her arms are wrapped around her body. My gaze drops to where her shirt was torn and another wave of anger rolls over me. "You're not fine. *None* of this is fine."

What if that asshole hurt her? What if he got any closer? What if I hadn't been there? Jesus Christ.

I touch her cheek. "You're freezing."

"I can't get warm."

"Then let's fix that." I guide her upstairs, into the bathroom, and crank on the shower until steam curls through the air. There's a tension between us. Something fragile and pulled tight. I can't take it and I clear my throat. "Are you... are you scared of me? After what happened out there? I know hockey players have a reputation for being violent, but normally, off the ice, I'd never hurt anyone."

Her eyes snap up to mine, wide and sure. "No. God no, Jefferson." Her eyes shine. "I'm not scared of you. No one who wasn't on the payroll has ever defended me like that."

Relief floods me so fast it makes me dizzy. I cup her face, my thumb stroking her cheek, damp from the steam. "I thought maybe I crossed a line."

"I'm not scared of you, but I hate that I brought you into this." She frowns. "There's probably going to be a huge stink about it, and that guy could even press charges..."

"Hey," I stop her. "I'm not worried about it or scared of him."

"It could affect your contract."

"Angel," I force her to look at me. "I'll deal with it. *We'll* deal with it. This is part of your life and something I'm willing to take on."

She nods, tension easing slightly out of her shoulders. The room warms around us, steam filling the gaps. There's a long beat, then she asks, "Did you mean it?"

"Mean what?" I search her face.

"When you called me your girl?"

The words lodge in my throat, but I nod. "Yeah. I meant it."

It shouldn't be a big deal, the declaration that I'm into this girl, that I want her to be mine and for everyone to know it. But it feels big and when she says, "Stay with me," softly, my heart hammers in my chest.

"I'm not going anywhere," I promise, stepping closer, helping her out of her clothes. Her torn shirt comes off first, then her leggings. I push her panties down her thighs and unhook her bra with careful hands, stripping her slowly, reverently, until she's bare in front of me. She's gorgeous–always is–but right now she looks fragile too, and all I want is to keep her safe.

Something soft flickers in her eyes before she steps into the shower, tilting her face into the spray. I strip fast, tugging off my clothes and letting them fall in a heap, then follow her in.

The heat hits us both, water sliding over her skin, washing away the last traces of the outside world. I take the soap and work it over her shoulders, her arms, down to her fingers, lingering there until they're pink and warm again. She exhales, a little sigh that tells me she's starting to come back.

I kiss her, gentle at first, just the press of my mouth against hers under the steady stream of water. She kisses me back, her lips parting, her hands fisting in my wet hair like she needs me closer. I press her against the tile, but carefully, keeping my body shielding hers. My hands skim her sides, her hips, the curve of her ass. Her skin is slick, soft, impossibly perfect under my palms.

"You feel so good," she whispers, arching into me.

I slide a hand between us, stroking her slowly, until she's ready for me to slide a finger inside, then another. She sets the pace, hips rocking into me, forehead pressed against my sternum. Every sound she makes goes straight to my chest, not just my cock, because it's not about taking her–it's about giving her back something steady when the whole world outside tried to strip it away.

"I want to come with you in me," she whimpers, the orgasm close. I pull out, then align myself with her slippery pussy and sink into her, it's slow, careful, like she's porcelain in my arms. Her leg hooks around my hip, and I pound into her as she clings to my body.

The hot water sprays over us both, steam fogging up the room. I kiss her temple, her jaw, her mouth, murmuring against her lips, "I've got you. Do you understand that?"

She nods, eyes closed, and the orgasm lets loose, the muscles clenching around me, holding onto me until I grunt low and come, spilling inside. The tremors wracking through her body are no longer about fear. They're from the release of knowing she's not alone in all of this. She's got me and fucking hell, that's not even the best part of it.

I've got her.

"Don't move." Ingrid's sitting in the middle of my bed with damp hair wearing my Wittmore Hockey hoodie and a pair of panties. I grab my phone and snap a picture. "Perfect."

"Seriously?" she asks, looking down at the ratty hoodie. I got it in high school, when I was recruited and signed to play on the team. It's soft and broken in and the band around the wrist is fraying, but Jesus Christ, she looks so fucking good in it.

"Angel, this encapsulates every teenage fantasy I've ever had."

I place my hands on the bed and kiss her, sliding my tongue into her open mouth. Even though we just had sex, I'm hard again, unable to get enough of this woman. Her hand curls around my neck and I get the feeling she's the same about me, and I'm thinking maybe we should just get naked again when her phone rings.

"Dammit," I mutter, nipping at her bottom lip.

She grins and says, "That's Madison. I'm going to have to take it."

"I'll grab some food downstairs," I tell her, letting them have some privacy. There's no doubt what she's calling about. Everyone on her team has surely heard about the incident at the arena by now. Fuck, depending on social media, the whole world may know.

There's not much to eat in the refrigerator, but I manage to cobble together a few sandwiches and a bag of unopened chips tucked in the back of the pantry. I'm halfway to the bedroom when I stop at the sound of Ingrid's voice, sharp with frustration. Madison's on speaker.

"You know how this looks?" Madison's voice is cool, clipped, the tone of someone already spinning damage control. "He hit a member of the press."

"He shoved him." Ingrid fires back. I can hear the shake in her voice, anger and maybe a little fear. "While defending me from being attacked."

Ignoring the specifics, Madison says, "You never should have been in that position in the first place."

"I'm not living in a box anymore, Madison. I want to live my life."

"That includes living it in real time, all over the internet, with zero privacy?" There's a pause, then Madison adds, "Someone put this on blast online. Are you sure it wasn't him?"

My grip tightens on the plate, jaw clenching.

"You're kidding, right?" Ingrid's laugh is brittle.

"It just seems like there are a lot of leaks lately. A lot of publicity. Much of it is about him—and more and more of it is about who he is, his upcoming career. It's building hype."

"I'm not even entertaining this," Ingrid snaps. "It's ridiculous. We were with one another the whole time."

Fucking in the shower, I want to shout, letting Madison know exactly how close we were, but I swallow it back.

"What's ridiculous is not covering every angle." Madison pauses, then her voice softens with authority, "I think it would be best if we started toward New York today instead of tomorrow."

"You want me to leave early?" Ingrid asks, incredulous. "Miss my last night with Jefferson?"

"How long do you think it'll be before the fans and press show up outside his house?" Madison presses. "You and I both know it's not secure. This is your safety we're talking about."

"I'm not leaving." Ingrid's tone hardens. "I'm not changing my plans. I'm not letting the fans win."

There's a sigh on the other end of the line. "You're being foolish."

"I'm being human," Ingrid bites back.

"No, you're dickmatized, and it's going to destroy everything you've worked for." Her voice turns harsh. "I can figure out a way to spin this and make sure it stays in control. I'll have legal reach out to the guy he pushed, but I thought you'd learned your lesson about allowing men to control your life. Obviously, I was wrong."

The call ends with a sharp beep.

Taking a deep breath to steady myself, I push the door open with my shoulder, setting the food on the bed with more force than I mean to. Her eyes fly to mine, wide and guilty.

"You heard…"

"Yeah, I heard." I drag a hand through my hair, tugging at the ends like it'll bleed off some of the frustration coiled in my chest. "Does she really think I'd do that? Put you at risk for a little publicity?"

"She's just paranoid," Ingrid says softly. Her voice is tired, worn around the edges. "We've been through a lot over the years, the good and the bad, the highs and the lows, and I know she wants the best for me."

"And she doesn't think I'm the best thing for you." I don't phrase it as a question.

Ingrid's eyes flicker. "She's protective."

"You've got a lot of excuses for her."

She sighs, shoulders folding inward. "It's hard when someone comes into my life. I haven't always made the best decisions, especially when it comes to men, and to be fair, she's the one who has to pick up the pieces."

I sit down beside her, the mattress dipping under my weight. My thigh presses against hers, grounding her, grounding me. "I'm not going to drop you, Ingrid."

"I know." The hesitation in her voice is so small most people wouldn't catch it. But I do. I hate the sound of it. Then she adds, "She's right about security, though."

"Then call Marv," I say immediately. "Let him sit outside the bedroom door if it makes you feel better."

A weak smile tugs at her mouth. But it's not the kind that reaches her eyes. It's the kind that says she's already made up her mind.

"This isn't about you," she promises, her tone low, steady, like she's trying to make me believe it. "It's about the reality of who I am and the life I lead. I can't put you, or the rest of your house, at risk. I can't open your neighborhood up to the well-meaning but often misguided Flock."

She's right. I know she's right. But I fucking hate it.

"You promise this isn't about me?" I take her hand in mine, pressing a kiss to the back of it, lingering there. "Because I would never do anything to jeopardize your safety."

"I know."

For a moment, it's just us, her hand in mine, the smell of shower steam still clinging to her hair, the warmth of her thigh against me. But the bubble we built tonight is already thinning, stretching too tight. And deep down, I know it's about to burst.

"If you're leaving," I murmur, sliding the tray of food out of the way, "then I'm spending every minute until you walk out that door worshipping you."

Her lips part, and before she can answer, I'm on her, pressing her back into the pillows, kissing her like it's the last oxygen I'll ever get. She clings to me, nails dragging over my shoulders, pulling me closer, closer still, until there's no space left between us.

It isn't slow this time. It isn't careful. It's frantic–mouths colliding, hands tangling, teeth catching on lips like we're both trying to memorize the taste of each other before it's taken away. She gasps my name into the kiss, and I swallow it whole, my palms sliding down her sides, hers fisting in my shirt like she'll never let go.

And she feels it too. I know she does. The urgency. The fear that every second is already slipping through our fingers. Because even as I kiss my way down her body, tasting, savoring, memorizing, I already feel it: that ache of missing her before she's even gone.

23

———————

I ngrid

IT'S like the moment I left the bubble of Wittmore and Jefferson's arms, I jumped straight into the fire. No more slow paced college town with their greasy bars with cheap drinks and quiet campus. I travel straight to New York and into the final leg of the tour.

There's no hiding now, not from the interviews, the media blitz, the endless headlines about ticket sales and broken records. They keep calling it the biggest tour of all time, the kind of event people will talk about for years.

I do my part. Teasing the surprise guests, hinting at a few legendary collabs. Every day, another celebrity posts about how they managed to score tickets, how they "wouldn't miss it for the world." It's dizzying, and if I'm being honest, I'm back in my limelight. The place where I shine.

Madison did her magic, getting the photographer that Jefferson pushed to back down, quelling the press with other, juicy teasers about the show that manages to distract them.

And then there's Jefferson.

He's caught in his own whirlwind–the rush of graduation week. Apparently, there are long-standing Wittmore traditions. A final night where they pass the torch from one senior class to the next, where everyone is decked out in black and gold.

I see it all secondhand–on their feeds, in tagged stories. Skin shiny with sweat, beer bottles raised high, wide grins and loud chants. The smiles are big, but there's a wistful edge too, like they know it's the last time they'll ever all be together like this.

It feels like something I'd write in a song.

I marvel at how Nadia looks effortless, the perfect shade of red lipstick flawless even at two in the morning. Twyler is in the middle of everything, tiny and wide-eyed, Reese always at her side. Even Shelby, who's younger and not graduating, pops up in photos, squeezed between them like she belongs there too.

And the guys... I've learned a lot about the men Jefferson thinks of as brothers. Reese with his type-A intensity. They all look up to him. Axel, his tattoos and piercings less about rebellion and more about capturing every moment with joy. Reid has a quiet steadiness, his personality showing up in his clothes or music, just happy to be with his friends. And then there's Jefferson, the center of it all, whether he tries to be or not.

"They look cozy," Madison remarks, peering over my shoulder at one of the photos. We're in the back of the SUV on the way from the hotel to the arena. She taps her nail against the screen where Jefferson has his arm slung over the back of a couch, a brunette tucked into the group next to him. "Who's that?"

"That's Craig's girlfriend," I remind her. "Remember, we met her in the bathroom at the Frozen Four victory party?"

"Oh, right. He's, what do you call it, second string?"

"Second line."

I'm not jealous of the girls, but there's a sting knowing that they aren't followed around by paparazzi or trailed by security guards.

With me gone, they can go out and live a normal life. And I can't help but wonder if Jefferson feels freer without me there.

Still, I ask, "Why do you do that?"

"Do what?" she asks.

"Assume Jefferson's doing something wrong?"

We've both done our best to pretend things between us are back to normal, but when she stirs up shit like this, it's hard to play nice.

"I didn't say anything," she replies innocently.

"You didn't have to. It's obvious that you think that just because Jefferson is standing by another woman, something sketchy is going on."

There's a beat that stretches between us that is only filled with the sound of a bus rattling by.

"Fine," Madison says, turning to face me. "I can ask you the same thing. Why do you always assume that a notorious campus player has changed his entire personality for you?"

The city blurs past the tinted windows of the SUV, yellow cabs weaving through traffic and neon signs flickering in the reflection on the glass. I tuck my knees closer, feeling the gentle bump of the car over the uneven streets, the hum of the engine under my thighs.

"He's done nothing to make me not trust him."

She rolls her eyes and mutters, "That you know of."

It's a loaded comment and I'm tired of the bullshit. "Receipts, Mads, or it's time to shut up."

She hesitates, leaning back into the leather seat as the SUV makes another slow turn down a crowded avenue. "Fine, Ing, you want to know who you're really dating?"

"Enlighten me."

"He has a list of people he wants to sleep with. He's carried it around for years, and you were number one on that list."

I stare at her, waiting for the bomb to drop, because what she just said isn't it. "It's no surprise Jefferson had a crush on me. He's admitted he's a fan. People have celebrity crushes. It's not a big deal."

The look she gives me makes it clear she thinks I'm an idiot. "Yeah, well, that's why he left you that note on your locker. He was shooting his shot, aiming for another notch on his hockey stick." She smirks at the gross innuendo. "It was the one and only time you'd be in town and he made a play. Thank god you didn't fall for it, although he ended up getting another opportunity."

The hum of the tires on the asphalt and the distant wail of sirens fill the space between us. She has no idea I met him that night, that I'd been curious enough to find out more. We hadn't had sex, but there's no doubt in my mind he would have if I'd wanted to.

Was that all I was? A celebrity conquest?

No. *No.* I don't believe that. We didn't have sex for weeks, and it was on my terms.

"Who told you this?"

"The girls," she admits easily. "After you two were snuggled up at the Frozen Four after party. They knew how much he was into you and were excited to see him actually make a move–although, from what I gather, not exactly surprised. According to them he's always been a huge player..."

My gut churns, and I turn away from her.

"I'm sorry, Ing," she says. "I just thought you'd want to know who you're dating."

"I do know who I'm dating."

But the words don't land as strongly as I want them to.

The SUV eases into the parking garage, the noises of the city falling behind. I don't look at Madison. I can't, not now. What I can do–will do–is focus on the night ahead and give my Flock the best damn show I can.

"THANK YOU," I breathe, ignoring the sweat dripping down my back. The crowd is a sea of moving bodies, all abuzz over my lyrics. My voice feels like it's rubbed raw, my legs weak, knowing it's almost over. "There would be no tour if it weren't for you."

"We love you, Ingrid!" The chorus of support and adoration bounces back at me.

The concerts have gone off amazingly. Huge stars showed up on stage, sharing the spotlight with me, filling the arena with energy and awe. Every night has been a whirlwind, but tonight–tonight is the last. Any lingering thoughts of relationships, the future, men, their motives, fade behind the roar of the crowd. He's texted me every night, telling me he watched the shows online. I send back thank yous, brushing them off with "busy" or "tired," whatever excuse keeps me focused. I need time to think, and right now, there's no time for anything but this.

The stage behind me has fallen dark, other than twinkling lights that mimic stars. A stage hand walks over and hands me my guitar, and I loop the strap over my head and shoulder. "I know you love the hits, and I love them too, but it didn't feel right closing down this show without giving you a little gift of something new."

The first chords vibrate in my chest. It's a familiar feeling, one that I experience every time I let one of my songs fly for the first time. It starts with an acoustic beat, then the band moves in quietly behind me.

"You walk me down the empty streets
Actin' like this could repeat
But I've been the girl in someone's dream
And I know how this ends
You've got charm, you've got the game
Silver tongue and a well-known name
I let you close, but not too far
You don't get to say you had me

I pulled you into shadows, gave you one good kiss
Your hands said maybe, but baby–
I told you what this is...

You can call it magic, call it fun
But when the sun comes up, I'm already gone

We burned for a moment, sharp and quick
But don't mistake it for a promise
Don't pretend it ever was his
You got a taste, but boy—
That's all this is

You LOOK like you're used to 'yes'
   Used to hearts and little wrecks
   But I'm not here to be undone
   By a jersey and a jawline
   So I told you not to follow me
   Told you go win your stupid ring
   I've got stages, you've got stats
   And we both know what that means

YOU CAN KEEP THAT MOMENT, seal it with a grin
   But don't rewrite it, don't spin it–
   You know what this is

YOU CAN CALL IT MAGIC, call it fun
   But when the sun comes up, I'm already gone
   We burned for a moment, sharp and quick
   But don't mistake it for a promise
   Don't pretend it ever was his
   You got a taste, but boy–
   That's all this is

DON'T LOOK BACK like we missed fate
   Don't paint hearts into empty space
   That was a kiss, not a vow
   And I'm not yours, not now, not ever

. . .

YOU CAN CALL IT MAGIC, call it fun
  Say I'm the one that slipped through your lungs
  We danced like fire, but I don't burn for this
  Keep the spark, not the wish
  You had your shot, now it's missed
  You got a kiss, but babe–
  That's all this is

JUST A KISS IN THE DARK…
  That's all this is."

THE FINAL NOTE hangs in the arena like a secret shared with a thousand strangers, who give me, give the lyrics a chance to breathe before the applause takes over.

"Thank you for everything!" I shout, handing over the guitar and striding to the back of the stage with the band lifting me up with their music. There's so much adrenaline thrumming through my veins. For a moment, I let myself feel untouchable, unstoppable, the spotlight mine and mine alone.

"THAT SONG."

That's all I hear for the rest of the night. From my mother who is waiting just outside the curtain backstage. From the dancers and members of my team. It's all the buzz at the after-party, the question that follows me–was that about Jefferson? Did he break your heart? Where is he?

I did it to myself, but that's how I operate. I put my feelings into the world, one lyric at a time, and hope that it hits home, hope that it allows me to heal.

This song? Apparently, it hit people right in the feels.

The party is a mix of celebrities, industry pros, my team, and everyone who made this tour legendary. I'm still riding high, half-delirious that it's over. That there are no more dates on the calendar. No more shows to prepare for. With champagne in hand, I am moving through the crowd, pushing aside any thought of what comes next.

And then I see him.

"Shit," I say aloud. Too loud. Madison glances over.

"Oh crap. Babe, I'll handle this."

"No. I've got it."

Jake.

He's leaning against the bar, the same thin frame I remember lying next to in the dark while we wrote music and pretended to be in love. His brown eyes scan the room nervously, well aware that he's crashing my party. Also aware that I'm not going to make a scene and kick him out.

And the cycle continues.

The last time I saw him, Jefferson had been there, shutting him down with ease. Jefferson isn't here tonight, something he also probably knew before coming in here. Now, he's here, and the air between us tightens.

Our eyes meet and he starts my way. I guess we're doing this.

"Hey," he says, voice low, threading through the music and chatter. "Big night." I nod, playing along. This isn't about a night. It's about the cumulation of *years*. "That song was something else."

"Thank you."

"Since we didn't get to talk last time, I thought maybe we could now."

"Sure, Jake, let's talk," I say, tired of the games. "What first? About the times you treated me like I was too much or not enough? Or maybe the way you used me to make yourself feel important. Or how you took my lyrics, switched them up, and pretended like they were your own?"

"Ing," he starts.

"What do *you* want to talk about? That's what's important."

"Look, I know I didn't handle things right." He runs a hand through his messy hair, the gesture once charming, now almost pleading. "I was jealous and insecure. I was a jerk, okay? I shouldn't have let you go like that. I... I was wrong."

It's an apology that, two months ago, would have had me swooning, but now, I just laugh, short and sharp. "Wrong? You were wrong for every time you belittled me, for every moment you said my music was trash and had no longevity. Where you tried to convince me that real art, real music, requires pain and sacrifice. That it has to hurt to get it down on paper." I feel a wave of emotion bubble in my chest. "So you're admitting all of this and what do you want? A round of applause?"

"I'm not asking for applause. I just needed to tell you I'm sorry. I should've tried harder, and maybe, there's the opportunity for us to try again."

"Seriously?" I shake my head, letting the high from the tour armor me. "You had your chance. You made your choice. I didn't stay, and I didn't look back. This," I gesture to the glittering crowd around us, my people, my night, "this is my life. You don't get to decide now that you want to be a part of it. Not after I've healed and moved on."

His jaw tightens, bitterness cutting through his words. "Moved on? Into another man's bed, sure. But where is he tonight, Ingrid? Where is he on the biggest night of your life? Because I'm here, babe. I showed up."

That's when the nail drives in that Jake will never understand me. I take an easy breath. "I'm not defined by a man and his support. I'm definitely not defined by a wanna-be hipster who spends more time on his hair than on his music." I lean in close, my voice low and sharp enough to slit. "Jefferson isn't here because he doesn't need to make my achievements about himself. He trusts me to stand on my own two feet–something you never could–and now that I've outgrown you, you can't stand it."

His nostrils flare, but I don't give him the chance to answer. I step back, raising my voice just enough that the nearby circle of guests turns toward us. "So, Jake, thanks for the apology, but you don't get to claim me now. You had your chance, and you blew it." I flash him the kind of smile meant for cameras, not ex-lovers. "But stay awhile, enjoy the free champagne, consider it my parting gift."

Pushing my shoulders back, I turn on my heel and head back into the fray. I don't look back, not even when it kills me not to watch him die a little inside, because the only direction I'm moving now is forward.

24

———

J efferson

The last week went by in a whirlwind, and now that graduation is over, it already feels like things are different. No more classes. No more practices. No more countdowns on the schedule that kept me anchored for four straight years.

My parents flew back home this morning. It was good having them here, showing them my world for a couple of days without interruptions. I promised I'd visit before I head to Florida and start the season, but the truth is that I don't want to think about hockey right now.

I want to see Ingrid.

The next date I've got circled is the fundraiser for the Flockton Foundation in Miami next week. I'd hop on a plane tonight if I hadn't promised Coach we'd spend time with the new players he recruited for the fall.

Ingrid and I have only texted here and there–short messages, both of us busy. I miss her. Badly. And not just her body or the way she feels in my hands. I miss her laugh and smile. Her quick wit and intelligence. And it sucks that I haven't even seen the final show on the tour. I know it was a spectacle, but the last twenty-four hours have been packed: the ceremony took up most of the day, followed by dinner with my roommates and their families. This morning I went to breakfast with my parents and then drove them to the airport. By the time I got home, I had to help the guys start cleaning out the kitchen.

I've done my best to avoid spoilers, although it's nearly impossible. Everyone's said it was insane, a total blowout, but the biggest thing I keep hearing, whispered in every recap, is that she sang a new song.

That alone is enough to keep me off the internet until I can see it for myself.

"Please don't tell me you're going upstairs to eat pizza and have phone sex," Reid calls as I pass through the kitchen, three greasy slices balanced on a paper plate. Half the kitchen is packed up in cardboard boxes.

"So what if I am?" I shoot back. God, if only. It's been a week since I've gotten off. My hand just isn't cutting it anymore.

"Stop." Shelby slaps her hands over her ears. "I don't want to hear it."

"Relax. I'm just going to watch last night's concert." I wink. "Pants on."

"Stop winking at my girl." Reid picks up a throw pillow and tosses it at me. I dodge it easily and grin.

"Oh, watch it down here," Shelby says, straightening on the couch. "I want to see it too."

I hesitate, then shrug. She's right. It's better on the flat screen anyway.

We settle in—me in the armchair, Shelby tucked under Reid's arm on the couch. She knows every lyric, even the deep-cut tracks. She's singing under her breath the whole time, and it's weirdly comforting, hearing someone else love Ingrid's music as much as I do.

When the lights on the stage dim, I sit forward. "I think this is it," I murmur. "The new one."

Behind the stage, the backdrop transforms into a midnight sky glittering with stars. A stagehand crosses to her and hands her a guitar. She adjusts the strap, lays her hand across the strings. She looks so casual–like this is second nature–but I can see it. The nerves, tucked just beneath the stage smile.

Her voice comes through the speakers, soft and certain: *"I know you love the hits, and I love them too, but it didn't feel right closing down this show without giving you a little gift of something new."*

Then she begins.

"You walk me down the empty streets
Actin' like this could repeat
But I've been the girl in someone's dream
And I know how this ends
You've got charm, you've got the game
Silver tongue and a well-known name
I let you close, but not too far
You don't get to say you had me..."

I FREEZE, the slice of pizza forgotten in my hand.

Shelby's voice cuts through, low and knowing. "This is so good."

I don't look at her. My eyes are locked on Ingrid, framed in light, spilling truth into a microphone.

Because then she hits the chorus, clear and sharp, every syllable a blade.

"That's all this is..."

Fuck.

I listen to the whole thing, my heart pounding harder with every lyric. A surreal, out-of-body sensation settles low in my gut, heavy and cold. Now I know what her exes feel like, but that's not me. Right? I'm not an ex.

This song isn't about *us*. Not the late nights, the way she laughed against my chest, the way we kept choosing each other again and again.

No.

It's about the night we met. About one kiss and nothing more. A flicker. A moment. Disposable.

The way she sings it's like that's where we began and ended.

But that night. That kiss. It hooked me for good, and my mind scrambles back through the last couple of days. The short replies. The simple emojis. *Busy. Tired. Talk later.*

I wanted to believe it was just the tour, just the chaos of her schedule. My family being in town and graduation.

But now...

The song ends, her voice fading out as the crowd roars. Shelby's still humming under her breath when I push to my feet, the pizza untouched, my body on autopilot.

"Jefferson?" Shelby's voice chases after me as I grab my phone off the table and head for the front door. "Are you okay?"

I don't answer. The porch air hits my face, cooler than the heat brewing inside me.

I scroll to her name. Hit dial.

To my shock, she picks up on the first ring.

"That song," I say, my voice rougher than I expect. "Why does it feel like a fucking goodbye?"

There's a pause on the other end, a soft rush of background noise. Then Ingrid's voice, low and sharp. "Is it true?"

"Is what true?"

I'm already wracking my brain searching for the answer before she says, "The list, Jefferson. The one with my name at the top. Is it true?"

"How do you..." I inhale sharply, my mind going straight to the wrinkled piece of paper I carried around for so long. "Who told you that?"

"So I was a conquest?"

"No. Fuck no, Angel–"

"Don't call me that. Jesus." Her laugh is brittle, humorless.

"People say I have a silver tongue, but you got me with yours. Hook, line, and manipulative sinker."

"That's not how it is." My mind is spinning, trying to sort out what she's asking. Why is she asking?I haven't looked at that list in months. "Yes, there's a list–"

"Thank you. That's all I need to know."

The line goes dead before I can form another word.

I drop onto the porch step, my phone heavy in my hand, fury burning through me. At myself. At life. At the goddamn timing of everything.

The door creaks behind me, and Shelby's voice floats out. "Jefferson? You okay?"

I don't look at her, fists tensing. "No."

I knew better than to think she'd go back inside. Shelby is the little sister none of us asked for, but got anyway. "She's mad. Somehow she knew about the list I made."

"Oh no." Shelby curses under her breath, coming down the steps. Reid follows, crossing his arms. Great.

"Your sex list?" he asks.

"Yeah, apparently she found out about it, and now she thinks I think of her as a conquest."

Shelby hesitates, shifting back and forth on her feet. "It might've been us," she blurts.

I look up at her, that sweet little innocent face, and ask slowly. "What does that mean?"

"The girls and I," she confesses. "We brought it up during the Frozen Four after-party. We thought it was funny, harmless. I swear we didn't think it mattered–it was the first night you two met. We had no clue it would turn serious."

"You brought it up to Ingrid?" Reid asks, already shaking his head. "Babe."

"Not Ingrid," she promises, looking between us. "Madison."

"Fuck," I mutter, running my hands over my face. "Well, that explains that."

"Explains what?" Reid asks.

"Why Madison spent the last month telling Ingrid that she thinks dating me is a bad idea."

"She does?" Shelby asks. "Why the hell would she think that?"

"I overheard them talking before she left last weekend. Madison even accused me of being the one to post about our location at the arena. She thinks I'm looking for attention."

"That's bullshit." Shelby slams her hand down on the porch railing, the sharp crack making Reid and me both look at her. "It is. First of all, you don't need to look for attention. It comes for you."

"True," Reid adds, smirking. "I think it's the pretty boy looks."

"Shut up." I lean back with a groan. "I would never do something like that, but none of that changes the fact that there is a list, and she found out about it. There's no way out of this: I look like I used her."

"Okay, I have to ask," Reid says carefully. "Did you pursue her just to say you banged Ingrid Flockton?"

My jaw locks, ready to punch Reid for even asking, but it's a fair question considering my past. I don't want to talk about it. Not about Ingrid, about us. About how the time we spent together was the best damn thing in my life. But I push the words out anyway. "No. I don't expect you to believe me, but there's more to this than you know." I swallow. "That first night I was looking for a hook up–a way to cross her off my list."

"At the Frozen Four."

I shake my head. "No, when she was in town for the concert. The night before we left for Chicago, I taped the letter to my locker. She DMed me. We met up–"

"What?!" Shelby shouts, holding her hands up. "Say that again, you did what?"

"I left her a note on my locker with her name on it. I had no idea if she'd get it or if it'd still be there when I got back, or, more likely, in the trash. But somehow she did get it. I'd offered to show her around, and she messaged me about the best place to get a burger–"

"The Jefferson Parks Special," Shelby says under her breath. "You mean she'd had it before."

"Yep, the night before. We met up outside the Den. I had a bag of takeout, and I took her on a tour of campus."

"And you kept this from me?" Shelby asks, her expression going from incredulous, to angry, to shocked, then rolling back again. "I thought we were friends!"

Her outrage is kind of adorable. "She asked me to."

"And that's all?" Reid asks, skeptically. "You had dinner and a tour that didn't include you taking off your pants."

"We kissed."

"Like the song," Shelby confirms.

"Yeah," I admit, my chest tightening. "Like the song."

"And you didn't try to sleep with her?" Reid raises an eyebrow.

I huff a dark laugh. "You know how I am, I wouldn't have *not* slept with her."

"Like a dog with a boner."

Shelby smacks him on the arm. "Gross."

But I can't help laughing too, even if it's bitter. "He's not wrong. I've never forced anyone–*ever*–but I usually don't have to do much to charm a woman. With Ingrid..." I trail off, the memory hitting hard. "She kissed me, but there was this hesitation. This mistrust and obviously some baggage. I respected that. Then she walked away." My throat feels tight, but I push on. "When she showed up in Chicago, I was shocked. I honestly never thought I'd see her again. Then we actually got to know one another. And I didn't even mind waiting."

Reid studies me for a long moment, then lets out a low whistle. "That's how you know it's real. You didn't care about getting laid. You cared about her."

Shelby nods, softer now. "Exactly. Ingrid's not just another girl on your list. She never was. That's why you wrote her name down in the first place, because she was different. She wasn't a conquest. She was a manifestation."

Her words dig deep, twisting in my chest. Different. Always different. That's why she's in my head every damn minute, why no one else even registers anymore.

But now? Now I may have run out of chances.

Because how the hell do you get to a girl like Ingrid Flockton when she doesn't want to see you?

REESE DRIVES, one hand draped on the wheel, the other flipping the radio stations until he lands on some old country song he hums under his breath. I stare out the window, jaw tight, phone facedown in my lap.

We're rounding the corner by campus, the arena coming into view, when a guy steps out from the sidewalk.

Reese mutters, "Shit," under his breath, slowing the truck.

I haven't opened social media since Ingrid hung up on me. The silence between us is bad enough–I don't need to scroll through a feed full of speculation, fan edits, and headlines dissecting every breath we've ever taken together.

The guy, different from the one I knocked to the ground a few weeks before, beelines for my side of the car, eyes sharp, mouth already moving as I open the door. "Jefferson, what do you have to say about–"

"No comment," I snap before he can finish.

He keeps pace as we get out, grabbing our bags out of the back, relentless. "No comment to the fact that Ingrid was seen with Jake Merchant at the post-tour wrap party?"

My foot slips like it forgot what it's supposed to be doing. The words hit me sideways, sharp and hot, like someone just shoved a live wire under my skin. Jake. Merchant.

Well. That was fast.

Reese reacts before I can. He circles the front of the car, his body a solid wall between me and the reporter. "He said no comment," Reese growls, his voice low enough to mean business. "And get the fuck out of here before I call security."

The reporter falters, but doesn't stop scribbling in his notebook.

I follow Reese toward the doors, but all I can hear is the echo of that sentence. Ingrid was with Jake. The thought coils in my chest like something mean and hungry, and for the first time since she hung up, the silence between us feels less like punishment and more like the end.

Were the rumors about Ingrid and Jake right all along? Does she really run back to him every single time? Maybe this time I was the rebound?

"I'm assuming you didn't know that," he says, pushing the door open.

"No."

"That sucks, man." I wait for the lecture or some kind of spirited pep-talk from my captain, but he just shakes his head and enters the arena. The lack of commentary from him is unsettling. Does that mean he thinks I should give up? That I fucked up so badly there's no chance Ingrid will ever speak to me again.

"I've just never had this happen before."

"Had what happen?" he asks.

"A woman ignoring me." The internal conflict is unbearable. "Or publicly using me as a rebound." I can't quite comprehend it or the mix of emotions in my gut. "There's the feeling of being used and, fuck, is this what she feels like? Did we use each other?"

"I'm not sure any of that is happening."

"Maybe not, but I don't even know how long I should wait before I try again. Or should I just let it go and cut my losses?"

"Maybe just give her time to cool off. Sometimes women need space."

Well that isn't helpful. Time is running out, each second speeding by faster than the last.

Music filters out of the weight room before we even reach the doors. A heavy beat, the kind of stuff Axel likes to work out to, filters down the hall.

"You ready for this?" I ask, not sure myself.

"It'll be fine. We don't have a dog in this fight," he says as a way to keep perspective. "All we're doing is smoothing the transition."

The year after a big win can be tough, especially when you're graduating out a lot of upperclassmen from the starting roster. That's probably why Coach is taking the risk on three guys from a junior college team. But the details–that they were part of the Serendee cult? There's no other excuse than Bryant has a soft heart. Right? He gave us a heads-up on the recruits: Holt and the Ward Brothers. Defense, center, and a right winger. He said they're rough, not quite as refined as the team we had this year.

The doors swing open and the music hits first–heavy bass that rattles in my chest.

"Jesus, did Axel leave his playlist up?" I joke. Four years of having to rotate through everyone's music, I could guess one of the guy's rotations in my sleep.

Three guys look up as we step inside, the kind of pause where everyone measures everyone else before deciding what to do next.

The one at the rack straightens, hand on the bar. Blond, built like a wall, sweat darkening the cut collar of his sweatshirt. The graphic on the front says, "Clinton Community College." His eyes cut toward us, gray and sharp, and it feels like walking into a spotlight.

"Jeb Holt," he says, voice low.

The guy on the bench peels tape from his fingers. Dark hair is plastered damp to his forehead, the fabric from his threadbare t-shirt stuck to his back. There's a restless energy rolling off him, like he's had too much caffeine or not enough sleep. "Gideon Ward," he adds, tossing the roll of tape onto the floor. His tone is lighter, but his gaze lingers too long, curious in a way that isn't entirely comfortable.

The last one doesn't move from where he's posted up against the shoulder press, arms down by his side, hands balled into fists. Black hair curls at his temples. He's leaner than the others, but no less ripped. His eyes locked on the ground in front of him, jaw clenched tight as he flexes his thighs and pushes up.

Gideon jerks his thumb at him. "That's my brother Noah over there trying to beat a personal record."

Reese clears his throat, stepping in. "I'm Reese and this is Jefferson.

I nod. "Welcome to Wittmore. Looks like you've got a head start on us."

The gym is kind of the perfect place for an intro like this. For athletes this is our language and nothing breaks tension like moving weight. Everyone falls into their own pattern. Reese and I spot for one another, like we've done for the past four years. There's a little small talk, and everyone's civil enough, but underneath, there's something else.

It's in the way these guys move: like a unit. Something deeper than just being teammates, which would track with Noah and Gideon being brothers. Twins? It's hard to tell since they're not identical, but there's enough similarities to see they're related. Shoulder to shoulder, even when they're on opposite sides of the room. I've only seen that kind of bond in brothers, or in guys who've been through some real shit together.

Holt racks his bar and wipes sweat off his face, casual as hell, asks, "So, the Frozen Four. What was it like?"

There's no doubt what he means. Winning. What was it like to win?

"Incredible," Reese says, "especially after coming up short last year."

"Vindication makes it sweeter," Noah says.

"So much fucking better," I reply with a laugh.

Later, Gideon leans over a bar and asks, "You're the one dating the pop princess, right?"

I pause, grip tightening on the dumbbells. "You know her?"

He shrugs. "Didn't grow up with access to electronics. But we do now. Everyone knows Ingrid Flockton."

Automatically, I picture telling Ingrid later that even guys who grew up off the grid know her name. She'd laugh and roll her eyes at me. But the smile slips almost as fast. Because the truth hits me square in the chest: she hasn't returned a call, hasn't answered a text, not since she hung up on me.

Why the hell does it hurt that much?

Thank fuck, Reese takes mercy on me and switches the subject. "You dating anyone?"

Something passes through the room at that question. Subtle. Silent. Unspoken.

Jeb shakes his head. "Nah. We're focused on this. Women are a distraction."

"Ah," I laugh. "The puck bunnies are going to love you."

Reese snorts in agreement, but the guys look uninterested. That kind of restraint is something I've never had to contend with. Four years. Four years of fucking my way across campus. Every girl in the stands or at a party, or at the bar. I gave all that up for Ingrid and have no regrets, but the way they lived with the arranged marriages and shit like the people in Serendee? Hell. Fucking. No.

As we go through the reps, I can't stop wondering how much baggage they're carrying from those years. From the documentary Twyler made us all watch, I remember the rules: no dating. Marriages were arranged by the cult leader–*if* he decided to grant one in the first place and not keep the women for himself.

I glance at them again. Jeb's arms are over his head, loosely holding the pull up bar, watching while Gideon lays on his back, with his brother sliding heavier and heavier weights on the edge of the bar. They're all quiet, but not closed off. It's more like they're communicating silently, through their eyes and actions.

Later, we lace up and move to the ice. The chill hits my face the second we step onto the rink, but it's welcome. Cleaner. Sharper. Less claustrophobic than the weight room.

They already have sticks in hand, gliding along the boards, testing edges, snapping passes between themselves with an easy rhythm that makes me pause. They're coordinated, tight, like a single unit despite having just met us.

I skate over to Reese, my shoulder brushing against his. "You see that," I say, watching as they run through a passing drill. "There's history in how they move together."

Reese gives me a look. "Yeah, I can see that."

I can't stop watching them. The subtle way they shift, the way Cross shields Ward from a check, the way Holt anticipates both of them before they make a move. It's the kind of connection that comes from more than just hockey drills. Whatever happens next year, it's going to be interesting.

25

I ngrid

My phone won't stop buzzing.

I should mute it, throw it across the room, let the battery bleed out until it's just a dead weight. Instead, I keep it face down on the table, every vibration rattling through me like a reminder that I'm the coward here.

When I finally give in and look, it's the same thing over and over.

Can we talk?

I need you to hear me out.

I'm sorry. Please call me.

I don't care if you're pissed, Angel, I just need to hear your voice.

Each one should make me feel powerful. Breakups are supposed to be my fuel. Heartache to chorus, betrayal to bridge. But instead of fire, all I feel is water pressing down on me. A slow, suffocating weight.

"Ingrid." Madison snaps her fingers in front of my face, dragging me back to the real world. "You're not even listening."

"I am," I lie. My voice sounds flat, even to me.

She narrows her eyes, arms crossed like she's dealing with a stubborn teenager instead of her boss-slash-best-friend. "Okay, then repeat back what I just said."

I can't. The only words in my head are Jefferson's. *"Yes, there's a list–"*

Madison sighs and pushes her laptop toward me, screen glowing with a color-coded spreadsheet. "Okay, listen. You need focus. Distraction. Forward motion." She taps one column with her nails, each click sharp as a metronome. "Studio sessions–we've got producers in L.A. begging to book you the second you're back. I said we'd keep it flexible, but if you want, I can lock in dates."

She scrolls. "The film adaptation is heating up again–remember that director who passed the first time? He's circling back. Wants to meet. Says he's finally got the financing lined up."

My eyes skim the list, but the words don't stick.

"Merch collab," she keeps going, relentlessly. "The fashion house wants to design a capsule with your name on it. Think edgy, European, runway crossover vibes. And," her voice lifts, like this is the clincher, "a publisher reached out about a book deal. Not a coffee table photo spread, a real memoir. People want the story behind the songs, Ingrid. Your story. That's legacy stuff."

I force a nod, though it all lands like noise. A hundred opportunities I should care about, should grab with both hands. Instead, I feel like I'm watching her from underwater–Madison's mouth moving, her eyes sharp, her voice cutting through, but all of it muffled, distorted.

She notices. She always notices. "I'm handing you the world here, and you're giving me nothing."

"I just got off an eighteen-month successful tour, Madison. What else do you want me to give?" My voice comes out sharper than I intend, clipped and fraying at the edges. "Fuck. That came out harsh."

Madison blinks, then quietly shuts the laptop. The click feels final. "I'm sorry. You're right. You're exhausted. I'll tell everyone you'll get back to them when you're ready."

I sink back into the cushion and stare at my nails. "No," I murmur after a beat. "I'm sorry. This isn't about work."

Work is my thing. It's where I thrive, where I prove myself, but it's also where I hide. Madison knows that as well as I do.

"Still stressed about him?" she asks carefully.

The question lands like a stone in my chest. "I'm more wondering why I always pick the worst guys. Like... how can I walk into a room, scan a hundred men, and go, 'yeah, that's the one. Give me the most toxic option available.'"

Madison lets out a brittle laugh. "I guess you have a type."

We both know it's not funny.

"I thought he was different." My throat tightens as the words slip out, softer, almost to myself. He *was* different–at least he seemed that way. Maybe because he never looked at me like a prize he'd already won, but like a fight he wanted to keep showing up for. Because he listened. Because he made me laugh. He made me feel so good.

Madison shifts beside me. "I shouldn't have told you about the list."

I lift my eyes to her, sharp. "Don't blame yourself."

But even as I say it, something prickles at the back of my mind. Madison *had* made a choice to tell me and only after I'd fallen hard. If she'd told me that night in Chicago, I could have kept walking. Why did she wait until I gave my heart to him? My body?

I shove the thought down before it can grow teeth. I'm too raw to pick apart motives, too tired to chase shadows. I'm the one that made the decision to pursue him and I'm the one that has to take the blame.

∼

THE BOUTIQUE IS LOCATED in Wynwood, tucked in a small, unassuming storefront. I'd been told about Bridgette's designs by my makeup artist and when she showed me her work, I'd been mesmerized. In person it's the kind of place where everything is curated down to the background playlist. Racks of gowns in muted jewel tones line the walls, while Bridgette keeps flitting around me with pins clenched between her teeth.

Madison had argued that I should have the dresses brought to the house with the excuse that it's easier and safer, more "controlled." But that's one thing Jefferson taught me. I don't have to hide all the time. I can go out, and I can live. If people see me, they see me.

It's not like I'm braving the streets alone. Marv positions himself out front, standing at the front door, even though it's locked for a private fitting. The material clings against my skin as I step into a deep emerald slip dress, bias cut so it skims along my waist and pools at my feet. The seamstress tugs the straps just so, then retreats, muttering something about the hem. I tilt toward the mirror, fingers grazing the fabric, imagining the ball lights scattering over me. The next image is one of Jefferson's hands, steady and sure, at my hips. My chest tightens and I push the thought away.

My phone buzzes on the velvet chair. I suspect it's him and almost ignore it, but I step off the platform and check. It's Shelby.

I swipe to answer, pressing the phone to my ear as I balance on one heel while the seamstress adjusts the other. I skip the pleasantries. "If you're trying to get me to take him back, don't."

"I'm not," Shelby says quickly. "I just wanted to check on you and see how you're doing."

It's weird, normally a call like this would get my hackles up. What kind of gossip are they looking for? Who is this benefitting? But the friendships I've made with these college girls are different. Shelby is so easy and genuine, which is only confirmed when she adds, "I also wanted to say I'm sorry for any part I had in this. And for what it's worth–I had no idea you two would start dating for real. Or fall in love."

I let out a dry laugh. "Falling in love is a bit of a stretch."

"Okay, sure," she concedes. "Let's call it deep like. Either way, I hate that it's come to this."

I glance at my reflection, the green silk hugging me fluffy and soft, when all I feel underneath is raw. Against my better judgment, I ask, "How is he?"

There's a pause before she says it. "A complete mess."

The seamstress steps back to study her work, head cocked, pins glinting between her fingers. My gaze stays fixed on my own eyes in the mirror as I whisper, "Good.'"

Shelby exhales softly on the other end of the line. "Look, whatever's going on with Jefferson, I just want you to know I'm still here. For you. Even though it's new, I value our friendship, and I don't want you to doubt that."

There's a pause, before she adds, quieter, "But here's the thing. You're mad about finding out the truth about what Jefferson said before he met you. I get it. But I'm hurt too, Ingrid. The way we met—it wasn't honest either. You'd already met him when you walked into the Badger Den that first night. You recognized the names on the back of our jerseys. You'd already eaten a Jefferson Parks Special. And I was the idiot who thought I was introducing you to someone new."

Her words settle heavy in my chest, an ache layered on top of the one already there. She's not wrong. I hadn't lied, not exactly, but I hadn't told the truth either.

"Shelby..." I start, then stop, because what am I supposed to say? That my whole world has been smoke and mirrors for so long I didn't even realize I was doing it? "You're right. I apologize."

"I don't blame you," she continues quickly, like she doesn't want me to spiral. "I just don't want either of us to pretend things were perfect from the start. It wasn't. But I still want to be your friend. That hasn't changed."

My throat tightens. For all the chaos between us, that lands. "I'm grateful for you, too, Shelby. For Nadia and Twyler, who are really great."

"They are great, aren't they?"

I laugh. "How have things been for you?"

She brightens a little, launching into it. "Busy. We've had graduations, and I've been meeting everyone's families. Parents, siblings. It's been good. But also kind of sad. Everyone's scattering to teams in different states. Just when I finally started to feel like I knew everyone, it's all shifting again."

Her wistfulness hums through the line, and I recognize it instantly. It mirrors my own. I guess that's why I'm drawn to her, why I keep answering when she calls. She's lonely too. And she must sense it back in me.

We say our goodbyes, and promise to catch up properly soon. I set the phone down, and the boutique is too quiet again.

The dress clings to me in the mirror, green and luminous, the kind of gown people expect me to wear. It's beautiful. Soft. Romantic. And completely wrong.

"Maybe something a little more form-fitting," I tell the seamstress, forcing brightness into my tone. My fingers smooth over the silk, like I can press confidence into it. "Less damsel in distress?"

Her gaze sweeps over me slowly, precise, mapping every line of my body like a tailor and a sculptor rolled into one. A knowing smile curves her lips. "I've got just the thing."

26

―――――

J efferson

"Is that the last one?" I ask, looking over the hood of the truck at Reid.

"Yep."

We've just finished the third trip to the donation center, dropping off the boxes we'd tossed everything we no longer needed into over the last week.

"How the heck did we accumulate so much stuff?" I drop into the passenger seat of Reid's truck.

"I want to know how we ended up with three fake Christmas trees?" he asks, cranking the engine of the old truck. "Or the seventeen coolers, although that one makes a little more sense."

"The bigger question," I remind him, "is how the hell did we end up cleaning the whole damn house by ourselves?"

"Yeah, that was a hard lesson to learn. Never be the last person to move out of the house."

The past few days have been long and hard. Seeing our best friends pack up their belongings and head out toward the future. I've just been dragging my feet a little since my plans changed. I was supposed to go down to Florida for the Foundation event, but now I'm not sure what to do.

My phone sits in the cup holder, and when I pick it up, the screen is dark, like it's mocking me. Her silence has weight, pressing down on me until it's hard to breathe. I tell myself to give her space, like Reese suggested, to not be the guy who hovers and smothers. I scroll back through the thread like an idiot, rereading what I've already sent, as if maybe the words will land differently the fifth time around. They don't. The silence stays the same.

But the longer I sit here, the harder it is not to reach for the phone. Not to try again.

"What are you doing, man?" Reid asks, breaking my spiral.

"Fuck if I know." I exhale and prop my elbow on the window edge. "She's done with me."

The streets of Wittmore fly by, and it feels weird to know this won't be my home anymore.

"Do you remember when Shelby went back to Texas?"

"Yeah." I know about it vaguely. They'd been seeing each other secretly because Axel couldn't handle the idea of his little sister having sex–especially with his best friend. "To break up with that dumbass of a fiance in person, right?"

"Kind of." His eyes stay trained on the road. "She gave me the brush off before she left. Like, not a goodbye but more about how she had to handle her life before we could move on."

"I don't think that's what Ingrid is doing." I didn't even get a good-bye. It was a solid click in the ear. A hard hangup. A fuck you.

"Maybe, but with Shelby I didn't just sit back and let her deal with it on her own. I flew out there, showed up at the door and supported her. I let her know I had her back even though the idea of facing her parents was scary as hell."

"Reese said I should give her some space."

He barks out a laugh. "Reese is full of shit. Remember how hard he pursued Twyler? Dude was relentless."

"True." There was a whole scene when she went to a team event with another guy. And then how he wooed her back with tickets to see the New Kings. He even drove down to Tennessee to get her back. "He didn't mess around."

"Nope. Just do what feels right, man. I mean, don't be a psycho, but also? She owes you the right to explain yourself."

"Yeah, but how do I get to her? This isn't as easy as showing up at her parents' house and holding a boom box over my head." Marv would have me face down in the dirt before I got past the gate.

"You gotta get creative, dude." He turns into the neighborhood. "Figure out what's your boom box and make it happen."

LATER, I'm sitting at a booth alone, half-slouched against the cracked vinyl seat, working through a Jefferson Parks Special. The burger is greasy in all the right ways, familiar, like a ritual I've repeated a hundred times before games, after wins, after losses.

After winning the Frozen Four, Mike, the owner, added a framed photo of the team to the wall. It's an honor to be up there among the old Wittmore jerseys, scuffed helmets, sticks signed in fading Sharpie. Every inch of the place smells like beer and fryer oil, sweat and nostalgia.

I should feel comfortable. Home. But all I can think is: this might be the last time I eat here. The last time I hear the hum of the busted neon sign or feel the sticky table under my elbows.

I take another bite listening to Reid's words that keep bouncing around in my skull: *Find your version of the boom box.*

This is the part I can't wrap my head around. Ingrid's rich, famous, untouchable. She can buy whatever she wants, go wherever she wants, be with whoever she wants. What the hell can I give her that she can't already get with a snap of her fingers?

"Want another beer to go with that heartattack?"

I look up to find Josie, the waitress who's served me since I was a freshman with a peeling fake ID. She's holding a tray cocked on one hip, hair escaping the messy bun on top of her head.

"Nah, I'm good."

She doesn't move. Just stares at me like she's trying to read the fine print on my forehead. Finally, she asks, "Okay, what's wrong?"

I force a smirk. "Why do you think something's wrong?"

"Because in the four years I've served you, every single time you flirt with me and check out my tits."

"I checked them out," I argue automatically. And yeah, I did. Josie's got a great rack. She wears this tight little cut off shirt with a V that leaves every straight guy in the bar drooling. But I know what she's saying. I've had a crush on her since the day I walked in here. She's older. Sexy as fuck. And completely out of my reach. Truthfully, I'm glad it never worked out. She's a cool chick and a good friend.

She sets her tray on the next table and slides into the booth across from me. I blink. I've never seen her sit before–not once.

"There's also a full table of Phi Nu's over there," she says, tipping her chin toward the group of girls in tight tank tops and even tighter shorts. "And you've completely ignored them."

"I came here to eat. Not to hook up." I shoot her a look. "*Or* get harassed."

"Well, whatever's going on, Parks, you need to get it together."

"Oh yeah? Why's that?"

"Because I've put all my money on The Surge to take the cup next year," she says, smirking as she leans back in the booth. "And they're gonna need you to do it."

That earns a real laugh out of me, short and rough. "You have a lot of faith in me."

Josie just grins, unbothered, and slides out of the booth. "You're right, I do. You're consistent, Jefferson. Determined. You came in here week after week and gave me your best shot, even when the odds were trash."

"Yeah, well, I took all those shots and never scored. Some people would call those the actions of a lunatic. What's the point?"

"Because someone had to be the one to tell you no." She shakes her head, amused. "I watched you charm your way into the pants of half this campus. Every girl walked away thinking she'd won the lottery."

"To be fair, everybody did leave happy." I wink.

"You're ridiculous."

"So I've heard," I mutter.

Her smile softens, just a fraction and she adds, "Jefferson, don't be afraid to use that mix of determination and charm to get what you want outside of hockey and getting off."

I watch her weave back through the tables, and for a second the noise of the bar hits me all at once–the clatter of pitchers on wood, the chant of some frat boys arguing over the game on TV, the low hum of everyone else just living. I've been part of this background noise for four years.

It's time for me to make something on my own.

I'm halfway back to the Manor when my phone buzzes in my pocket.

For a split second, every time the phone rings, my heart leaps straight into my throat.

The screen lights up with an unfamiliar number. I swipe to answer anyway. "Hello?"

"Jefferson Parks?" A clipped, professional woman's voice comes through, crisp like someone who has no patience for wasted time. "This is Lila Harris, player-manager for the Surge. I'm calling to go over logistics for your arrival in September."

"Ms. Harris." My back straightens like she can see my posture through the line. My pulse is hammering so hard it's almost stupid. "Yeah, that sounds great."

"Good. Let's start with your housing placement. As you know, the team often pairs rookies with an established veteran during their first season. You're being placed with Grant Pierce."

I sit forward so fast my knee knocks into the coffee table. "Seriously?"

"Yes. Grant is one of our most reliable players."

Reliable. That's one word for the guy. The man's a machine–top scorer for the Surge, absolute beast on the ice. He's the reason the team made it to the finals last year. I'd watched him through high school and college, tried to mimic his power play drills, studied how he found open ice like it was instinct. The idea of not only sharing a rink with him but also living with him? Unreal.

"That's–" I can't help the grin that spreads across my face. "That's awesome."

"I thought you'd approve." She doesn't sound amused, just efficient, as if she checked a box confirming my enthusiasm. She moves on, rattling off details like she's reading from a prepared script. My flight information. What time I'm expected at the training facility. The schedule for my physical, and training appointments. She's covering so much I feel like I should be taking notes, but all I've got is the phone in my hand to try to keep myself grounded.

Because this is real. It's happening.

Then she launches into PR obligations.

"It's important for the team to maintain a good reputation within the community," she says. "So you'll be expected to attend certain events, like school or hospital visits, charity fundraisers, meet-and-greets. We have longstanding partnerships with several organizations throughout Florida."

I shift the phone from one ear to the other. "Sure, that makes sense. Wittmore has us do the same thing."

She doesn't pause. Just keeps rolling, her voice even and clipped: media training sessions, paperwork for W-2s, direct deposit, housing arrangements. Somewhere between the HR talk and a mention of pre-season press photos, my brain starts to fog. It's not that I don't care–it's just a lot, and the steady stream of business talk feels a little like being back in class with Professor Hawkins droning on about financial systems.

Then something sparks.

An idea. An opportunity.

"Lila," I interrupt before I can stop myself. "What if there's an event I'd like to attend before the season starts?"

"An event you *want* to go to?" she repeats with a hint of incredulousness. "*Before* the season starts?"

"Yes, ma'am."

It's obvious no one has ever asked her this before, but no one has been me. No one has had, what did Josie call it? 'Determination and charm.'

No one else has had everything on the line.

27

I ngrid

BY THE TIME the sun starts sliding down over the green waves of the Atlantic, the house is already buzzing like a hive. The Foundation Ball is tonight, and my mother has been in full command mode since dawn–shouting directions, rearranging florals, stopping just short of making some poor event planner cry in the driveway.

"You know how she is," I say to Madison as I climb into the vanity chair. The stylist behind me separates a section of hair, winding it into a curling iron. "This is where she thrives."

Madison snorts, perched on the velvet chaise across from mine, with her ever present laptop in front of her. "I wonder where you get it."

I don't bother answering. The truth is, she's right. My mother loves this part–the planning and execution of a big event, setting the stage for a night to remember. I think it goes back to those real estate days, where designing and prepping a home were part of the job. And me? I've been trained for it since I was old enough to hold a microphone.

The room smells like hairspray and perfume. Two makeup artists hover with brushes and palettes, waiting their turn. My gown hangs on the back of the door, glittering under the recessed lights. The whole thing feels less like getting ready for a fundraiser and more like prepping for the Grammys. Except this time, it's not about who wins, it's about generosity.

I close my eyes as the heat from the iron brushes my neck. I'm almost relaxed when Madison clears her throat.

"So," she says casually, too casually. "He's in town."

My eyes snap open. In the mirror, I catch her watching me. "Who?"

"Jake."

"Why would I care if Jake's in town?" It's a genuine question. The excitement that I used to feel in my chest just at the mention of his name is no longer there.

She shrugs, an escaped tendril of hair grazing her shoulder. "He could be your date."

The stylist makes a soft, awkward sound and focuses harder on the curl. My stomach knots.

"Why would I want Jake to be my date?" My voice comes out sharp enough to sting.

Madison doesn't look away. "It's an option. A safe one. People already know him, they like the story. It'd be good PR."

PR. The word tastes like poison on my tongue. I stare at my reflection, my lashes half-done, hair half-curled, and suspicion starts prickling in the back of my skull. Why was he at the after-party in New York? He hadn't been invited, not by me. And the Atlanta concert–he'd gotten backstage without a badge. Sure, Marv asked if he could come back, but even to get to the private area, somebody had to grease that door.

Somebody like Madison.

"Why do you even know he's in town? Are you keeping up with him?"

"I keep up with everything," she snaps. "And *everyone*. Including all of your exes. It's my job."

There's a territorialness in her tone, one that makes me uncomfortable. My pulse ticks faster as the pieces start falling into place, ugly and undeniable. The photos that always seemed to leak. The gossip columns with just enough detail to sting. The times Jake magically appeared where he shouldn't have been.

"Your job is to be my assistant, Madison. It's not to push narratives in the press about my dating life," I say slowly, testing the shape of the accusation. "Especially with men I've deemed aren't healthy for me."

Or, I wonder, men who *are* healthy for me and seem like a threat.

Madison's expression doesn't shift, but she closes her laptop with a snap that makes the stylists flinch. "All of this is bigger than love and broken hearts. It's business, all of it, even if you can't see it."

"Maybe you've forgotten, Madison, but I'm not just your brand. I'm a person."

Madison doesn't flinch. She tilts her head, lips pressed into a thin line. "Am *I* the one who forgot that, or are *you*? Because it's hard to tell where one stops and the other begins. You spent years playing games with Jake—writing your little lyrics and teasing audiences, playing hide and seek with the paparazzi. And now you want me to believe you suddenly don't want to bring him back in? Like I haven't had to clean up after every other breakup you've had and spin it into something new?"

The words land sharp, and I feel them in my chest before I can even form a response. "Or do you mean every breakup you've orchestrated?" My voice shakes, but doesn't break. "Because that's what happened with Jefferson, isn't it? You decided it was time for us to end. For me to go back to Jake. Why? Because what I had with Jefferson was real? Because for once I was happy and could see a way out of the toxic cycle I was caught in?"

"You deserved to know the truth," she says flatly, like she's explaining a business strategy.

"On your timeline," I snap back. "For maximum effect."

The room seems to shrink around us. Stylists pretend to busy themselves, curling irons paused midair, eyes cast anywhere but at us. Madison and I just stare at one another, a different kind of heartache cracking me open from the inside.

It's not the breakup with Jefferson that ruins me–it's realizing Madison chose it for me.

THE HOUSE HUMS WITH LIFE. Laughter, glasses clinking, the low swell of a string quartet warming up out back. The Foundation Ball is always the one night a year when we open our doors, when our home becomes something other than a private place for family. The lavish gardens are dressed with lanterns, velvet ropes keeping the curious at bay, while moonlight reflects off the water. It's flawless. Of course it is. My mother wouldn't allow anything less.

Everything sparkles under the lights, from the polished marble floors to the towering floral arrangements she's fussed over for weeks. It's the kind of perfection that takes armies of assistants and endless hours of planning. When I stop at the bottom of the stairs, catching my reflection in the gilded mirror, I almost don't recognize the girl staring back at me.

I, too, look perfect. The hair is perfect. The gown is perfect. The smile–the signature red lipstick, plastered on, practiced–perfect too. But inside, I feel hollowed out. My chest aches with the effort of holding it all together, and the only thing I want in this moment is to crawl back into my bed upstairs, bury myself beneath the covers, and pretend none of it exists.

I want to call Jefferson. I want to hear his voice steady me. But I can't. Not after everything. Not when Madison's fingerprints are still smeared all over the wreckage of what we were.

I want answers too–about how much of the last few years was real, how much was orchestrated, manipulated, staged for cameras and headlines. About whether I've been living my life, or simply living the story Madison chose for me.

But none of those wants matter tonight.

Tonight isn't about me. It's about the Foundation, about the girls and families we support, about the charities that will benefit from every dollar pledged and every photo splashed across glossy magazines tomorrow morning. It's about my mother, who has poured herself into this cause with relentless energy.

So I inhale, let the air fill my lungs, and fix that smile in place until it feels like part of me. The show must go on.

"That dress," I hear over and over, from every guest I stop to smile at. "Absolutely gorgeous. Who is the designer?"

I supply them with the answer, gushing over Bridgette. She'll be on every blog by midnight. The hallways are filled with actors wearing expensive watches and surgically smoothed faces. Athletes in custom fit tuxedos that accentuate the bulk of their shoulders. Socialites dripping in borrowed diamonds, laughing too loudly, their perfume clouding the air. Everyone has the same statement when they see me: *that dress.*

And it is something to talk about. Not like me, not what I've worn in the past–the soft silks, the frothy skirts that made me look delicate, approachable, a doll to be posed for photographs. This one is slinky, liquid silver that clings like it was poured onto me. The fabric catches the light and throws it back like sparks. It looks like metal. Like armor.

Armor I didn't even realize how desperately I'd need tonight, until I was standing here, holding myself together under a hundred hungry gazes. While I'd been vacillating between heartbreak and anger, word was spreading about my love life. And now I know why.

The smile starts to ache, so I duck away, sliding past a velvet rope into one of the side gardens. It's roped off to the guests, but the party noise still trickles in, muffled by hedges and fountains. I draw in a deep breath of warm Miami air, willing my lungs to unclench.

That's when the faint curl of cigarette smoke drifts toward me.

My father.

He's leaning against the stone balustrade, one hand in his pocket, the other loosely cradling his cigarette. The glow at the end flares as he takes a drag, his eyes finding me in the shadows. He smiles the way only he can—wry, knowing, amused that he caught me slipping away.

"Hey, Daddy."

"Hiding out?" he asks, smoke curling from his mouth in a slow exhale. His voice is softer than the world inside the ballroom, stripped of all the pretense. If my mother knew that he was hiding, *and* smoking, she'd throw a fit.

"Just needed a minute," I admit.

He nods in quiet understanding. My father's always been more comfortable in the wings than in the spotlight. He studies me now, his gaze moving past the dress, past the diamonds, past the perfect hair. Past the armor I've strapped on just to get through the night.

And I can tell—he sees me. The real me.

"What happened?" he asks.

"That obvious, huh?"

"Probably not to all those people in there, but to me? Yeah." He frowns. "You're hurting. Talk to me."

"I don't even know where to begin." Madison? Jefferson? Jake? The last five years? It's all a blur of manipulation and half-truths, leaving me gaslit, twisted up, and completely out of control.

"Start wherever you want." He pulls another cigarette from his pack, balancing it between his fingers. "But I'll warn you—we've got maybe half a cigarette before your mother sends out a search party."

I laugh, a quick, startled sound. He's always had a way of breaking tension without even trying. So I tell him. A condensed version, quick and messy, spilling out before I can stop myself. He listens without interrupting, just takes a long drag when I finish.

"Out of all that," he says finally, smoke curling into the night, "what makes you the most upset?"

"Losing Jefferson." The words slip out before I can filter myself.

"Then focus on that."

"I'm not sure if it's that easy."

"Nothing worth fighting for is easy, Ingrid. You know that better than anyone."

He's right, of course. I've fought to be seen and to be taken seriously in this industry for years. I've fought to be represented, to have ownership. But this is different, isn't it?

"I'm the one that didn't allow him to explain himself." I swallow, throat tight. "I've been ignoring him all week. Full-on ghosting. Except now, he hasn't called in twenty-four hours, so... he probably took the hint. I may have completely screwed this up."

My father looks at me, steady and certain in a way I'm not. "That's the thing about love, Ing. If it's real, it'll keep finding you. You just have to be ready to receive it."

"I don't know if that's true."

"With the actors and musicians, maybe not, but a man who chases pucks for a living? Who wants to win more than anything else? I wouldn't give up on him yet."

He stubs out the cigarette and hides it under a planter to come back for later, then crooks his arm for me to link with his. I slip mine through, grateful for the quiet solidarity. Maybe I've lost my grip on love, maybe I don't know who to believe anymore–but at least tonight, I know I'm not alone.

28

Jefferson

I'VE BEEN in big arenas, staring down an opponent twice my size, sweating so hard it stung my eyes, but walking up the marble steps to Ingrid Flockton's mansion in Miami is a whole different kind of pressure.

The Flock Foundation Ball. The place is glowing like it's alive with floodlights cutting across the manicured lawns, cameras flashing from behind the velvet ropes, valets in white gloves opening doors for athletes, actors, models, the kind of people I used to see on TV. I can feel the eyes on me before I even tell the woman at the door my name.

"Good evening," she says, drinking me in. At least I look the part.

"Jefferson Parks, Surge Hockey," *My name is on the list*, I want to add, but hold back, just giving her a small grin. I still can't believe Lila pulled it off, greasing wheels and sliding my name onto the guest list like it belonged there.

Clean suit. Pressed shirt. Tie I redid three times before I got in the Uber. I'm not unfamiliar with dressing up. I've escorted women to all kinds of team and sorority events. I'm a good-looking guy, that's a fact, and maybe I should feel out of place, but I don't. This is where a career in hockey will take me, and I'm ready for it. I'm okay with the spotlight. The only problem is that, for this specific event, I'm not sure I'm welcome.

I'm waved through with a quick grin, and inside the air-conditioning hits me with a rush of chilled air, carrying perfume, champagne, and money. Everything is polished to perfection–the chandeliers, the white and gold floral arrangements, the endless champagne flutes balanced on silver trays. My heart hammers against my ribs, because I know she's here.

And then I see her.

Ingrid Flockton, center of the universe.

The metallic gown clings to her like it was poured over her body, molten steel that shifts under the lights with every move she makes. Her hair is pulled back sleek, exposing the line of her neck. It's dyed a shade darker than the last time I saw her. More violet than lavender. Just seeing her is electric. Like sticking a fork in a socket. Every nerve in me sparks alive, screaming that this–*her*–is what I've been starving for. She's who had me spun out.

And now that I'm here, there's no doubt in my mind: This is it. This is the chance. My boom box moment.

"Good evening, Mr. Parks."

Fuck.

Marv appears from nowhere, solid as a wall, doing his best to be an obstacle between me and Ingrid.

"Hey, Marv. Long time."

Ingrid's security guard is good. Way too good.

"You know you can't be here." His tone isn't angry, just flat, like I'm already one wrong move away from being tossed out on my ass.

I wince. "I have a ticket. I swear. Ask the lady at the front."

"Just because you have a ticket doesn't mean you're welcome."

True. Dead true. My mouth goes dry. "Look, man, I just–I want to talk to her. Just for a minute. I'm not here to cause problems."

"No can do." Marv clamps a hand around my elbow. Not rough, but firm enough that the message is clear: walk, or I'll make you. My pulse kicks up.

"Marv, wait."

We both turn at the voice and my savior isn't who I expect. Madison sweeps up in a floor length beaded blue gown, hair piled on her head like a beauty queen. Her eyes narrowing the moment they land on me.

"I have no idea how you pulled this off," she mutters under her breath.

"I swear. I'm not here to—"

"Save it." She cuts me off, crossing her arms. For a second, I brace for her to tell Marv to haul me out by the collar. Instead, she sighs, heavy and frustrated. "Let him go."

Marv raises a brow. "You sure?"

"I'll take responsibility."

I stare at her, blindsided. "You will?"

Marv's expression asks the same question, but he releases me and says, "Okay. Call me if there's trouble."

He takes a step back, but I feel his eyes still on me. I turn to Madison. "Why are you doing this?"

Her jaw tightens. "Because I already fucked up once, and my friendship with Ingrid means more to me than anything else. If I can give her the chance to get closure, I'm going to take it." Her eyes bore into mine. "Just don't hurt her. She can't go through any more heartbreak."

I nod. "I don't plan on it."

She studies me one last time before jerking her head toward the French doors. "Out there. Patio. Five minutes. That's all you get."

The doors open, and cool night air rushes over me, salt curling in with the sound of the ocean. The waves crash steady against the beach, a rhythm that seems to sync with my pulse. I pace once, twice, trying to catch my breath, when the door clicks again.

And Ingrid steps out.

I let my gaze sweep over her curves, I can't stop it. The dress, the armor. "Prepared for battle, Angel?"

Her lips curve, but it's not really a smile. "It appears so."

"Well, you look beautiful." My fingers twitch with the urge to brush the hair off her shoulder.

"How did you get in here?" she asks, looking over my shoulder. I have no doubt Marv is nearby.

"Legally," I confirm. "Turns out there are perks to being a professional hockey player other than fame and glory."

She exhales, eyes flicking back toward the ballroom like she's already planning her exit. I can feel her pulling away, and panic flares hot in my chest.

"Ingrid, wait. I need to explain."

Her arms cross, defensive, diamonds flashing at her ears. "How do you explain that list as anything other than proof that I was just another name to screw your way through?"

Fuck. This isn't going how I wanted, but I'm not ready to give up. I reach into my pocket and pull out the folded piece of notebook paper. The thing is battered, edges worn soft. I hold it up like evidence. "This. Yeah, it's real. It's stupid and shallow and exactly what you think it is. Freshman-year me thought it was clever to write down every girl I thought was hot, every girl I wanted to hook up with before graduation. Models, sorority girls, puck bunnies. You name it."

"Classy," she mutters, eyes sharp.

"I know." My voice cracks. "But what you don't know is this–your name? It's at the top. And it's the only one not crossed out."

Her brows pull together, suspicion warring with confusion. "If you're trying to impress me with something, I'm missing the point."

I step closer, lowering my voice. "The day I met you, you stopped being a name. You became real. Too real. And I couldn't reduce you to a checkbox. Couldn't risk losing what I felt for the sake of bragging rights."

The silence that follows is heavier than the waves crashing

against the shore. She looks at me, searching, like she wants to find a crack in the story.

"I left it on my desk that day, shoved between the pages of a history assignment," I say, holding the page out. "And I never looked at it again. Because the list didn't matter anymore. You did."

Her throat works as she swallows, gaze darting from the paper to my face. "You expect me to believe that?"

"No. I expect you to believe me." The words come out harsher than I want, but fuck it. I'm going all in, because that's what I want from her–all of it. I step forward and take her face in my hands. "I expect you to believe what you've seen when I look at you. When I'm with you. When I'm *in* you." Her eyes widen. "I'm not perfect, Angel, but I swear to God, you were never just a name on a piece of paper."

Her lips press together, trembling at the edges. For the first time tonight, she doesn't look like steel. She looks like Ingrid–the woman who took a chance on me for no real goddamn reason other than curiosity.

And I realize I'm waiting for her to decide if she's going to walk away or let me back in.

"I want to believe you," she whispers finally, her voice raw. "But you don't know what it's like to always wonder if you're just another conquest. Another headline for Madison to spin." Her throat works as she swallows. "I've spent years being told my value is in what I can do for others, not in being loved. And then you–" she breaks off, shaking her head. "You were supposed to be different."

I step closer, slow, like approaching a wild animal I don't want to spook. "I *am* different."

Her eyes flash, pained. "But then I found out about that list. And Madison..." Her jaw trembles, but she clenches it shut before tears can fall. "Madison knew. She let me think, she let me *fall* for you, while keeping that in her back pocket, waiting for the moment it would hurt the most. And it worked. Because it hit the one fear I can't shake."

"Which is?" I press gently.

Her gaze lifts to mine, shimmering but fierce. "That no matter how strong I pretend to be, I'll always just be someone's prize. Someone's win on the way to building themselves into something more."

The words gut me. I want to crush the list in my fist, burn it, bury it, anything to erase the proof of who I was before her. But instead I hold her gaze steady.

"I've got trophies, Angel. They're shiny and the victory feels amazing, but it's fleeting. Once it's over, there's another game, another match, another championship on the horizon. You're not a conquest or a prize. You're the person that I want to come home to every single day. You're the woman that makes life less about me and more about what I can be for you."

Her breath catches, shoulders rigid, and for a moment I think she's going to bolt back inside. But she doesn't. She just stands there, letting me see the cracks in her armor.

It's time I showed her the cracks in mine.

My chest is tight. "You think you're the only one who's scared here?" My voice is low, rough. "I've never cared about anyone like this. Not the girls before you, not my teammates, not even the game. I spent my whole life thinking that monogamy wasn't something I wanted, and then you show up and turn that upside down. And that scares the shit out of me." I shake my head, swallowing hard. "The thought of losing you fucked me up."

Her eyes flicker, softening, but she doesn't speak. She just studies me, like she's trying to decide if she can trust what she sees. I lower my hand to her hip, anchoring her to me. "I don't want to play games with you, Ingrid. I don't want to chase headlines or elevate my image. I just want *you*. All of you." I let out a breath, finally saying what I should've said weeks ago. "I love you."

Her lips part, her breath uneven, and in the silence that follows, I feel like I've laid my entire soul bare at her feet.

It's absolutely fucking terrifying.

For a second, the only sounds are the strains of the party from inside and the ocean crashing against the shore, steady and relentless. That and the thundering of my own pulse. I've said the words, put myself all the way out there, and it feels like standing on the edge of a cliff waiting to see if she'll jump with me.

Her lips tremble. She blinks fast, like she's fighting tears. "I love you, too."

The words slam into me, knock the air straight out of my chest. I didn't realize how much I needed to hear them until now. I never even knew I needed them. Not until Ingrid walked into my life and walked right back out.

She exhales shakily, eyes shining. "That's why it hurt so much. That's why I was so angry. Because the thought of being nothing more than a name on your list–just another story–it would've destroyed me. You could destroy me."

My fingers curl around her waist. "I'd rather destroy myself first."

She licks her bottom lip, plump and red, and I bend, capturing her mouth with mine. The kiss isn't gentle. I'm taking back all those unanswered calls and sleepless nights, of wanting her so badly it bordered on madness. She gasps against me, and I take advantage, sliding my tongue against hers. Jesus, she tastes so good.

Her hands fist in my lapels, yanking me closer, pressing that molten-steel dress against me. The fabric is cool, her body is hot, and I can feel every curve, every shiver as she arches into me. I let her feel me back.

"Jefferson," she whispers against my lips.

"I missed fucking you so much."

"Yeah, well, I missed you fucking me too." She eyes me, a look that goes straight to my balls. "You wear the hell out of a suit."

I groan, dragging my mouth down the line of her jaw, tasting the salt of her skin. My hands skim her hips, the gown slipping under my palms like liquid metal, and I swear I'd set fire to the entire ballroom, donate my first year's salary, if it meant keeping her right here, just like this.

Her nails scrape the back of my neck, and I nip at her lower lip, pulling back just enough to look at her. Her pupils are blown wide, lips swollen, chest rising and falling like she's run a marathon. "How long until I can get you naked?"

A throat clears, deep and gravelly. Ingrid reacts before I do.

"Daddy," she says quickly, voice higher than usual.

Her father's gaze drops to where my hand still rests on her hip. I make no move to remove it–Ingrid isn't something to hide, and neither am I.

"You must be the hockey player," he says, taking us both in.

"I am." I extend my hand, firm shake, eyes steady. "Jefferson Parks."

Before he can say more, Madison pops her head out of the glass doors. She approaches the three of us. "Sorry for interrupting, but it's time for your speech."

She squeezes my arm, gives me one last searching look, then slips back into the house, the noise of the party swallowing her whole.

That leaves me standing face to face with the man whose opinion suddenly matters more than I'd like to admit. I run a hand through my hair. "This isn't how I expected to meet you but–"

He cuts me off. "My daughter deserves a man who can meet her on every level. Perseverance–that's key. You showed up. That's what's important to her and to me." He slides a hand in his pocket. "Being with Ingrid means you get all of her. The ups and downs. The manic writing highs, and the spiral when the bad reviews come in. Are you up to that?"

His words land heavy, not like a threat, but like a line being drawn in the sand. "I know a little bit about wins and losses, sir, but I know that no matter what happens, I want her by my side."

Then he grins, claps me on the back with surprising force and starts inside. I follow, taking a deep breath, ready for everything that comes next. Hockey, fame, prestige. None of it meant anything, until I got Ingrid back. And now that I did, I'm never letting her go.

29

———————

I ngrid

It's after midnight when the party finally winds down. As the guests trickle out the door, the musicians pack away their instruments and the bartender shuts down the bar. It'll be another day or two before the house gets back to normal but for now I marvel at the handsome man next to me. Jefferson has stayed by my side all night, never once straying, his presence solid and steady.

He held firm through the small talk, shaking hands with family, old friends, and faces so famous they're practically carved into the Hollywood skyline. He acclimates easily, no different, I assume, than at a frat party. Less beer from a keg and more champagne. But what surprised me most was how they looked at him, not as my arm candy or some temporary distraction, but as Jefferson Parks. He's more well-known than I realized, his reputation as an all-star hockey player preceding him. They asked him about winning the Frozen Four. They asked what it's like to play with Reese Cain. They asked him about the chances for the Surge next season.

He answered every single question with that easy grin that melts me from the inside out. At one point, his fingers threaded through mine, anchoring me, and he said, "I'm just excited about life right now."

Swoon. Literal swoon.

Slowly, the final guests drift out, the house strangely still. My mother slumps against the banister, exhaustion written all over her, though she's still smiling, still glowing.

"Thank you. You're amazing," I tell her. "I heard it was a record year for fundraising."

"I love doing this," she sighs, kicking off her heels with a relieved sigh, "but now I need a vacation."

"That's why the plane leaves in two days," my father reminds her, tucking her arm in his. "Then we'll be in our own private cabana overlooking crystal clear water. A reward for a job well done."

"Good night, sweetheart," my mother calls. "And nice to meet you, Jefferson."

"Thank you for an amazing evening," Jefferson replies with that charming grin, and I know my mother is won over.

We watch them climb the stairs before I turn my attention back to the man next to me. Jefferson lost his jacket two hours ago. His tie sometime after that. The top of his shirt is unbuttoned giving a small peek at his broad chest underneath. "I like them," he says quietly. "They suit one another."

"Some days, yes," I admit, fighting back a yawn. "But they're also really different. I think that's why it works. They meet each other's needs."

"Right now, I'm ready to meet your needs." He tilts his head and sucks a hot kiss on my neck.

"Yeah? What is it that you think I need?" I ask, preparing myself for a filthy response.

"My tongue in your pussy, followed by my cock." He doesn't

disappoint. "You need me stretching that tight little cunt of yours until you can't take it anymore."

My breath hitches. "I've missed you and your dirty mouth."

"And my magnificent cock?" he teases.

"It's magnificent, huh?"

"I'll just have to prove it."

God, he's so sexy, so much fun. I'm not kidding about missing him, it's only having him this close that makes me realize how much.

In a swift move, he lifts me off my feet, cradling me under my back and legs. "Jefferson!" I squeal, but I love being in his strong arms. He strides toward the steps, but before we make it to the stairs, Madison steps into our path.

Her eyes flick between us, how he's holding me, and her expression tight. "I was hoping we could talk?"

Jefferson eases me back to the ground, hands never leaving me. Grounding. Steady.

I need it for what I'm about to do.

"Not tonight."

"Please." Madison swallows, eyes shining. "I thought I was doing the right thing. After everything–your breakups, the rumors, the press always circling...I thought it was my job to protect you. To keep you safe, even if that meant stepping in where I shouldn't have." Her throat bobs as she swallows. "I crossed a line. I went too far. And I hurt you, which is the opposite of what I ever wanted."

The words hang heavy between us, a mix of guilt and something close to relief, like finally saying it out loud is breaking her open. Tears slip down her cheeks, and she doesn't even bother wiping them away.

For a long moment, I don't know what to say. My chest is tight, my mind spinning back through the months of tension, the silences, the mistrust. "I'm glad you're thinking about your actions and how hurtful they were, but like I said, I'm not talking about this tonight."

Madison blinks hard. She nods, lips pressed together, then steps aside, giving us a clear path up the stairs. I don't look back. My hand tightens around Jefferson's as we climb the stairs, heart hammering. "I know that was harsh, but–"

"Hey," he tells me, "you don't have to make excuses for people when they upset you. She can wait another day." He pulls me against his body. His erection is thick and hard against his leg. "Me, on the other hand? I can't wait another fucking minute."

His mouth dips, capturing mine in a kiss that's all hunger and need, hot and unrelenting. It steals my breath, leaving me dizzy and wanting more. My fingers tangle in his hair, and he groans, a sound that makes my stomach flip. Every inch of him presses against me, and the world outside ceases to exist.

I lead him upstairs to my bedroom. The massive room sprawls around us, vast and luxurious. The canopy bed dominates the space, swathed in silk and velvet, soft lighting casts shadows on the walls. I step back just enough to catch a glimpse of him, my body aching in anticipation, and he grins, teeth brushing his bottom lip, eyes dark with intent.

Jefferson's hands are gentle when he pushes the silver straps off my shoulders, letting the fabric pool at my feet. His eyes drink me in, skimming down my body. I don't feel self-conscious. I feel worshipped.

"Touch me," I beg. When he does it's teasing, a rough thumb grazing my nipple, mouth dipping down to take the other in his mouth. He works me into hard, aching peaks, a slippery heat building between my legs.

"Fuck, I missed you, Angel."

There's no doubt that he wants me. It's in his every touch and kiss. It's in the hard erection threatening to tear the seam of his pants. Reaching between us, I unbuckle his belt and take him in my hand, heavy and hot. Giving him a long stroke, he growls low in his chest and snaps, lifting me up and throwing me on the bed.

I land on my back and look up at him as he removes the rest of his clothes. His body is a temple of hard cut muscle. I watch him closely, his cock swinging heavy between his legs, yelping in surprise when he grabs my ankles and pulls me to the edge of the bed.

"This first time is gonna be fast, but after that we can take it slow."

He says it like there's no discussion, and I realize how incredibly hot that is. Someone taking charge that isn't me. He strokes himself, and I do the same, touching myself between the legs. Getting myself ready for him.

"That may be the hottest thing I've ever seen." He groans watching my fingers turn slick. Flattening his palm on my inner thigh, he spreads me apart, then eases a finger inside, curving it in the most deliriously, delicious way. "You're so fucking tight, I want to feel you around my cock."

Impatiently, he withdraws his fingers and crawls over me, lining himself up and grazing the tip of his cock against my entrance, giving me what I crave.

It's fast. Hard. A punishing thrust inside that I feel in my bones. I wrap my legs around him and he pulls me close, fucking into me like I'm the answer to everything.

I circle his bicep with my fingers, marveling at how solid and warm he is under my hands. How good he feels inside me. At the urgency that builds between us, the need and the raw, unfiltered connection. I'm on the edge, one blink away from falling apart, when he looks down at me, gray eyes steady, and says it again, "I love you."

It's those words that trigger the spiral, the shatter of my body, my psyche, my soul. The orgasm rushes through me, pulsing and hot around him. I barely have time to think, time to *breathe*, because the muscle in the back of his jaw draws tight and his body seizes up. I'm still spiraling when he thrusts into me one last time and groans.

I'm addicted to this man. To his face and body and, yeah, magnificent cock. I'm obsessed with the way he touches me, holds me, carries me like my weight and the burdens that come with Ingrid Flockton are light as a feather. I'm completely consumed by the way he looks hovering over me, dick twitching inside, making sure that I take every drop of him, and fuck, I just want more.

He pulls out, and we tumble back across the expanse of silk sheets, mouths fused, bodies greedy after too many days apart. He kisses me like he's been starving, like he's afraid I'll vanish if he stops.

My nails rake down his back, pulling him closer. Skin against skin. I flatten my hand over his chest, feeling the hammer of his heartbeat. It matches mine.

"I love you," I tell him, pushing a lock of that blond hair out of his eyes. "You, and your magnificent cock."

"Yes!" He grins, fist pumping like a dork. "I knew it."

He's so silly, but that's what makes this so incredible. Love doesn't have to be painful and fraught. It can be fun and respectful. Sexy and confident. It can be a long moment, where we lie there, tangled together, the night silent except for our breathing and the distant crash of waves.

Love can be a place where the outside doesn't matter—only this bed, this room, and the man who showed up for me.

I LEAVE Jefferson tangled in my sheets, his chest rising slow and steady, the exhaustion of the night finally catching up to him. He looks peaceful, unguarded—satiated by our night together. I brush my fingers over his shoulder, then slip out quietly.

Some things can't wait.

By the time I've made it through the drive-thru and parked outside Madison's place, the weight of two large coffees in my hand feels less like a peace offering and more like armor. She answers the door in sweats, her hair twisted up, eyes already glassy with guilt. Relief flickers across her face when she sees me.

"Ingrid," she breathes out, like she wasn't sure I'd ever show up.

I hold out the coffee. "Figured we'd both need caffeine for this."

She takes the offering, but I'm not feeling overly generous. I'm not joking about the caffeine. I'm going to need to be sharp if I'm going to handle this the right way, because Madison has been my friend since we were kids, but what she's been doing? It's not okay.

I step past her and enter the kitchen. My voice is sharper than I mean it to be, but I don't back down. "We need to figure this out."

Madison twists her fingers in her sleeves, then blurts, "I'm sorry. Again. For all of it."

I fold my arms, holding her gaze. "Sorry doesn't cover pushing Jake in front of me at every turn even after I told you that our relationship was toxic. Or telling me about Jefferson's list when you knew how much it would hurt me. You've been pulling strings in my personal life, Madison. Why?"

She flinches and I think for a moment she's not going to answer me, but she sighs and says, "Because I was tired, Ingrid. Not just physically but mentally. Tired of being in the shadows. Tired of always being the assistant, the sidekick, the one cleaning up after whatever guy you were with took the spotlight. Jake, Jefferson, whoever the boyfriend was sucking up all of the oxygen in the room. They took precedence, always, and I guess I thought that if I stirred things up, if I controlled the narrative a little, I could matter." Her voice cracks, and she wipes her cheek with the back of her hand. "I told myself it was helping you by keeping you relevant, distracting the press when you needed cover. But somewhere along the way, it stopped being about you and started being about me."

The coffee sits between us, untouched, steam curling like the last fragile thread of patience. "But why Jake? You know how much he hurt me and how hard it was to get over him."

Guilt flickers in her eyes. "I guess I knew that Jake wouldn't take you away from me. That it wasn't ever going to be long term, and every break up kind of brought us closer. You know?"

The admission sends me reeling, so much so I'm unable to speak. She was pushing us together so that I would get hurt. So I would need her.

"I hurt you. I know that. I'm sorry."

"You did more than hurt me. You made me question someone I love. That's not your place. It was never your place." I try to manage the emotions stampeding through my veins. "I trusted you, Mads. Implicitly. I gave you access to every part of my life and in return you used it against me."

"I know. It got out of hand." Madison's voice cracks, tears finally spilling free. "I just don't know where we go from here."

For the first time in weeks, something like clarity settles in my chest. I set my coffee down and fold my arms. "I think we start with a break. The tour is over, and other people can handle my schedule for a minute. I think we both need to take a little time off to rest and recover. The past two years have been insane."

Madison lets out a tired laugh. "Absolutely insane."

I smile back because we both feel that exhaustion down to our bones. "Once we have space to breathe," I continue, "maybe we can try again. But with different boundaries for both of us."

She nods, slow and earnest. I mean more than the words. Madison needs help. She needs boundaries, therapy, a team that isn't run entirely through her own fear of being invisible. But that's not the same as tossing her aside. Professionally, I have access. I can get her the help she needs and keep her close while putting rules in place. Personally, we'll have to rebuild trust.

I stand, slipping my bag over my shoulder. "Jefferson told me you helped him last night, that you got Marv to stand down."

She looks startled. "I felt like it was what you would've wanted me to do."

"I appreciate that." I mean it. "He does too."

She searches my face. "So you're back together?"

"We are." I grin, feeling the truth in my chest like heat. "He's important to me. I love him. If you want us to be friends and work together in the future, you're going to have to accept that."

Madison's mouth flattens for a second, then she nods, quicker this time. "I can. I *do*. This was never about Jefferson."

Her words are earnest; I believe her. It doesn't erase everything, but it's a start.

I step toward her and, impulsively, pull her into a hug. She stiffens, then melts, and for a breath we're not boss and assistant, not the pop star and the fixer–just two people who've been splintered and are trying to stitch themselves back together.

When I pull away, the late morning light slants across her kitchen table. "Tomorrow," I say, "we'll make a plan—therapy, PR guidelines, a clear line you don't cross."

Madison swallows. "Thank you. For not throwing me away."

"We've been friends for a long time, Mads. I'd never throw you away."

She watches me head for the door, a mix of relief and guilt in her face. I close the car door, breathe in the warm air, and drive home feeling raw and tired and, for the first time in weeks, like I'm steering my own life again.

30

———

Jefferson

The door clicks open and I glance up, heart already lighter just seeing her silhouette in the doorway. Ingrid slips inside, quiet as ever, and kicks off her shoes by the dresser. They tumble over each other, a careless little heap that makes me smile because she's here, not on a stage, not on the road, but here with me.

She crosses the room in one of those sexy little tennis skirts that show off her legs and a crop top. Without hesitation she crawls back under the covers, sliding into my side like she belongs there. Which she does. My arm goes around her automatically, like my body has been waiting for her weight against me.

"Thought maybe you'd be up by now," she says, pressing her ass into the curve of my body. My dick twitches in appreciation.

"I thought if I stayed in bed, maybe there'd be a shot you'd get back in."

"Smart boy."

"How did it go?" I ask, my voice low, not wanting to break the spell of this moment.

"Okay, I think." She nuzzles into my chest, her hair tickling my chin. "I hope so. I think maybe having some space will be good for us."

I kiss her temple, breathing her in. I didn't realize how much I needed the quiet of her, how good it feels to have her pressed close without the roar of a crowd or the pressure of a game between us. "I spent the last four years spending just about twenty-four-seven with three roommates. We lived together, played together, traveled together, partied together... things changed when they started dating someone seriously. Everyone was happier, well, almost everyone."

Her head tilts back so she can look at me. "You weren't happier?"

I run my thumb along her shoulder, tracing lazy circles on her skin. "At the time it felt like I was losing something, my wingmen, I guess, but looking back? They weren't leaving me behind. They were just...growing up. Moving forward. I guess I didn't realize I wanted that too, until you."

Her lips curve, soft and knowing. "So, what are you saying?

I tug her until she's on top of me, legs straddled over my hips. She's a goddess and I'm the fucking luckiest man in the world. "You're it, Angel."

Her hand rests over my chest, right above my heart, and I know she feels how hard it's beating. "Good," she whispers. "Because you're it for me too. Even when it's messy. Even when I'm on the road and you're playing halfway across the country."

"We'll figure it out," I say, certain in a way I've never been about anything. "Calls. Flights. Off-season trips. Hell, I'll even learn how to live out of one of those sparkly suitcases of yours if it means being with you."

She laughs, quiet but genuine, and kisses me slowly. When she pulls back, she doesn't move far, her forehead resting against mine. "That sounds like a plan."

"But I've got a month off, what about you?"

She grins. "I've got a little free time coming up."

The hem of her skirt brushes my thighs, light as a tease, "Any idea what we should do with it?"

"A few." She laughs softly, then leans down to kiss me–slow at first, then deeper, until the world narrows to just the press of her lips and the weight of her body against mine. My hands slide lower, over the soft curve of her thighs, gripping just enough to draw a little gasp from her.

Her lips part against mine, that tiny gasp turning into a sound I feel all the way down to my balls. I grip her tighter, pulling her closer, until there isn't an inch between us. The skirt rides higher as she shifts in my lap, and I curse the stretchy shorts underneath.

"You drive me fucking insane," I murmur against her mouth, nipping at her bottom lip before letting her take it back in a kiss that leaves me dizzy. Grinding down on me with that hot, little pussy, I groan, the thin barrier of my shorts doing nothing to hide how hard I am for her. My hands slip under her skirt, palms gliding up the backs of her thighs, settling on the curve of her ass. She shivers at the contact, pressing closer, like she can't get enough.

"Angel," I whisper, and it's half prayer, half plea.

"Yeah?" Her voice is pure sin, soft and taunting all at once.

"How pissed are you going to be if I tear this skirt?"

Her smile curves against my jaw as she kisses her way down to my neck, teeth grazing my skin just enough to leave me aching for more. "Impatient?"

"If I could fuck you all day, I would. Strip you bare, keep you naked, wear you out." The words snap the last thread of restraint I have. I grab the hem of her crop top and pull it up and over her head in one swift move, tossing it to the floor. She sits back just long enough for me to take her in—hair a little mussed, lips kiss-swollen, chest rising and falling fast. Her nipples are hard peaks, tits that fit perfectly in my palms. She's a queen, my lap her throne, and that sexy smirk on her mouth tells me she knows exactly how much she owns me.

"Beautiful," I say, because anything less would be a lie. Heat, softness, and the electric shock of being skin-to-skin again after too damn long. I can't stop kissing her. Hard, deep, desperate. Every kiss is a claim and I roll us over, pressing her body into the mattress, letting her feel how fucking much I want her. But showing her isn't enough. She needs to hear it. "I love you, Angel."

"I love you too, Jefferson."

I rise up, peel off that skirt, not giving a fuck if it tears or not. I'll buy her a new one. Kissing my way down the length of her body, she arches beneath me, every sigh and shiver pulling me deeper under her spell. By the time I settle between her thighs, she's trembling, whispering my name like it's the only word she knows.

When I finally push into her, it's everything–heat, home, *salvation*. Her nails bite into my shoulders, her legs wrap tight around me, and I lose myself completely. Every thrust is a promise, every groan a confession, until we're both unraveling together, nothing between us but love and fire.

After, she melts against me, skin damp, heart racing against mine. I hold her close, kissing the crown of her head, and for the first time in my life, I don't want or need anything else.

Because she's it. My Angel. My future. My forever.

EPILOGUE

J*efferson*
Two months later

I LOG onto the video session, and within seconds my screen fills with the familiar chaos of my old roommates. Different cities now, different lives, but the same loud energy. After we all moved out, the group chat turned live when someone obnoxiously titled it *Men of the Manor.* We try to meet weekly.

"How's New York?" I ask Reese and Reid. Same city, different teams.

"Good, although I didn't expect feeling like a rookie all over again," Reid says with a grimace.

"Yeah," I agree. "I know the feeling."

"But the city is great."

"Incredible," Reese adds. "Check out this view." He lifts his laptop, giving us a glimpse out the window. It's mostly the brick wall of the building across the way, but if he tilts the camera just right, you get a sliver of downtown skyline. "The coaching staff is good, and so far everyone has been pretty receptive. And the facilities?" He whistles. "Unreal."

"Right?" Axel pipes up from where he's sprawled shirtless on his bed, tugging at the hoop in his eyebrow. His hair is freshly dyed platinum, like he's leaning into the villain arc. "I thought we had it good at Wittmore, but the pro's are on another level."

Reese smirks. "At least you're not freezing your ass off yet. Wait until January."

"Shut up." Axel flips him off, grinning, but we all know he and Nadia are born and raised in the south and are going to miss the warm weather.

"How about you?" I glance at Reid.

"Not bad," Reid says, leaning back in his chair. Behind him, I can see his sketch pads stacked high, a marker tucked behind his ear. "My team in New York is competitive as hell, but I'm holding my own. Balancing ice time with design gigs isn't easy, though. The athletic department at Wittmore gave me a contract I couldn't refuse–new logos, merch lines, all of it."

"Guy can't stay away from art if he tried," Axel teases.

"Also a good excuse to visit Shelby."

"How is she?" I ask, although Ingrid and the other girls keep up better than we do.

"She's good. Still at the Den, taking a couple classes. She moved into the Teal House after Twyler and Nadia left. Oh shit," he adds, running a hand through his ginger hair. "You won't believe who moved into the Manor."

"Emerson said they tried but it was already rented," I say.

"Yep. It's those guys from Serendee. Coach set them up, I think. There's some girl with them too."

"A girl?" Axel perks up immediately. "Living in the Manor?"

The blasphemy.

"Yeah, a sister or something? I'm not sure. She's got that vibe, you know."

Everyone nods. 'That vibe' means long hair and dresses. The Serendee vibe.

Reid shrugs. "Shelby's pretty wary of anything religious or culty after the way you guys were raised." He nods toward Axel's box. "Honestly, they kind of freak me out too."

"They're good players, though," Reese notes. "But we all know it takes more than talent to be a good teammate and compete at the highest levels. Hope they don't fuck up our legacy."

Axel leans forward, camera flashing over his pierced nipple. "What about you, Parks? How's Florida?"

"Like you give a shit about Florida," I challenge. "You want to know about Grant Pierce, right?"

"Obviously." Axel smirks. "I want to know everything. What does he eat, what type of deodorant does he use, the kind of jockstrap he prefers."

"Stop being a psycho," Reese tells him, but he's leaning a little closer too, like he wants all the details himself.

I don't give them much–just that preseason's started, I'm putting in hours with the trainers, getting into routine. They don't need the details; they know how it goes.

"And Ingrid?" Reid asks, clearly prompted by someone just off screen. His girlfriend, no doubt.

"She's good." I can't stop the smile that pulls at my face. "The Vegas residency announcement was huge. Six months on the Strip. Which means for once we're both in places we actually get to stay awhile. No buses, no hotel hopping. Just...home bases."

There's a beat of silence before Axel whistles. "So, Parksy, let me get this straight. You've got a pro contract, your pop star girl's got a Vegas residency, and you're living in Florida sunshine. You really did win the damn lottery."

I laugh and look across the room. Ingrid's curled up on the chair in the corner, notepad balanced on her knee. She's been writing and the whole process is fascinating to watch. She looks up at me and gives me one of those smiles that bottoms out my stomach. "Feels that way."

And for the first time, it doesn't feel like I'm chasing the next thing. It feels like I've already found it.

. . .

*

Three Months After That
Ingrid

THE WAGs SECTION IS BUZZING, though most of the women sit in their polished coats and perfect makeup, more focused on sipping wine than the game. It's a home game, so Twyler is a little out of place in her *Cain #15* jersey among the Florida fans, but nothing's going to stop her from supporting her man.

I'm wearing a custom Reid Wilder-designed hockey jacket. Team colors stitched across the sleeves, Jefferson's name and number bold across the back. When he presented me with the sketch, I was amazed and immediately sent it off to be made. He'd outdone himself with the detailing; it feels like both a fashion statement and a declaration.

My phone buzzes, and I check the screen. A laugh slips out before I can stop it.

"What?" Twyler leans over, ponytail brushing my shoulder.

"It's Reid." I tilt the screen so she can see. "He says the second the cameras caught me walking in, the internet exploded asking about the jacket."

Almost on cue, another buzz. I grin. "Shelby this time. She says thank you for making her boyfriend so happy. Apparently, Reid's already getting messages about expanding the design. People want one of their own."

"I bet they do," Twyler says knowingly. "It doesn't hurt that Jefferson's having an amazing rookie season, or that anything Ingrid Flockton touches turns to gold.

"Not sure about that, but I do know that Reese is doing great too."

"My man doesn't do less than great." She smirks, and the smugness is absolutely warranted. Reese is already making headlines for his record-breaking stats.

"How are Ax and Nadia?" I ask. "Any updates?

"Chicago suits them, I think," she says, eyes tracking the ice. "Nadia seems to really like her job in logistics. Axel isn't starting yet, but he's getting some ice time, which is all he needs to prove himself."

We settle back into our seats just as the puck drops again. The energy in the arena hits me like a cascade of thundering sticks and skates cutting across ice, the crowd rising and falling with every play. It's both different and familiar, fun but stressful, being on the other side of the stage. Down below, Jefferson throws his weight into a body check against Reese, and Twyler practically launches out of her chair.

"Careful with that shoulder, Parks!" she shouts, hands cupped around her mouth. The other women glance at her, startled, but I laugh. Always the trainer, always looking for an injury before anyone else. "He knows Reese's weak spots."

"I don't think Jefferson would intentionally injure his friend."

She rolls her eyes, like I'm naive. "He just needs to mind himself or he's going to have to deal with me." She flops back down but can't stop bouncing her knee.

The puck slides loose at center ice, and suddenly the game explodes with speed–Jefferson fighting for control along the boards, Reese swooping in with that lethal quickness of his. Skates screech, sticks clash, and the roar of the crowd spikes as the two of them battle it out. Reese breaks away first, driving toward the net, only to have Jefferson barrel in from behind, muscling him off balance just enough to force a wide shot. The goalie snags it clean, and the arena erupts again.

I find myself more invested–*deeply* invested. "How do you handle the stress?" I ask Twy after another just missed shot. My heart pounds so hard and fast, I think it may crack my ribs.

"Not well," she admits, pointing to her hairline. "Do you see that? Gray hair already."

I laugh because I don't think I see any gray, but I understand the feeling. I try to distract her and myself by asking her about work with the Wolfpack, the minor league team she's working with up north.

Between plays, she gives me the rundown, but overall ,she seems happy with her new job.

When the buzzer signals intermission, Twyler finally turns her attention back to me. "So, how's residency in Vegas?"

"It's going well." I pause, searching for the right words. "Intense, but in a good way. The venue is great and it's nice to perform on a smaller scale. Between rehearsals and shows, I've finally figured out a rhythm." I shift a little. "Are you guys still coming out for New Year's Eve?

"Yes! I can't wait. I've never been."

"Vegas is loud, chaotic, full of lights and strangers, but—don't worry—I'll make sure it's memorable for us. I've got something special planned for after the show."

"I don't doubt it." She tilts her head, like she's weighing her words. "You going to invite Madison?"

The question makes me pause, then nod. "Yeah. I figured everyone would like to see her."

"So you two patched things up?"

That's a loaded question. After some time apart, Madison was the one who came to me and said she wanted to resign. I can admit that I felt panicked. We'd worked together for so long, but she meant what she said. Our friendship was more important.

"Things are definitely better now that we're just friends and not working together. She's actually working with one of the acts that opened for us on the tour, Leslie Morgan. She's up and coming, *fast,* and needs someone with a lot of experience. I think it's going to be a great fit." I lift an eyebrow. "She's also dating someone."

Twyler's huge eyes widen. "Oh, really? Who?"

"The sister of one of my dancers. Cassie. I really like her. She's grounded, sweet. It works."

"Good for her."

The buzzer cuts our conversation short. We rise as the guys skate back onto the ice, helmets low, sticks tapping. The whole place roars when Jefferson takes position, his shoulders broad and sure, his every move radiating confidence.

I press a hand to the embroidered letters across my jacket, warmth rising in my chest. Music, the stage, the adrenaline of touring–it's still mine. But now I have this too. The chance to watch him chase his dream, to share these ridiculous, joyful moments with new friends.

The best of both worlds.

*

Much to Twyler's frustration, Florida takes the win, and the whole arena practically rattles with noise. I hug her and Reese goodbye after the game, confirming the plans again for New Year's Eve. By the time we pile into a convoy of SUVs toward the team's after-party, the mood is electric.

The club is packed–music thumping, drinks flowing, everyone high off adrenaline. I'd worried, once, about slipping into Jefferson's world, about being *the girlfriend* in a sea of women and men who've known me since childhood for my fame and career, but they've welcomed me, pulling me in like I'm one of their own.

"Ingrid!" Grant Pierce grins when he sees me. He gestures to one of the guys, Conrad Wilkins, who presses a drink into my hand. His wife pulls me in to show me a picture of their new baby. There's no hesitation, no guardedness. Just open, rowdy acceptance.

And Jefferson, watching it all, looks like he might explode with pride.

Later, we're on the dance floor, bodies pressed close, sweat-dampened hair clinging to my temples. It's just like that night after the Frozen Four victory, the two of us lost in the music, victory glittering in the air around us.

I lean up, my mouth brushing his ear, and whisper, "Brilliant Sunrise."

He stiffens slightly, pulling back enough to frown at me. "What?"

"The song." My voice is almost swallowed by the bass. "Was it *Brilliant Sunrise*?"

For a moment, he just stares down at me, eyes dark and unreadable. Then his mouth quirks, equal parts fond and exasperated. "Angel, are you still on about this?"

"Yes." I lean closer, refusing to back down. "I deserve to know which one it was."

He exhales a laugh, low and rough, then shakes his head. "I could tell you, but I don't want anything tainted between us."

"It won't," I promise, but I kind of get what he means.

"That girl, way back then," he pushes my hair over my shoulder. I'm letting the color fade out, slowly going back to my natural blond. "I won't say she didn't mean anything to me. That's disrespectful to the moment. But what I remember–other than popping off in about forty seconds flat," he grimaces, "is that every time I hear your voice, a switch flips. I get hard and horny. Not because of that disastrous first time, but because it was always you, Ingrid. And when I hear the song, any song by you, and hear your incredible voice, all I think about is how much I love you."

I stare at him, my heart so full it almost hurts. And I know he means every word. I also know he's completely full of shit and loves nothing more than keeping me in suspense.

"So you're not going to tell me," I challenge.

His grin widens, lighting up the whole damn room. "Not a chance."

I laugh, helpless against it, and let him pull me closer. The music swells around us, bodies pressed tight, the rest of the world blurring and fading until it feels like it's just us.

AFTERWORD

Don't miss the bonus scene and future take from Enticing the Enforcer! Grab it HERE!

Thank you all so much for reading Jefferson and Ingrid's book! When I first started Wittmore Hockey, it was the summer of 2023. The Lawson Family had been in the middle of a firestorm for two years at that point (F*ck Cancer) and my daughter was headed to work at camp. I suggested she get herself a fake boy friend (as a joke!) before she left for college in the fall. Of course, that amazing idea was shot down *immediately*, but as with all of us writers, once a little idea worms its way into my brain it can be impossible to shake.

Reese Cain, Axel Rakestraw, Reid Wilder and Jefferson Parks have been a fun palate cleanser between my darker content. Contemporary Hockey Romance has been my life preserver during the hard times over the past few years, something I go to over and over when I want to read something that I know will make me feel safe, happy and give me all the feels. When things got hard, that's when it felt right for me to write some of my own, so that I could maybe offer that to others out there needing a safe harbor.

I need to thank a few people that helped me with this process:

Anna & Chelsey-the women that keep me on track and moving forward. Lisa, Nicole, and my other early readers! Beth for being a rock during all my drama, Taylor Swift, sports, and book discussions. I know I'm missing people. I apologize. My brain is Swiss cheese.

If you don't know, Wittmore is larger than the hockey boys. The college is the home to my darker frat-bully romance, Blacklisted, and it's also the town my dark cult romance, The Cult of Serendee, is located. As you may have noticed, I left a few teasers in this book, introducing future players from Serendee, yes, that was on purpose, and yes, that is where I will be headed next with my solo work. Hockey x Cult Survivors? This sounds like only something I would think is a good idea—I hope you'll join in for the ride!

Pre-order *The Way We Break* today!

They say you can't outrun the past—but maybe you can fake it.

After everything that happened in Serendee, the survivors swore they were done letting anyone close. Wittmore was supposed to be a clean start—new school, new team, new rules. But trauma has a way of catching up, no matter how fast you move.

On the ice, there's order. Noise. Purpose.

Off it? There's guilt. Flashbacks. Temptation.

The quiet understanding that second chances are never as simple as they seem.

Wounds are still raw. Old habits—*rituals*—creep back in.

And maybe it's easier to follow *The Way* than to ever let it go.

The Way We Break is book one in the angsty, reverse harem, Wittmore Hockey x Cult of Serendee crossover series.